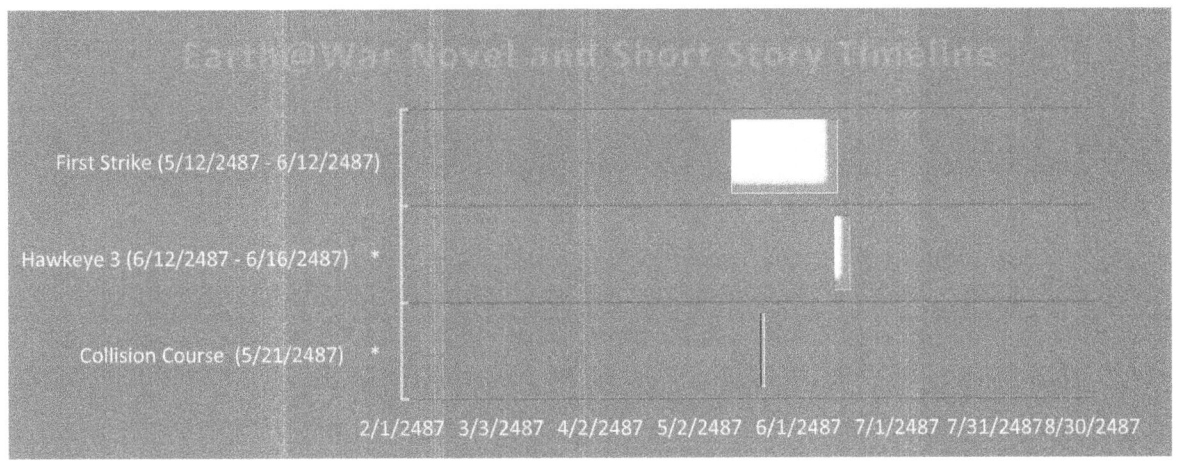

First Strike

An Earth@War Novel

By John J. Knox Jr.

PROLOGUE

Cargo Ship Vladimir
In route to Kylar II, near Omar
May 12, 2487, 0130 UT

James McVeigh, Third Officer of the Cargo Ship *Vladimir*, stood on the bridge gazing out into space. The 32-year-old was on his third journey doing the Earth-Kylar-Omar run on *Vladimir*. He had been working for SDK shipping for almost ten years, after serving as a Quartermaster in the navy for four. McVeigh liked the work, enjoyed being in space and liked SDK shipping.

The ship was 1400 feet long, with a 650-foot beam. The bridge was at the aft end of the ship, allowing McVeigh to see the eight cargo holds along with dozens of containers secured to the ship. *Vladimir* was painted a bright white, with running lights spaced every 100 foot along each side of the ship. The four GX engines, located in the two engine rooms pushed the ship along at 14 AMU, just slightly slower than its maximum fully loaded speed of 16 AMU.

McVeigh walked over to the sensor display on the starboard side of the bridge to check for other ships in the area. The ship was currently on its night cycle, so the only people on the bridge were McVeigh and a helmsman, a crewmember whose name McVeigh couldn't recall. The helmsman was seated at a console at the forward part of the bridge. After checking the sensors, McVeigh move over to the navigation table on the port side of the bridge to check the ship's position. The ship was in the middle of the shipping lane, perfectly on track for the Kylar system. *Vladimir* would arrive at Kylar II, a mainly tropical planet that was home to Naval Base Oscar, the largest base in this sector and the home to the Navy's Fourth Fleet on May 28th. While unloading cargo, the officers and crew of *Vladimir* would have two weeks of liberty on the planet known for its warm weather and beautiful women. Then it would be on to Earth to unload the remainder of the cargo and back to Omar with fresh cargo from Earth. It was an easy, safe journey, with well-marked shipping lanes and a well-protected sector, despite the war between Antron and Batron, though Batron was at times threatening Earth who was selling weapons to Antron. Still, Earth had a large Army and Navy and no one would dare attack it. Besides, Earth was over 12,000 AMU from Batron.

A beep from the sensor console caught McVeigh's attention. He crossed the bridge and stepped up to the console and saw a blip moving at an angle, crossing the shipping lane and not following it. It was labeled "UNK" indicating an unknown ship. That was strange since most ships broadcast their identity for safety reasons. Fifteen seconds later, several other unidentified ships appeared on the console, all traveling in the same direction at a speed of 22 AMU. McVeigh peered out of the angled windows of the bridge as his mind struggled to find an explanation for what he saw seeing on the console. In the distance McVeigh saw three bright flashes, then streaks of light causing his heart to race. He understood now and reacted immediately.

"Helm, disengage auto, bow thrusters down full! Increase speed to flank! Right thrusters to full!" McVeigh ordered as he quickly crossed the bridge to the internal communication station.

"Bow thrusters down full, right thrusters to full, increase to flank, aye, sir," the helmsman responded, not knowing why the order had been given, but hearing the urgency in the officer's voice. His hand moved over his console using the touchscreen to carry out the orders.

"Very well," McVeigh replied as he pressed the button that sounded the collision alarm. The alarm consisted of three loud beeps, a pause and then repeated for a fifteen second pause. The helmsman's eyes grew wide at the sound of the alarm.

McVeigh moved back to the sensor console which was now sounding an alarm also. On the display three dots were closing in on *Vladimir*. The dots were red and labeled "MIS" indicating inbound missiles. Looking out of the bridge windows, McVeigh saw the view was shifting up and to the right. "Secure the bow thrusters," he ordered.

"Secure bow thrusters, aye, sir," the helmsman replied as he carried out the order.

"Speed?"

"15 AMU and increasing, sir."

Not enough, McVeigh though, quickly moving ack to the internal comm station. He pressed the button that activated the ship's public address system. "Brace for impact," he announced calmly and professionally to his own surprise. Then he pushed the button for the collision alarm for the second time.

"Secure right thruster," McVeigh ordered the helmsman a second before the first missile hit near the communications shack located directly aft of the bridge. The explosion from the impact destroyed the communications shack and the ensuing fireball engulfed the bridge, killing both McVeigh and the helmsman. The destruction of the communication shack cut off any communication from *Vladimir*, and therefore Vladimir was unable to send a message. Seconds after the fireball consumed the bridge, the fire went out as the air was vented into space.

The second missile struck the bulkhead separating Engine Rooms One and Two, venting both engine rooms into space and instantly killing the six people on watch in the engineering spaces. The impact and explosion twisted the ship, causing electrical power to fail throughout the ship.

The third missile struck the keel of the ship near Cargo Bay 3. The ship broke in two. By now, almost all the air throughout the ship was gone and the six officers and 33 crewmembers were dead. The stress on each section of the ship as it twisted and shook began tearing the ship apart. Compartments imploded and bulkheads failed. The remains of *Vladimir* drifted away from the shipping lane.

CHAPTER ONE

Naval Assault Forces, Recruit Training Command
Naval Base Bravo, Mars
May 13, 2487, 1320 Local, 1420 UT

Naval Base Bravo was the Navy's primary training facility and housed the Recruit Training Commands for both the Navy and the Naval Assault Forces as well as numerous schools for technical training. The training station consisted of a series of domes connected by tunnels, with each dome housing a specific command. Dome 3 housed the Recruit Training Command for the Naval Assault Forces, the ground assault troops for Earth's Navy.

Max Finley, in his fifteenth and final week of boot camp, was sweating. The dome for the Naval Assault Forces boot camp was intentionally hot and the gravity generators set to 1.2 G's, forcing new recruits to excel under adverse conditions. Many recruits couldn't handle it and quit. Max Finley, however was not a quitter.

Max tightened his grip on his L-29 assault rifle and belly crawled to cover behind a large boulder. He looked to his right and saw Phil Moore, originally from Atlanta, and another recruit named Lou on their bellies, L-29s at the ready. To his left was Dave Roberts and another recruit named Joseph using a shallow crater for cover. Max, Dave and Phil had met on the shuttle from Earth to Mars and had become close friends as they went through training together. They were all 19 years old, tough and willing to do whatever it took to make it into the Naval Assault Forces.

Max repositioned his L-29. The assault rifle was the standard for the Naval Assault Forces, replacing the L-27. At nine pounds, it was lighter than the L-27 and had a range of 200 yards. It fired 8-mm bolts in single fire, three bolt bursts or fully automatic modes. Max currently had single fire mode selected with the safety off. The laser was set on low power mode for this live fire exercise which still stung and often stunned you if you were hit. The low power mode only existed on the training version of the weapon, since in the field, you only fired if you intended to kill the enemy.

Max was the fire team leader for this team exercise. A fire team consisted of four team members and a team leader. As team leader, Max would maneuver his team through a two-mile course, engaging enemies played by various drill instructors. He did this from the middle position, with two members of his team on each side. He would signal his teammates to move, cover or hold depending on the situation.

"What are you ladies waiting for? The enemy to come to you?" the Company Drill Instructor yelled through the ear piece Max was wearing. *Easy to say advance when it isn't your ass on the line*, thought Max. Still, this was his mission to lead and he wasn't about to fail, especially after almost 15 weeks of training. Failing this course would mean moving back in training if you were lucky, and being removed from recruit training and returning to civilian life if you weren't, meaning the last three months of your life was wasted.

He wiped the sweat from his forehead and signaled to the left for Dave and Joseph to advance approximately 100 yards to some boulders they could use for cover. He sighted his rifle down range, covering for the two of them. Once Joseph and Dave were in position, he signaled for Phil and Lou. They advanced to a trench approximately eighty yards from the previous position. Finally, he signaled for the fire team to cover for him as he advanced to a mound that he would use for cover.

As he began to move, half squatting as he ran, a bolt hit in front of him, blowing red Martian dirt into his face. He instinctively dropped and rolled right as he heard return fire from his team. Pressing his body to the ground, he moved his rifle into position and fired two rounds blindly downrange. Another bolt flew above his head. This time Max located the source of the incoming bolts. The enemy was behind the same mound he intended to use for cover. He waited, L-29 sighted just above the mound. Thirty seconds later, although it seemed to be a lot longer than that to Max as he laid in the dry Martian dirt with his heart racing, a head appeared, peeking over the mound. Max double tapped his trigger sending two bolts into the head of the instructor who had fired at him, dropping the instructor. Max considered swapping out the power cell of his L-29 but realized that he still had at least 26 rounds left.

"Lucky shot. How about moving along? We don't have all day," the Company Drill Instructor, Sergeant Blake, yelled in his ear causing Max to smile. Max moved quickly behind the mound of dirt that the instructor had been behind, keeping his head low as he went. In the distance, he could see a low wall. It took almost thirty minutes to make it to the three-foot-high wall. The team engaged two more instructors along the way with Phil and Joe each scoring a "kill". So far, the team was performing great, working together. Max didn't feel it was necessarily his leadership and was thankful that he had great recruits on his team.

The wall presented a unique challenge. While being great for cover, the team needed to get over it and into a safe position without getting hit. Max attempted to peek over the wall, but a barrage of bolts forced him back down. *Damn, now what do I do?* Max asked himself. He knew he needed to find a solution quickly or Sergeant Blake would be on his ass. Max signaled for Phil and Dave to join him. Staying low, they made their way over to Max who sat leaning against the wall.

"We have to get a look over this wall and figure out what to do when we go over it," Max began. "When I signal, the three of us are going to look over the wall, firing five or so rounds as we do, and then drop back down."

The three men turned, kneeling behind the wall. Max counted to three with his fingers and the men raise up above the wall firing rapidly, using the top of the wall to steady their weapons. Each man fired five rounds, then quickly dropped back down behind the wall.

"What did you see?" Max asked as bolts hit the wall behind him.

"A lot of enemy," Dave replied, wiping the sweat from his face.

"And nothing for cover," Phil added. Max too had noticed there was no cover. Once they went over the wall, they would have to move quickly or they would have no chance. *This isn't going to be easy*, Max thought. Of course, nothing about bootcamp had been easy. To become a member of the Naval Assault Forces, you had to show strength and determination. If you lacked either of those, you would never make it as a trooper.

"The way I figure it, this has to be the end of the course," Max told the others who nodded their head in agreement as all three men changed out the charge packs on the L-29s. If it wasn't the end of the course, Max didn't know how they would make it. He assumed that going over the wall was going to cost him some of the team. What remained afterwards probably couldn't go much further. Bolts continued to hit the wall behind them with a loud smacking sound. "Okay, go back to your positions. When I signal, we all go over the wall. Start firing as soon as you hit the ground. Full auto, don't conserve your charge. Once you're over, advance rapidly."

"Aye," Phil and Dave replied in unison. They returned to their positions and filled the other two fire team members in on the plan. Max just hoped the plan worked. If it didn't he could imagine how Sergeant Blake would act. And worse would be facing his team, the loss would be his, but they would lose as well. And all of them would have to face the consequences.

A minute later, all five men were in position, kneeling behind the wall. Max signaled and scrambled over the wall dropping on the other side. Dropping to one knee, he began sweeping his L-29 right to left, sending a dozen bolts down range, not aiming at anything, but attempting to force the enemy to stop firing. He rose up and began to cautiously advance, continuing to fire as bolts passed by him. With his eyes downrange, he concentrated, attempting to pinpoint enemy positions. A blast from an explosion to his left added to the confusion of incoming and outgoing fire.

Max heard a yell and out of the corner of his eye saw Lou fall, hit by an incoming bolt from an instructor. Max hit two instructors and, in his peripheral vision saw three others fall. He changed his charge back out, toggled his selector switch back to single round and began to sweep left and right looking for any remaining instructors. He fired, double-tapping at center mass as he had been instructed during initial training on his weapon, and watched the instructor fall as Joe hit one to his left.

"Cease fire," ordered a voice over the comm unit. Relief filled Max's body as the exercise ended. *That was intense,* Max thought, adrenaline still pumping. Medics came out to check on the people who were hit but no one was seriously injured. To Max's surprise, Lou was the only one on his team that an instructor managed to hit. The three other members of the fire team ran to Max celebrating their victory.

A squat, muscular Drill Instructor came out on field. "Clear out!" he ordered in a loud, firm voice.

Max walked off with the rest of the team proud of their performance. His fire team joined the other teams who had completed the exercise on a set of bleachers near the course where they could observe other members of their company as they came through the course. He grabbed an energy bar, ate in quickly and drank from his canteen. It took another two hours for the rest of the recruits in his company to complete the exercise, the men in the bleacher enjoying a brief break from training.

Sergeant Blake walked up to the company after the last fire team finished. "Now let's go for a little run," Sergeant Blake ordered. Max was not surprised. If there was anything he had learned in bootcamp, it was that there was never a long break. Finish one thing and it was off to the next. He stood up, sweat dripping from his body. *I love this job*, he told himself only half believing it as he rose.

* * * * *

Headquarters Fourth Fleet
Naval Base Oscar, Kylar II
May 14, 2487, 0658 Local, 1338 UT

Admiral William P. Morris, Commander of the Fourth Fleet, arrived at his office at almost exactly 0700 as was his habit. The 6'2" Admiral had 33 years of service. Medium built at 215 pounds with cropped graying hair and wearing a clean and perfectly pressed uniform and a booming voice that commanded obedience, he was the poster child of what a high-ranking officer should be. As Commander of the Fourth Fleet, he was responsible for the entire Young-Wise sector.

The sector stretched from Masic Point to Omar and then on to Kylar and finally reaching Batron and Antron, a total of 76 systems with approximately half of them populated, mainly by humans as far as Omar and other species beyond that.

With tensions mounting between Batron and Earth over Batron's war with Antron, his job was becoming more difficult. Even though Earth had declared itself neutral, mainly to avoid becoming involved in another war, Earth continued to sell arms to Antron despite Batron's strong objections. Tensions were increasing in the sector, with Batron threatening Earth's cargo vessels, attempting to cut off Antron. Between the tensions with Batron and continued cuts to the fleet's budget, the stress on the Admiral was building.

Admiral Morris' office was large. Opposite of the door was a large dark wood desk with two chairs that sat empty in front of it. On top of the desk was a computer display and three comm units. One connected him to his Administrative Assistant, one was a general comm unit and the last was a secure unit when the purpose of communication was sensitive. A couch ran along one wall with pictures of the various ships that the Admiral had serve on hanging above it, including *ESS Charleston (D-614)*, his first ship, which the Admiral had served on as a Lieutenant during the War at Masic Point, the last war that Earth was involved in. The war had started in 2464 and ended in 2467 and resulted in Earth using far less automation on her ships. Computers now assisted the crews of ships, but did not control the ships themselves.

The walls in the office were painted white with beige carpeting, standard colors for naval offices. Two flags were behind him to the left the Naval flag and to the right the flag of the United Nations, Earth's primary governing body. Painted on the wall behind the desk was the large seal of the Fourth Fleet. The Admiral had barely settled in behind the desk when the door chimed.

"Enter," the Admiral commanded.

Yeoman Second Class Andrew Wilson entered the room holding a stack of papers. The 5'10 African-American from Miami was the Admiral's Administrative Assistant in charge of the Admiral's busy schedule, screened visitors and comms, maintained records for the Admiral and served the Admiral in whatever other way that was needed. He was a tremendous asset to the Admiral and a very dedicated individual. Since his boss arrived at 0700, Andrew was here at 0530.

"Overnight dispatches, sir," Andrew said placing the papers on the desk. He had sorted them, of course, with the one's that needed the most needed the Admiral's attention on top.

"Thank you, Wilson," the Admiral responded.

"And Rear Admiral Kilgallon is here, sir."

"Send him in."

Rear Admiral Kilgallon was Commander of Destroyer Squadron Ten (DesRon10) and assigned to Fourth Fleet. His command included 29 destroyers, 17 cruisers, 21 supply ships and 2 repair ships. He still occasionally grumbled about having cruisers assigned to his squadron, but with budget cuts came the elimination of Cruiser Squadron Four, and the cruisers assigned to other squadrons, including Destroyer Squadron Ten. Many years ago, as a newly commissioned Ensign, Kilgallon had become the junior officer on *ESS Charleston*, replacing a then newly promoted Lieutenant Morris in that role, just before the war at Masic Point. The two served together and remained good friends throughout their careers.

"Have a seat, Frank," Admiral Morris said as Kilgallon entered.

"Thank you, Admiral," Kilgallon replied as he sat down.

Admiral Morris pushed a button on the Comm Box. "Bring us some coffee Wilson."

"Aye, sir," came the reply.

"So, what's on your mind?" the Admiral asked.

"Well, I'm becoming concerned with my squadron's state of readiness. We aren't getting enough training time between deployments and it's beginning to show," Kilgallon said. "Mistakes are being made and new officers and crew just don't know what they are doing."

"What's the status of your ships?" Morris asked.

"Of my destroyers, seventeen are here, three are deployed to Omar IV, six are at Masic Point and three are in the lunar shipyards. I have eight cruisers here that haven't been underway in almost a year, two are at Earth in the process of being decommissioned, one is in the lunar shipyard, one at Mars and one at Omar IV. Admiral, almost half of my destroyers haven't been underway at all in over six months."

Andrews entered the office carrying two coffee cups and a pot of coffee along with cream and sugar. He silently poured a cup for each of the officers and stepped out of the office.

"The carriers haven't been out for nine months. I've been warning the United Nations that we need time underway, but they say budget problems are limiting the funds they can give the fleet, "Admiral Morris said as he watched Kilgallon add cream and sugar to his coffee.

"All I'm saying, Admiral, is that my crews are going to need training if we are going to maintain any level of readiness."

Admiral Morris looked thoughtfully at Kilgallon and took a sip of his own coffee before speaking. "Tell you what, Frank. I'm going to take the initiative here. Let's deploy half of your ships and all the carriers for a 12-day workup starting tomorrow. Keep this information to only necessary personnel and we'll do a rapid, emergency deployment drill and sortie. Divide the ships into black and gold and run a combat exercise. I'll take the heat, but you get the men ready. Do me a favor and inform the commanders of the other squadrons involved. I'll have the orders prepared."

"Thank you, Admiral," Kilgallon said sincerely. "It's the right thing to do."

"So how is Evelyn?" Morris asked.

"She's great. Excited about the grandbaby coming. And Rose?"

"Same as always, wanting me to eat healthier," the Admiral said with a laugh. "We ought to get together this week. Maybe play a round of golf, then barbeque with the wives."

"Sounds great, sir," Kilgallon said as he sipped his coffee. Ten minutes later, he stood. "Well, sir, I better inform the Squadron Commanders."

"Very well. I'll get the sortie order ready," the Admiral said as he stood and shook Kilgallon's hand. "Make it worth it Frank."

"Aye, sir," Rear Admiral Kilgallon replied as he left the room

* * * * *

Office of the Secretary General
United Nations Headquarters, Earth
May 14, 2487, 1446 UT

When humans realized they were not alone in the universe, things changed. It was quickly determined that a planet wide system of government was needed. Although individual nations retained their sovereignty, Earth's political affairs were centralized and the United Nations changed to managed those affairs and represented Earth in intergalactic matters.

The United Nations was made up of elected representatives from its 193-member nations. With the discovery of extra-terrestrial life, the United Nations quickly determined that an executive branch of the U.N. would be needed. But a worldwide general election was not feasible. So, the representatives select the Secretary General from among its members to serve as head of the Executive Committee. Vincent Colón was selected the position in 2484 and won the respect of people around him. The heavy set, yet remarkably fit man from Mexico City endured the triumph of his selection just three years after his wife Maurice had passed away. His poise during her year long battle with cancer, while still serving as a representative was well publicized and earned him much respect.

The Secretary General entered the conference room in the newly refurbished executive wing of the United Nations. This room had a small conference table. Three chairs sat on one side of the table, the two on each end currently occupied, while the center chair was empty. On the other side of the table was an empty chair. The Secretary General walked over and sat in the chair between the other two people.

"Good afternoon," the Secretary General said.

"Good afternoon, Mr. Secretary," replied Carol Anderson. The former embassy worker who had served on Batron and considered by many to be the leading expert on Batronian affairs. She was one of only a few dozen humans fluent in their language and understood their customs and culture. She had become increasingly valuable to the Secretary General as tensions increased between the two planets. She had a silent demeanor, preferring to silently observe what was going on and offering her opinion only when asked.

"Good afternoon, sir," Alex Weber, the Minister of Earth Defense Forces said. A war hero during the War at Masic Point, twice wounded, Alex had been born in London and accepted his appointment out of sincere respect for Vincente Colón certainly not out of a desire to become entangled in politics. As former Commandant of the Naval Assault Forces, he had seen politicians in action and had little respect for the games they played, often placing their own desires ahead of what was necessary for security.

"Send in the Ambassador," the Secretary General ordered an orderly at the door. Thirty seconds later, the Ambassador from Batron entered the room. Like most Batronians, he was tall by human standards at 6'8", had gray skin and a thin, wiry form. His large, dark eyes were set apart by a strangely shaped flat nose.

"Mr. Secretary, Miss Anderson, Minister," the Ambassador said in heavily accented English, the standard language for most of Earth, nodding to each person as he greeted them.

"Mr. Ambassador, please have a seat," the Secretary General said. The Batronian sat at the table opposite of the humans. "I am under a great deal of pressure from our shipping companies because Batronian warships have been threatening our cargo ships in interstellar space."

"I'm sorry, but my government does not keep me up to date regarding military operations," the Ambassador replied carefully. "Perhaps they are concerned about weapons being shipped to Antron."

"Earth has the right to engage in free trade," Colón said.

"We don't see it as free trade. We see it as Earth arming our enemies," the Batronian replied.

"Mr. Ambassador," Alex piped in, "we are looking for a way to deescalate the situation between our worlds. Threatening to board our cargo ships or to fire on them is going to force us to send armed escorts with them. And that increases the chance of someone firing a shot, which I know neither of our worlds want."

"Mr. Weber, as long as your government continues to sell weapons to our enemy, there will be tension," the Ambassador replied.

"That, Mr. Ambassador, sounds like a threat," the Secretary General said.

"It was not intended as a threat. But I ask you, how would you feel if we armed your enemies?" the Ambassador asked. He looked at each of the humans who remained expressionless. "Your weapons are killing us!" he shouted, slamming his fist on the table in frustration. The sudden outburst caught the humans at the table off guard, but years of practice allowed Colón not to react in kind, but to remain in control of himself and the situation.

"Mr. Ambassador, please inform your government that any attempt to board any ship from Earth, or to fire on any ship from Earth in interstellar space will be considered an act of war," Colón said firmly. "That is something we are trying to avoid."

"Very well. I will pass on your message," the Batronian said.

"Thank you, Mr. Ambassador," the Secretary General said rising. The Batronian had been on Earth long enough to know that this signaled the end of the meeting, so he stood as well and then moments later left the room.

"Well?" Colón asked taking his seat again.

"He isn't bluffing. He feels they are right and if it was up to him, I think we'd already be at war. Let's just hope his government is a little more level headed," Carol Anderson said. The more she thought about the situation, the more concerned she became. She knew that the Batronians would never accept anyone assisting the Antronians in any way.

"What is the state of our military?" Colón asked turning to Alex.

"The only real forces in that sector are the Fourth Fleet and the Third Naval Assault Division. The Third Regiment is forward deployed to Omar IV and the remainder of the division is on Kylar II. Admiral Morris has decided to conduct a training exercise involving approximately half of his ships. They haven't had any real training in some time and he's concerned. I don't know where we can get the funds, but I recommend we allow the exercise," Alex said.

"Do it. We'll get the funds from somewhere," the Secretary General said as he stood. "We need to be ready for anything," he added.

"Yes, we do, Mr. Secretary," Alex answered.

* * * * *

Headquarters Fourth Fleet
Naval Base Oscar, Kylar II
May 14, 2487, 1710 Local, 2350 UT

Andrew Wilson left work just five minutes after Admiral Morris left for the day. Stepping out into Kylar's bright sun, Andrew took a breath. Kylar II was tropical year-round. The trees on Kylar II were similar to palm trees found on Earth but with black trunks. The planet consisted of two large land masses: one in the northern hemisphere and one in the southern. Naval Base Oscar was located on the smaller northern land mass and was the larger of the two naval bases in the Wise-Young sector, the other naval base being located on Omar IV. Naval Base Oscar encompassed 140 square miles. In addition to being the headquarters of the Fourth Fleet, the Headquarters of Third Division, II Corps of the Naval Assault Forces was located on Kylar II.

Walking across the lot, Andrew headed for his personal vehicle, one of the perks for working for Admiral Morris. Few single enlisted personnel on Kylar II had their own vehicle or their own apartment. But given the responsibilities he took on each day, the Admiral thought that his Administrative Assistant deserved a little comfort while off duty. It was 86 degrees out, but with the humidity it felt several degrees warmer and Andrew was sweating by the time he got to his vehicle. He got in, set the temperature to 72 and drove to the Communications Center for Naval Base Oscar just five miles from Headquarters. He parked the vehicle and waited only ten minutes before a blond-haired woman in uniform made her way from the center and got into his vehicle.

"How was your day?" Andrew asked as she got in.

"Busy," Kaitlyn Ryder, a third-class Communications Specialist assigned as a clerk in the Communications Center said. At 21, she was three years younger the Andrew. Originally from Baltimore, she was slim and attractive. Andrew and Kaitlyn met at the base club six months ago and had been together since. They were well suited for each other, both preferring quiet nights at home over partying. "With everything we have going on with Batron, we have more traffic than I've ever seen. Just sorting through it takes forever. I can imagine how crazy it must be at Fourth Fleet."

"Yeah, we've been swamped," Andrew said as he pulled out and headed toward the apartment he obtained two miles from the center. "I don't think anything will actually happen, but nothing happening seems to be creating a lot of work."

"Do you have to deploy for the exercise tomorrow?" Kaitlyn asked.

"No," Andrew said, knowing he could speak openly with Kaitlyn since she, like himself, was cleared at the highest security level. "It may require a couple of extra hours here and there but nothing else."

"Good," she replied, taking his hand. Andrew had been out on deployment only once since they started dating. It was only a month-long deployment, on a carrier in orbit above Kylar II, not even out of the system, but it was something she was in no hurry to repeat.

"So, I was thinking," Andrew said, "that we should go on a small trip this weekend. Maybe get one of those little cottages on the beach and get away from the base."

"Really? That would be great," Kaitlyn said with a smile on her face as they arrive at Andrew's apartment.

CHAPTER TWO

ESS Argentina (D-868)
In Orbit, Kylar II
May 15, 2487, 0728 UT

Above Kylar II, a series of docks orbited the planet. Each dock was a two-story rectangular platform that could handle between one and four ships depending on the size and type of the ships. Four clamps held each ship to the dock and two tunnels connected the ships to the dock allowing the transfer personnel, food and parts to and from the ships. A separate series of lines allowed the ship to refuel. Additionally, the docks provided power to the ships allowing them to shut down their engines for maintenance. Shuttles ran down from the docks to Naval Base Oscar to provide officers and crew the ability to take liberty on the planet, as well as pick up supplies to bring back to the ships.

Currently docked at dock 12A was *ESS Argentina*, a 24-year-old *Spain* class destroyer. The 680-foot-long ship, with a 125-foot beam and armed with a 125-mm main gun, six 75-mm twin gun mounts for defense against spacecraft and a total of eight missile platforms, four forward and four aft. The ship, assigned to Destroyer Squadron Ten, had a top speed of 34 AMU, just slightly faster than the carriers it protected. *Argentina* was nearing the end of her career as the navy began replacing the older *Spain* class destroyers with the newer *Norway* class.

Ensign Albert Singleton was a 2486 graduate of the Naval Academy and with only four months aboard *Argentina*, the junior officer of the ship. Currently, he was serving as Supply Officer. It was a job that fit well with his organized nature and attention to detail. For now, though, he was on watch on the quarterdeck as Officer of the Deck. The quarterdeck was where the crew entered the ship through the dock when returning to the ship and was the control center of the ship while it was docked, performing the same functions as the bridge did when the ship was underway.

By 0728 on the morning of May 15, members of the crew had returned to the ship from liberty to begin the workday. At 0730, the Petty Officer of the Watch, a second-class Communications Specialist made an announcement over the intercom.

"Quarters. Quarters. All hands to quarters for muster, instruction and inspection," the Petty Officer of the Watch announced. This was part of the normal "Plan of the Day" on the ship. At 0800, the ship would commence routine work for the day, ending the workday at 1600.

Thirty minutes until we are relieved, Albert thought. He was already planning for the day ahead. It wasn't going to be very busy, which would allow him to work on his qualifications. A voice from the comm unit interrupted his thoughts.

"Quarterdeck, Communications Central."

"Quarterdeck, aye," Ensign Singleton replied as he pressed a button on the unit.

"We have flash traffic," the voice over the comm unit reported.

"Okay. The Messenger of the Watch is on his way," Al said, nodding to the Messenger, a junior enlisted woman recently out of boot camp. Great, Al thought, with only thirty minutes to go. That thought vanished when he read the message five minutes later.

```
150524870718U

From: Commander Fourth Fleet
To: ESS Argentina (D-868)
Subj: Emergency Underway

1. Get underway immediately. Move to Grid 084
   172.
2. Report to Commander, Carrier Squadron One
   to participate in an exercise on Black team.
```

Al reached over to the Comm Unit and switched it to broadcast over the ship's intercom. "All hands prepare for emergency underway. Set the normal underway watch. On deck condition four, officers section one, enlisted section one," he said. Then he switched the Comm Unit over to Engineering. "Main Control, Quarterdeck. Light off engines and shift to internal power."

"The Officer of the Deck has shifted the watch from the quarterdeck to the bridge," a voice announced a few minutes later officially relieving Ensign Singleton and moving command of the ship from the quarterdeck to the bridge. Al began making his way up to the bridge. Like approximately a quarter of the crew, Albert had never been underway on *Argentina* and since he had no other duties at the moment, he decided to watch the operation from the bridge.

Al entered the bridge, where the Captain, Rayford McCollum, was ensuring that the ship was prepared to get underway. The Captain, a 46-year-old veteran of the War at Masic Point, always impressed Al with his seemingly unshakable confidence to command. Al watched as various crewmembers communicated to each other. The tubes withdrew from the dock, engines were brought online and thrusters readied. The navigation station, helm and sensor stations were all manned.

"XO, get us underway," the Captain ordered.

"Aye, sir," Commander Pete Williams, the Executive Officer and second in command replied. Turning to the enlisted woman on the Comm Unit, he ordered, "Unhook the docking clamps."

"Aye, sir," the woman replied. A half a minute later, she announced, "all clamps are clear."

"Very well," the XO said, then turning to another crewmember, "Boatswain's Mate, over the intercom, 'Underway'."

"Underway," the Boatswain's Mate said, the intercom carrying his voice so that everyone aboard the ship was aware of the change in status.

"Right thrusters one-third," the XO ordered the helm.

"Aye, sir," the helmsman answered, his fingers tapping the appropriate buttons on the helm. "Right thrusters are at one-third."

Looking out of the bridge windows, Al could see the ship begin to drift away from the dock.

"Secure right thrusters. Main thrusters ahead full," Commander Williams ordered. Until *Argentina* was out of the Kylar System, she would be restricted to thrusters only. The main engines were for interstellar space travel only.

Ensign Singleton watched as the ship was handled skillfully and wondered how long it would take for him to gain that level of competence.

It took almost an hour for *Argentina* to clear the system. Once cleared, Commander Williams ordered, "Secure main thrusts. All engines ahead full. Make your speed 28 AMU."

* * * * *

Naval Space Center
Naval Base Oscar, Kylar II
May 15, 2487, 0150 Local, 0830 UT

As *ESS Argentina* was leaving the Kylar system, a scramble order was issued to the spacecraft stationed at the Space Center at Naval Base Oscar. The Naval Space Center was located just two miles from Andrew Wilson's four-story apartment building.

One of the wings that scrambled was the 18th Fighter Wing consisting of 20 SF-112 fighter spacecraft. The wing was divided into four flights (Alpha, Bravo, Charlie and Delta). Lieutenant Commander Chris "C-Dog" Davenport was the newly appointed flight leader for Charlie Flight. Chris and the other pilots in his wing suited up and made their way to their fighters that were waiting on the tarmac where their crews were finishing prepping the craft for flight.

The SF-1112 was the Navy's newest fighter. Designed to intercept enemy spacecraft, the fighters were tasked to defend carriers, to escort attack spacecraft to targets and to provide air cover during assault operations. The SF-112 had a maximum speed of 125 AMU and a range of 500 AMU. It carried up to twelve missiles, either the short-range AM-2s or the long-range AM-6s. Additionally, it had a 35-mm laser gun mount and for defense, 20 decoys to fool incoming missiles.

"Any bets that I bag more kills during this exercise than you, C-Dog?" Lieutenant Donald "Dreamer" Franklin asked. Don was Chris' best friend even though Don was two years younger than the 27-year-old Flight Leader.

"There you go dreaming again," Chris teased. Don had earned the callsign "Dreamer" in flight school when he stated it was his dream to fly fighters. Chris slapped Don on the back. "This should be fun. We haven't been on a carrier in a long time."

"We sure haven't," Don replied. The 18th Fighter Wing was assigned to *ESS London* (SCV-7). The carrier had just cleared the system and was awaiting the arrival of its spacecraft.

"Time to fly," Chris said as he arrived at his fighter. The SF-112 was painted gray with "Chris 'C-Dog' Davenport" painted in large letters underneath the cockpit on both sides of the craft. A small black star beside his name indicated that he was the Flight Leader. Since the spacecraft had to fly both in space and in an atmosphere, it looked like an aircraft with a needle nose and large wings with the engines located under each wing. The body was constructed of strato-steel to prevent overheating when the craft reentered the atmosphere.

Chris climbed the ladder and lowered himself into the familiar cockpit. He pulled the straps, securing himself into position and donned his helmet. He flipped switches, checking the status of the spacecraft's system. Finally, he started his spacecraft's powerful LX-15 engines. The shipped hummed as the engines came to life. He keyed his comm unit. "Charlie Leader to Charlie Flight, comm check."

One by one, the rest of the flight replied with a "loud and clear" including Charlie Three, Don. With all systems looking good, Chris contacted the control tower. "Charlie Flight requesting permission to takeoff," Chris said professionally.

"Charlie Flight, you are cleared for takeoff. Contact SCV-7 on 186.6 when clear of Kylar II," the voice from the control tower replied.

"Roger control. Charlie Flight, Charlie Leader, takeoff pattern delta," Chris ordered the Flight. Chris toggled a switch that brought the spacecraft eight inches off the ground and retracted the landing gear, then advanced the throttle slowly. The fighter surged ahead and Chris pulled back on the control, pulling the craft into a steep 70-degree angle. He glanced left and right, spotting the rest of the flight as he accelerated into the sky. In the atmosphere, the SF-112 used control surfaces similar to an aircraft to control the spacecraft. In space, thrusters were used to simulate the control surfaces, such as the wings and rudder, and allowed the spacecraft to be handled similarly in space and an atmosphere.

Two minutes after launch, the spacecraft exit Kylar II's atmosphere at a speed of .8AMU. "SVC-7, Charlie Leader, requesting vector," Chris said changing his comm unit to 187.6

"Charlie Flight your vector is 125 by 217," came the reply.

"Roger," Chris said, turning his craft to the new heading. He watched as the rest of the flight formed up on him.

It took a half an hour to arrive at the carrier. *ESS London* was the lead ship of the London-class carriers, the only class actively serving in the Navy. To describe her as large was an understatement. She was 1700 feet long and 750 feet wide. She consisted of sixteen decks and could hold 144 spacecraft: 72 fighters, 48 attack craft and 24 miscellaneous and support craft. Painted dark gray, the ship was moderately armed with twelve 75-mm gun mounts and sixteen 35-mm anti-spacecraft guns, not a lot of firepower, but with her embarked spacecraft to defend her, a formidable target.

Chris watched as his wing began landing on the carrier. After everyone else in the wing had landed, Chris circled around and lined up for his approach to the rear of the massive ship. The flight bay was on the eighth deck. The large doors were open, extending most of the width of the ship. Using his rudder and control stick, Chris lined up with the two lights in the bay that guided him in.

"Charlie Leader, speed 26, heading 227 by 168," the control said reporting *London*'s course and speed. Chris looked at his HUD, verifying his heading was also 227 by 168 and his speed was 26.05 AMU. It was a perfect setup for final approach. As he approached the carrier, he could see red lights running across the deck of the flight bay. This line of lights indicated the beginning of the carrier's gravitation field. As he crossed the line, he activated thrusters on the bottom of his fighter that would compensate for the gravity of the ship, keeping his fighter from slamming onto the deck of the carrier. He flew into the bay, into the landing area, extended his gear, throttled down and touched down gently on the deck. As he shut down his engines, he felt the telltale sign of the clamp that ran along the deck latch onto his fighter to move the SF-112 to the parking area. A red light, changed to a flashing yellow as the bay doors closed. Once the flight bay was repressurized, the light turned green and crewmembers entered the bay to assist pilots out of the spacecraft and to begin maintenance and refueling.

* * * * *

Cargo Ship Alexander
Approaching Antron System
May 17, 2487, 1430 UT

Captain Robert Wise was the Commanding Officer of the Cargo Ship *Alexander* and was on the bridge observing his newest officer who had the conn. Captain Wise was a veteran with SDK Shipping having served as an officer on the company's cargo ships for 32 years. At 52-years-old, it wouldn't be long before Captain Wise would retire, something his wife seemed to look forward to even more than he did. As the ship, sister of the Cargo Ship *Vladimir*, approached the Antron system, the young Fifth Officer continued to order reductions in speed. "Helm, reduce speed to three AMU," he ordered.

"Reduce speed to three, aye, sir," the helmsman replied.

"Captain, we have multiple contacts moving to intercept, bearing 115 by 010," the Third Officer who was monitoring the sensor display announced.

"I have the conn," the Captain stated quickly, taking control of the ship. The ships, three Batronian destroyers, were moving into view. "All stop," the Captain ordered the helm.

"All stop, aye, sir," the helm replied.

"Earth Cargo Ship, this is Batronian Warship 90B. You are approaching a blockade ordered by the Batronian government. Reverse your course. Do not attempt to enter the Antron system," a voice announced over the short distance voice comm.

The Captain walked over to the Comm Unit and pressed a button. "Batronian Warship 90B, this is Cargo Ship *Alexander*. We have a cargo shipment destined for Antron. We are operating under an Earth charter and demand to be allowed to enter the system," he said firmly.

"Cargo Ship *Alexander*, do not attempt to enter the Antron system or you will be fired upon," came the reply. Like all civilian ships, *Alexander* had no weapons and the Captain realized he was in no position to argue.

"Helm, come to 290 by 170, speed 4 AMU," he ordered reluctantly. Turning to his Fifth Officer, he said, "You have the conn. Maintain this heading and speed. I'll send a message to corporate informing them of the situation." The heading would take them away from Antron while someone figured out what to do.

* * * * *

Office of the Secretary General
United Nation's Headquarters Earth
May 18, 2487, 0915 UT

"They what?" Secretary General Colón asked in a raised voice.

"We don't know when they set up the blockade, but they intercepted one of SDK's cargo ships, the *Alexander*, and refused to allow it to enter the Antron system," Alex Weber said.

"What do we do?" Colón asked.

"I have requested that Admiral Morris dispatch two destroyers from Omar to escort *Alexander* back to Omar. We could use them to escort the ship to Antron instead, but that would escalate the situation. I just don't want *Alexander* to think they are out there by themselves. The Admiral said he would cut the orders to the destroyers," Alex reported

"Okay. I think I'll have the Batronian Ambassador over for a chat this afternoon. Remind him of our position in this matter."

"Another issue that may or may not be related. The Cargo Ship *Vladimir* hasn't been heard from since the thirteenth when she left Omar to Kylar," Alex said.

"Have we had any incidents on that side of Omar?"

"No, sir. I think *Vladimir* may be having comm issues. That's a long way from Batron and Antron. Still, I'm having the fleet monitor the situation."

"Very well. When is she due at Kylar?"

"The 28th," Alex answered.

* * * * *

ESS London (SCV-7)
Black Team, Training Near the Kylar System
May 18, 2487, 1030 UT

The training exercises between the black and gold teams were entering their third day and were going well. Commander of Carrier Squadron One aboard London led the black team. The gold team was led by the Commander of Battleship Squadron Three aboard *ESS Dallas* (SCV-9). Rear Admiral Kilgallon was assigned as scorekeeper on Kylar II. So far both the gold and black teams had performed well, attacking and counterattacking professionally, despite the lack of experience of many members of the crews on most ships.

Lieutenant Commander Davenport and Lieutenant Franklin were the alert fighters waiting to be launched to defend *London* on a moment's notice. They sat in their fighters in the flight bay, canopies open, but ready to close and launch if needed. They had been on alert for three hours with only one more hour to go before they were relieved. If they were launched, the rest of the flight would be launched in five minutes and the whole wing could be spaceborne in fifteen. Chris was reading a book. Being an avid reader helped when you sat in a cockpit for hours at a time. Don would undoubtfully be working crossword puzzles, his favorite alert fighter pastime. Since both sets of bay doors were close and the flight bay was pressurized, *London*'s crewmembers walked freely through the bay. A light, green in color, indicated the bay was pressurized and the doors were closed.

"You awake Dreamer?" Chris asked, keying the comm unit to Charlie Flight's frequency.

"I'm with you, C-Dog. One more hour to go," Don replied. Chris smiled as he pictured Don in the cockpit. The two had a great friendship, both on duty and off. They drank and chased women on Kylar II together, hung out on the beach on weekends and trained together during the week. The two of them led the flight in "kills" during the exercise, with Chris leading Don by just two. Donald, of course, promised that would change by the time the exercise was over.

"Launch the alert fighters," a voice announced over the flight bay's intercom and was repeated on the fighter's comm unit. Chris dropped his book into a pouch hanging from his seat and toggled the switch to close the canopy without thinking about it as his instincts, sharpened by training took over. The ship's crew began to move to the clear plastic enclosures, referred to as bubbles, that would remain pressurized during flight operation and allow the crewmembers to see and direct the launching of spacecraft. The formerly green light now flashed amber and an alarm sounded directing the crew to clear the flight bay.

One crewmember, already in a bubble to Chris' right, twirled a finger in the air, signaling Chris. Chris pressed the engine start button and heard the whine of the SF112's LX-15 engines as they came online. The cockpit pressurized and Chris rotated the stick to check the directional thrusters. Then, Chris throttled his engines up and then back down. He looked at the information on his HUD checking power, fuel pressure and thrust. Everything was in the green. One of the best things about the SF-112 fighter was its reliability.

Satisfied, Chris keyed his comm. "Charlie Leader is ready to launch," he said.

"Charlie Three ready for launch," Chris heard Don say two seconds later.

The flashing amber light stopped flashing remaining on now as a steady amber light. Chris' spacecraft vibrated, almost like it was trembling as the flight bay was depressurized, the air being pumped from the bay into storage tanks to prevent it from being vented to space. The light changed from amber to red as both sets of flight bay doors opened.

"Bay ready," a voice announced over the comm. Chris focused his attention on the Signalman, who was female, in the bubble. He felt and heard the clamps release his fighter. The Signalman saluted and pointed toward the open bay door at the forward end of *London*. Chris tapped a button lifting his fighter eight inches off the deck. He throttled up sending the spacecraft down the bay and out of the door. He exited *London*, accelerated his fighter to 100 AMU, broke right and climbed up relative to *London*. He saw Don exit the ship and break left as he climbed. Coming out of the turns, the two fighters joined each other "over" *London*. It had been just thirty seconds since the launch order had been given.

"Charlie Leader, Flight Control, vector 217 by 284, distance 90 AMU. Four attack craft escorted by two fighters," the voice on the comm said. "Clear to engage."

"Roger, Control," Chris said. "Charlie Three break to vector in three…two…one…now," Chris said. Chris shifted his stick left and down, coming quickly to his new heading. The two SF-112's swung in perfect formation, Don showing his skills by precisely matching Chris' movement. The fighters closed in on the approaching spacecraft from *ESS Dallas*. The HUD identified the fighters as SF-112s and the attack craft as SA-18s. "Engage the SF-112s first," Chris told Don. Removing the fighters first would make picking off the defenseless attack craft easy, even though the attack craft were the real threat to *London*. Still, attack craft without their escorts were easy pickings.

"Roger that, C-Dog," Don replied.

"Select AM-6s," Chris ordered. The AM-6 had a range of 50 AMU and Chris desired to engage the other fighters from as great a distance as possible. Since firing a missile at another spacecraft in a training exercise was impossible, for the training exercise, a pilot "killed" another spacecraft by maintaining a weapon lock on it for two seconds.

The other fighters accelerated toward Chris and Don, leaving the attack craft behind and taking up a position between Don and Chris and the attack craft they were protecting. Chris engaged the spacecraft to the right leaving Don the one to the left. Chris got a lock on the enemy but lost the lock as the other spacecraft banked sharply fooling Chris. An alarm warned him that the enemy now had a lock on him. He broke right and pulled up, releasing a decoy and was relieved to hear the alarm stop.

He rolled hard to the right and located the enemy again. The other pilot must have been relatively inexperienced as he released two decoys before Chris attempted to engage him. Chris locked onto the SF-112 and held the lock this time.

"I have lock," Chris announced over the training comm.

"Acknowledged," the gold team pilot replied admitting defeat. It took Don nearly another minute to "destroy" the second fighter.

"Attack craft are bugging out. Switch to AM-2s and let's get them," Chris told Don.

"Roger that, C-Dog," Don replied.

The fully loaded SA-18s had a maximum speed of 100 AMU, so Chris and Don's SF-112s had no trouble catching up them. Staying out of the range of the 35mm guns on the SA-18s, Chris and Don used the AM-2s to lock on and "destroy" all four of the spacecrafts, gaining a clear victory for the black team.

"Flight Control, Charlie Leader. Vape six. Returning to the nest," Chris said proudly.

* * * * *

Naval Assault Forces Recruit Training Command
Naval Station Bravo, Mars
May 18, 2487, 1430 Local, 1530 UT

"Eyes right!" Sergeant Blake ordered as Company C051 passed in front of the inspection stand. The men and women of the training company turned their heads to the right as Sergeant Blake saluted the Reviewing Officer, the Commander of Naval Station Bravo. This was graduation day for the 48 remaining members of Company C051. "Ready, front," Blake ordered.

The company marched from the parade grounds and was dismissed to enjoy their first weekend of liberty since joining the Naval Assault Forces. Boot camp was over for these former recruits. Max Finley, Dave Roberts and Phil Moore headed to the barracks so they could change to their class B uniforms and explore the Martian city of Johnstown. When they arrived at the barracks, they found their orders were ready. Each man was handed a copy of his orders.

Phil Moore was the first to open his orders. "Third Division, Third Regiment on Omar IV," he yelled. The orders confirmed what the Pass-In-Review ceremony symbolized. He was now a member of the Naval Assault Forces. This was a huge accomplishment for the young man who had escaped the slums of Atlanta to become a trooper assigned to Omar IV.

Dave Roberts opened his orders. "Oh shit! Third Division, Third Regiment on Omar IV, baby," he said celebrating with Phil. They would continue to serve together to the surprise of the two men. Max was reading his orders quietly. "You're going too, right, Max?"

"Third Division, First Regiment, Kylar II," Max said. He was shocked that after starting their journey together, he would be leaving his friends. Like Phil, he had grown up in Atlanta. Unlike Phil, he was white and grew up not in the slums, but in a wealthy subdivision. On Earth, it was unlikely they would have ever met, but now it was hard to imagine being on duty without him.

"Oh man, I thought we'd all be station together," Phil said, his excitement suddenly gone.

"Where? Omar IV? Hey, better you two than me. I'm going to Kylar II. Women and more women!" Max said trying to change the mood. "Let's get out of here."

The three men caught a shuttle over to Johnstown. They hit the nearest bar and drinking reminiscing about bootcamp as they did. Already, their stories were taking on a larger than life feel. As they drank and talked, Max was thinking about how hard it would be not to have them around.

"At least we'll be on the transport together," Dave said.

"Yeah," Max replied trying to be strong.

* * * * *

Headquarters Fourth Fleet
Naval Base Oscar, Kylar II
May 18, 2487 1705 Local, 2305 UT

Kaitlyn had surprised Andrew by waiting for him outside of Fourth Fleet Headquarters. Admiral Morris was satisfied with the results of the fleet exercise so far and made a mental note to thank Kilgallon for the idea while they were golfing the next day. Andrew, on the other hand, had his own plans this weekend and Kaitlyn saved him time with her surprise of meeting him here.

Andrew greeted her with a light kiss on the lips.

"Surprised?" she asked.

"Very, how did you manage to get here this early?" Andrew asked.

"I have 65 days of leave I hadn't used, so I decided to burn some. Besides, if I didn't use

some soon, I'll start losing days," she replied as he led her toward his vehicle.

"65 days! Don't you ever take leave?" Andrew asked.

"Not since Comm School," Kaitlyn said with a giggle. "So now I'm on leave until the 28th."

"I wish I would have known. I could have put in for leave, too."

"It's okay. They wouldn't have approved your leave with the exercise going on anyway.

So, I figured, if it's okay, I'll stay at your apartment and you could find out what it's like to home

to your girlfriend every night," Kaitlyn said. Kaitlyn had just 18 months left on her contract and

the decision to stay in or get out depended on where Andrew and her relationship stood. The idea

of being a stay-at-home wife or mother was appealing to her, but so far, any discussion of the

future the couple had was vague, consisting of more "if's" than "when's".

Andrew opened the door and found the vehicle packed and ready to go. "You packed

already?" Andrew asked surprised by Kaitlyn.

"Yep. I didn't want to waste any of our time together," Kaitlyn said with a smile getting

in. "I've never been to a beach before," she said as Andrew pulled out of Fourth Fleet's lot.

"You grew up in Baltimore. How could you have never been to a beach?" Andrew asked.

"I don't know. I grew up in the suburbs and just never got around to it."

"Well, it will be great," Andrew said as he turned toward the exit of the base.

An hour and a half later, they pulled up to a cottage near a small village on the Eastern Ocean. Kylar II had three oceans: The Northern, Eastern and Western. The larger resorts on the Northern Ocean catered to tourists from Earth and Earth's settlements. These resorts featured nightclubs, parties and lots of drinking. The cottages on the Eastern Ocean were more private with less flash, geared towards romantic getaways and used almost exclusively by residents of Kylar II.

The cottage Andrew and Kaitlyn stayed at was small and cozy. It consisted of a large room with a kitchen area and a loft bedroom. The ocean was just 100 yards from the back door with a sandy beach covering the entire area between the cottage and the ocean. Palm trees surrounded the cottage and beach ensuring privacy. Andrew and Kaitlyn brought their bags in and set them down in the main room. Andrew was about to carry them up to the loft when Kaitlyn said, "Before we unpack, let's go for a swim." They changed into their bathing suits, then ran down the beach toward the water holding hands.

* * * * *

ESS Argentina (D-868)
Near Kylar System
May 19, 2487, 0915 UT

Ensign Albert Singleton stood alongside Commander Pete Williams on the Bridge. Onboard *Argentina*, the Captain had assigned the XO the job of training new officers for bridge qualifications. So, the XO was standing watch as Officer of the Deck while Al stood watch as Officer of the Deck Under Instruction. The two officers were studying the sensor display on the port side of the bridge. They were a contrast in appearance. The XO was short at 5'6", Ensign Singleton taller at 6'. The XO had black hair, the Ensign sandy brown. And the XO at age 46 was double the age of the 23-year-old Ensign.

"So, to protect carriers and battleships, we must detect stealth ships. But it isn't easy. In stealth mode, they are invisible both to our eyes and our sensors, unless they are traveling at a speed of say 7 AMU or more. And then they appear only as a distortion. That's why most stealth ship Captains stay at a speed of 5 AMU or less when they are in stealth mode," the XO said.

"But they cannot stay in stealth mode forever?" Al asked.

"No. The stealth ship cannot produce enough power to run the stealth system and power the ship. So, while they are in normal mode, they charge a large bank of power cells. Then, when they enter stealth mode, those cells supplement the power from the engines. But eventually, the power is used up and the ship will return to normal mode."

"How long can they stay in stealth mode?"

"Two days, maybe three if the Captain conserved energy," Commander Williams replied.

"Why not just build more powerful engines? Or larger ones?" the Ensign asked.

"Because the amount of energy required for stealth mode is proportional to the ship's mass. Bigger, more powerful engines have more mass so it doesn't solve the problem. Stealth ships are designed using as little mass as possible. That is why the armor of a stealth ship is so thin; it reduces mass."

"That's why we have the M-7 missiles?"

"Exactly. The standard M-4 anti-ship missile would pass right through a stealth ship before exploding. The M-7s are slower and have a shorter detonator," Pete told the junior officer. "If there is a stealth ship in the area, locating it and destroying it is the top priority, even over enemy spacecraft."

"Yes, sir," Al said, the lesson obviously over. Al looked around the bridge. Unlike civilian ships, the bridge of naval ships was manned heavily. In addition to the Officer of the Deck, there was a helmsman, a Quartermaster of the Watch who handled the navigation systems, a Boatswain's Mate of the Watch who was a carryover from ocean going ships and maintained the ship's log and made announcements over the intercom, and a Messenger of the Watch who ran errands for the Officer of the Deck. Additionally, there were various people on comm units to communicate with other spaces on the ship.

Commander Williams and Ensign Singleton walked over to the Navigation Station. The Quartermaster of the Watch acknowledged the XO's presence and then said, "Sir, we are ready for the turn."

"Very well," the XO replied. "Make the turn Ensign."

"Aye, sir. Helm, come right and down to new course 165 by 207," Al ordered.

"Come right and down to 165 by 207, aye, sir," the 21-year-old female helmsman replied, her hands moving over the controls executing the order. "Thrusters activated. Coming to course 165 by 207," she said.

"Very well," Al said, watching the stars shifting outside the bridge windows.

"Steady on course 165 by 207," the helmsman said a minute later.

"Very well," Ensign Singleton replied amazed that he could control *Argentina* with just his words. Of course, in reality, dozens of men and women were controlling every aspect of the ship. Crewmembers standing watches in the engine rooms, communication shack, combat information center and other spaces in the ship, worked together to keep the ship functioning. All 21 officers and 307 crewmembers had a job to do.

At noon, the Executive Officer and Al were relieved. Al grabbed a quick bite to eat and headed for the supply office, where he would try to do a full day's work by 1600.

* * * * *

Golf Course
Naval Base Oscar, Kylar II
May 19, 2487, 0820 Local, 1500 UT

The ball bounced almost perfectly in the center of the fairway, 280 yards from where Admiral Morris was standing in the tee box at the 7th hole. The ball bounced and rolled another 20 yards, stopping in the middle of the fairway, setting up an easy second shot.

"Nice shot, sir," Kilgallon said as he admired the shot. His own shot had been thirty yards shorter and in the light rough just left of the fairway.

"The gravity helps," Admiral Morris replied as Kilgallon and he began walking down the fairway. He was referring to the fact that Kylar II's gravity was only 97% of Earth's.

"The gravity doesn't make the ball go straight," Kilgallon said with a smile. The two men walked together heading for Kilgallon's ball.

"Frank, the exercise was a great idea. You made the right call," Morris said.

"Thank you, Admiral," Kilgallon replied

"We're on the golf course, knock off the Admiral stuff," Morris said. Although he currently outranked Frank, the Admiral thought of Frank more as a friend than as a subordinate. After all, they had served much of their career together and even when not serving together, still managed to stay in contact. Hell, they even met their wives together at a base club on Earth's moon while *Charleston* was being repaired at the lunar shipyard from damage sustained a little less than halfway through the War at Masic Point.

"Okay, Bill," Kilgallon said, reverting to the Admiral's preferred name. He remembered that the Admiral had once preferred Will back before Masic Point. But for many years now, it had been Bill. Bill never told Frank why the change in preference, but Frank suspected it somehow reflected the changes that both men had gone through during the war.

Kilgallon pulled out his seven iron after estimating he had about 190 yards to the flag. Morris watched him as he hit the ball. He sliced the ball causing it to land 30 yards to the right of the green, but, at least, missing the bunker.

"Not bad," Admiral Morris said. He started walking with Kilgallon toward his own ball. "Has the exercise helped?"

"Yes. Just the boost in morale alone has helped."

Admiral Morris pulled out his nine iron. He hit the ball, bouncing it on the green and leaving it just nine feet from the hole.

"Incredible," Kilgallon said shaking his head in disbelief.

"Practice," Morris said.

Later that afternoon, the two men sat on the deck of Admiral Morris' home drinking a beer. "Frank, do you think that Batron will attack us?"

"I don't think they would attack us here. Omar IV maybe," Kilgallon replied.

"That's my gut feeling too. Still, Intelligence has no idea where their fleet is. We have a cargo ship missing and another one that was turned away from Antron. Frank, the fleet is not ready. If I was Batron, I would take advantage of that," Admiral Morris said sipping his beer.

"Then, we should thank God that you're on our side," Kilgallon responded with a laugh.

Admiral Morris took a long drink. "I don't want a war, Frank."

"Me neither, Bill."

"Masic Point still haunts me," Morris said looking off into the distance. "We were just kids. Just like the crews on our ships today. Remember Ronald Allen?"

Kilgallon closed his eyes remembering the red-headed friend of theirs that was a practical joker. "Yeah, I remember."

"He was only 24. He died in my arms."

"I know. But it isn't within our ability to stop a war. We can just give these boys the best chance we can," Frank said.

"True. Well, let's get them ready, Frank," Admiral Morris said.

"We are. The exercise is helping," Frank replied as the door from the house opened and the two wives stepped out on the porch. Rose and Evelyn had been friends long before they married Frank and Bill.

"You better stop talking shop on my back deck," Rose told the Admiral sitting on his lap as Evelyn sat on Frank's.

"Aye, ma'am," Morris said with a laugh knowing his wife was the boss here.

* * * * *

Cottage
Eastern Ocean, Kylar II
May 19, 2487, 1925 Local, 0205 UT

Andrew and Kaitlyn strolled along the beach as the sun set opposite of the ocean. Kaitlyn, wearing a blue bathing suit was nicely tanned even before she came to the beach. As they walked, together, the smile never left her face. Kaitlyn looked so different without her uniform, Andrew noticed, softer and more feminine. He never tired of seeing her this way.

"I am so happy," she said. She looked it. Not only the smile, but her body language in general showing a perfect continence that made Andrew pleased that they were able to make this trip.

"So am I," Andrew replied. They stopped and he kissed her on the lips. His heart was pounding and his hands were clammy.

"What's wrong?" Kaitlyn asked. *Don't let him be deploying*, Kaitlyn silently prayed.

Andrew looked into her eyes and took her hands in his as he got down on one knee. Tears streaked down her face as she answered his question.

* * * * *

Naval Space Center
Naval Base Bravo, Mars
May 21, 2487, 1300 Local, 1200 UT

A total of twenty troopers boarded the transport spacecraft destined for Kylar II, including Max, Dave and Phil. Dave and Phil would catch an additional transport to Omar IV from there, while Max would report for duty on Kylar II. The men passed their duffle bags to a cargo handler, then boarded the spacecraft, the three sitting together for one last time.

"You know, we're all assigned to Third Division. We'll probably all end up on either Kylar II or Omar IV together eventually," Phil said. Ever since they had read their orders, Phil had been trying to focus on the three of them together again.

"Yeah," replied Max even though he had a gut feeling that they would never serve together again. He was not wrong.

The TP-5 Transport Craft (Personnel) could carry roughly a hundred people. However, counting the crew, there would only be 27 people on this flight to Kylar II. The spacecraft had a maximum speed of 80 AMU and a range of approximately 2400 AMU before needing to refuel. Since Kylar II was only 1452 AMU away, the craft could make the trip without refueling even though the trip would take approximately eighteen hours. Because flights on TP-5s could be so long, each craft had two crews. Each crew consisted of a pilot, copilot and two cabin stewards. One crew slept in a small cabin just off the flight deck, while the other crew operated the spacecraft.

A few minutes after boarding, the spacecraft lifted off. The twenty troopers fresh from boot camp were nervous and the nervousness showed itself as the troopers talked and joked into the night, while the eight troopers who were not fresh out of boot camp slept. Few of the new troopers

slept at all during the eighteen-hour trip.

CHAPTER THREE

Naval Space Center
Naval Base Oscar, Kylar II
May 21, 2487, 2330 Local, May 22, 2487, 0600 UT

The TP-5 landed at Kylar before midnight locally, making it still the 21st although for the troopers arriving on the transport, it felt like it was a day later. The twenty former recruits grabbed their duffle bags and headed to the terminal. Eight of the troopers, including Dave and Phil would board another TP-5 in twenty minutes to take the 28 ½ hour flight to Rankus where they would refuel. After that, they would fly another 28 hours to Omar IV.

Max said goodbye to Dave and Phil, and then headed outside with nineteen other troopers that were reporting for duty either with the First or Twentieth Regiment of First Division. The night air was humid, especially after fifteen weeks in the dry Martian air, though it was significantly cooler. The sky was clear and Max could see the Hammond Nebula cluster in the sky above Kylar II. Palm trees seemed to be everywhere in contrast to the very few trees that had been planted in the Recruit Training Command for the Naval Assault Forces dome on Mars. The troopers noticed a man standing beside a transport vehicle outside of the terminal.

"Okay, I'm going to take you over to the division headquarters. So, load up," the duty driver, a nameless corporal ordered. The twenty troopers boarded the ground transport and ten minutes later, they headed forHeadquarters Third Division, II Corps of the Naval Assault Force.

The transport took a road north on the naval base. Twenty minutes later, they entered a gate with the Third Division's crest on top of it. The entire Third Division complex was surrounded by a fence, separating it from the remainder of the naval base and providing security for the troopers. Third Division's headquarters was a large four-story building two hundred yards and directly in front of the main gate. It was painted bright white, with well-maintained landscaping and the largest building in Third Division's complex. To both sides and behind headquarters were clusters of T-shaped buildings, three buildings in each cluster. Each housed a battalion of troopers, one company to each floor, and one platoon in each wing. The First Regiment's barracks were the ones to the left of headquarters. Third Regiment's, to the right, sat empty since it was forward deployed to Omar IV. The Twentieth Regiment's barracks were behind the headquarters.

Max and the other troopers went into headquarters and turned in their orders. They were processed quickly, unlike when arriving in boot camp, where processing took many hours. Max was assigned to Second Platoon of Company A, Second Battalion. After the twenty troopers were processed, another corporal took them around, dropping each of them off at the proper barracks.

Max enter the building for Second Battalion. Company A was on the first floor and Second Platoon was in the north wing. It was just after 0100 local time when Max entered the barracks. It was a standard setup with twelve cots on each side of a long open room, with footlockers at the end of each cot. Two long tables separated the two rows of cots. At the far end of the barracks was a door that led to the head and one that led to an office where Max could see a Sergeant standing at the door, signaling for him to come. Max walked down the barracks to the Sergeant and followed him into the office. The Sergeant shut the door and sat at a desk in front of Max.

"You are Private Finley?" the Sergeant asked.

"Yes, Sergeant," Max replied formally.

"I'm Sergeant Wesley. I'm your platoon sergeant." Sergeant Steve Wesley was the poster child of a Naval Assault Force Trooper. At 5'10", he was a fit 180 pounds, toned, muscular and tanned from his time on Kylar II. He was a "lifer" with eight years of service already and recently signing up for his third four-year hitch. He had a firm demeanor, with a set jaw and tattoos covering both arms. He presented himself like a Sergeant you would see in the old Masic Point movies. The only thing the Sergeant lacked was combat experience.

"Nice to meet you, Sergeant," Max said.

"Well, it's too late to do anything tonight. Your bunk is the only empty one. Linen is in the footlocker. Why don't you get some sleep? Revile is at 0600 and we'll go over everything then."

"Aye, Sergeant," Max said. He left the office and went back into the dimly lit room. He opened his footlocker quietly, removed the linen and made his cot, perfectly tight, with hospital corners as he had been doing everyday since joining the Assault Forces. Then he went to the head, brushed his teeth and returned to his bunk and went to sleep.

* * * * *

Apartment Building 14
Naval Base Oscar, Kylar II
May 22, 2487, 0445 Local, 0925 UT

Although Kaitlyn was on leave, she still got up early to help her fiancé get ready. *Her fiancé*, she thought with a smile as she cleared the breakfast dishes. Andrew was dressing in his freshly pressed uniform. Andrew had offered to help clear the dishes, but Kaitlyn was enjoying doing the domestic duties. *I'm going to be his wife*, she thought looking down at her engagement ring.

"So, what are you going to do today?" Andrew asked as he came back into the room. Being on the Admiral's staff, his uniform was kept in perfect shape. He was always clean-shaven and had his hair cut to exact military standard. Two rows of ribbons were on his chest, mostly unit citations. The only two individual awards he had were his good conduct medal and his space service ribbon.

"I want to go to the exchange and see about getting new dishes," she said. As part of their engagement, she would be moving in with Andrew. Like most bachelors, Andrew had few dishes and none that matched, a point that Kaitlyn had teased him about on numerous occasions since they had started dating.

"Okay," Andrew said with a chuckle holding his hands up as if surrendering. "Do you want to use the vehicle today?"

"Yes, if it's okay," she asked. She had only borrowed his vehicle on one other occasion, although Andrew had offered on several other occasions. Now that she was moving in, Kaitlyn felt more comfortable borrowing it. After all, by the time her leave was over it would be their apartment and their vehicle.

"Yes. You can just drop me off and pick me up at 1730. I'll comm you if anything changes," Andrew said as he poured one last cup of coffee. The couple sat together enjoying the last few minutes alone as Andrew drank the coffee.

They left the apartment at 0515 and Andrew walked into the office at almost exactly 0530. He started the coffee and retrieved the overnight dispatches. He knew it was going to be a long day when he saw the first one. *Why wasn't I informed?* he thought, not for the first and unfortunately, not for the last time.

When Admiral Morris arrived at 0700, Andrew immediately handed him that dispatch. Admiral Morris read it and ordered, "Get me Rear Admiral Kilgallon."

"Aye, sir," Andrew said. He walked out to the reception area and using his comm unit contacted Headquarters Destroyer Squadron Ten and told the Duty Officer to locate Kilgallon and have him report to Admiral Morris immediately. While waiting for Kilgallon to arrive, Andrew anticipated the next thing the Admiral would want and prepared a message for all Fourth Fleet ships. Rear Admiral Kilgallon showed up at 0735 and Andrew led him into the Admiral's office.

"Have a seat, Frank," Admiral Morris said, "and read this." Kilgallon read the dispatch in stunned silence. A ship, *ESS Mexico (D-866)* had collided with a stealth ship operating in stealth mode inside of the Omar system.

"Wow. I assume it wasn't one of our own stealth ships," Kilgallon said.

"No. We are assuming it was Batronian. No one else in this sector has stealth ships, and we can think of no one who would travel out here from anywhere else that has them," the Admiral said. "Of course, the bastard blew up so we can't say for sure."

"So, what do we do?" Kilgallon asked.

"If the Batronians were operating a stealth ship in the Omar system, they may be operating them anywhere. A stealth ship, hell, a warship of any kind, operating inside of any of our systems is a violation of our territory and we would be justified to fire on it."

"Yes, we would, sir," Frank replied. As much as he didn't want the situation with Batron to escalate, Admiral Morris was correct. Moving a warship of any type into another planet's territory was certainly an aggressive act. And a stealth ship, whose entire purpose was to remain hidden, raised all kinds of red flags.

"Wilson, come in here," the Admiral ordered through the comm unit. Andrew enter the office. "Prepare a message for the fleet to be on the lookout for any stealth ships in any of our systems. If they are detected, they are free to engage it."

"Aye, sir," Andrew said and then handed Admiral Morris the message he had already prepared.

"You're good, Wilson," the Admiral said signing the message.

* * * * *

ESS Argentina (D-868)
Near Kylar
May 22, 2487, 1415 UT

Commander Williams assembled the officer of *Argentina* in the wardroom. The officers reported in over a period of fifteen minutes, most arriving in groups of two or three. Ensign Singleton, like most of the officers, assumed that the officer's call was regarding the ongoing exercise. Albert was nervous hoping that he had not performed too badly. His ship handling skills, he admitted to himself, weren't the best, but he was improving. He felt he was good at navigation and his skills with the sensor equipment had become excellent. Still, Al was hoping that he wouldn't be singled out for any deficiencies.

"Gentlemen, have a seat," the XO ordered as he entered the wardroom. The officers took their seats around a large table with the XO sitting at one end. After everyone was seated, Commander Williams passed around copies of the dispatch the ship had received. Al carefully read the message. Like most of the officers at the table, he had to read it twice to make sure he was reading it correctly.

```
220524871402U

From: Commander, Fourth Fleet
To: All Fourth Fleet Ships
Subj: Update of Rules of Engagement

1. On 5/21/2487, ESS Mexico (D-866) collided
   with a stealth ship operating in stealth
   mode in the Omar system.
2. The stealth ship was not part of Earth's
   fleet.
3. Any stealth ship, not belonging to Earth,
   operating in any of Earth's systems is to
   be immediately challenged and engaged.
```

"Wow," the First Lieutenant said, reading the message for a second time.

"Our assumption is that it was a Batronian ship operating illegally in the Omar system. They are the only beings in this sector that have stealth ships other than us. We will be returning to Kylar II on the 25th. When we approach the system, we will be keeping our eyes open. We are setting extra watches," The XO said. "The First Lieutenant will be the Officer of the Deck and have the conn. Ensign Singleton, you will supervise the sensor techs and monitor the sensors. Forward missile launchers will be loaded with M-7 missiles and Fire Control will be manned. Any sign of a stealth ship and we will pursue it, understood?"

"Yes, sir," the officers of *Argentina* said together.

* * * * *

Home of Admiral Morris
Naval Base Oscar, Kylar II
May 23, 2487, 1930 Local, May 24, 2487, 0210 UT

Admiral Morris sat on his front porch smoking a cigar and drinking a glass of ice tea as he watched the sunset. His wife Rose sat beside him as she had done so many times over the years watching him closely. She could see the stress clearly on her husband's face. She knew this was one of the times he couldn't tell her exactly what was going on, but it was clear something was bothering him.

"Can you talk about it?" Rose asked softly.

"I don't think we can avoid a war," Bill told her puffing on the cigar. He couldn't tell her about the collision that led him to that conclusion, but the conclusion itself wasn't classified.

"That isn't a failure of yours," Rose said in a soft voice.

"No, but it's my boys that will have to go into harm's way. And I can't help but think of what I would do in Batron's place. What if they were the one providing weapons to a planet we were at war with? Wouldn't we be upset?"

"I remember once when you were a Lieutenant during Masic Point, one of your men asked you a question regarding the war. You said that those decisions were above your paygrade. Bill, there are some decisions that aren't yours to make. You can only do your duty and let your boys do theirs," Rose said placing her hand on his arm.

"You're right," the Admiral said. He took a drink of his ice tea and puffed on his cigar, pausing to flick the ash. "But, I remember what it was like. War is much different than what these boys think. It is a terrible burden."

"You were where they are now and when war came, you adapted."

"I had no choice. And neither will they. Just the same I wish I could spare them the lesson."

"So, do I," Rose replied. "And I hate to bear the nights alone again, wondering where you are and are you hurt. It's tough, but I married you knowing that the Navy was in your blood. So, if we must do this one more time, we'll do it together," Rose said with such sincerity that it touched the Admiral.

What a great wife I have, Bill thought. He took one last puff of his cigar, put it out and then swallowed the last of his ice tea as he rose from his chair.

"I think we've talked enough about a war. Besides, I know something better we can do than talk," he said with a twinkle in his eyes.

"Aye, sir," Rose teased, getting up and walking inside.

* * * * *

Naval Space Center
Naval Base Quebec, Omar IV
May 25, 2487, 0136 Local, May 24, 2487 2236 UT

The TP-5 arrived less than five minutes behind schedule, impressive considering the long flight and stopover. After three days on transports, Dave Roberts and Phil Moore, as well as the other six troopers, were more than ready to get off the transport.

Omar IV was a terraformed planet that had no indigenous life. In fact, when it was discovered in 2239, it barely had an atmosphere. Shortly thereafter, it was selected for terraforming and became a very earthlike planet with a variety of climates across its single land mass. But despite its similarity to Earth, it was never heavily populated. There were only four major cities with populations of about 75,000 each. With the smaller towns and villages, there were still less than a half of a million people on the planet that had a land area roughly twice that of Asia. But that was why the few people who lived there chose it. Even the largest cities were not as crowded as any of the major cities on Earth were.

Naval Base Quebec was the only naval base in the Young-Wise sector beyond Kylar. It was less than a quarter of the size of Naval Base Oscar. It had eight orbiting docks that could support up to 32 naval ships, although only four ships were currently docked there. It had been a long time since the navy kept more than a dozen ships at Omar IV. The base could support a regiment from the Naval Assault Forces and currently the Third Regiment of the Third Division

was posted there. The Twentieth Regiment was scheduled to relieve them in eighteen months.

The eight troopers left the transport and found a Sergeant waiting for them. He quickly

separated them by Battalion, then Company and finally by Platoon. Then, he marched them to the

appropriate barracks. Dave and Phil were both assigned to First Platoon of Company C, First

Battalion. Each barracks building was a single-story hut with twelve sets of bunkbeds. Dave and

Phil went inside and were met by a Corporal who took their orders and pointed out their bunks.

"You better grab some sleep," the Corporal said. Despite their exhaustion, Dave and Phil

grabbed a shower before hitting their bunks. Three days on transports without access to a shower

meant that the shower was even more important than sleep.

Reveille came at 0600 for the Platoon. The troopers quickly introduced themselves to Dave

and Phil. Dave and Phil quickly used the head, made up their bunks and were dressed for breakfast

within fifteen minutes, quicker than the troopers around them. It was a sign of men fresh out of

boot camp. They were so used to being constantly pressured to go faster, that when arrived in the

field they were still moving as if in boot camp.

First Platoon marched over to the chow hall, then headed back to the barracks to get their

L-29s and headed out to the firing range.

The Platoon Sergeant, Pavlo Pachenko was a 27-year-old Russian. He was solidly built at

6'2" and 215 pounds. "Let's see what you two can do," he said to Dave and Phil. They took up

their positions on the line, placed new charge packs into their weapons, ensured their weapons

were in single-fire mode and flipped the safety off.

"Ready on the left…ready on the right…ready on the firing line, "Sergeant Pachenko said.

"Fire!"

Dave focused on a target 175 yards away and fired off five rounds, all five hitting the center of the target. He switched to another target at 100 yards and again fired off five rounds. This was followed by targets at 150, 125 and 200 yards. Every round that Dave fired found its target. Phil managed twenty-six hits, missing twice at 200 yards and once each at 150 and 175 yards. While not perfect, it was certainly respectable.

"Cease Fire!" the Sergeant ordered. He turned to Dave and said, "Nice shooting."

"It's easy compared to shooting on Mars. The heat makes everything miserable," Dave said.

"Ain't that the truth," Sergeant Pachenko said with a chuckle. Dave and Phil removed the power pack and put their safeties on. They fell back and watched the next set of troopers' fire.

"That was impressive," Phil whispered to Dave.

"Thanks. More luck than anything," Dave replied modestly. "Not bad yourself."

"Yeah," Phil said looking around. The planet was so green after seeing the rusty color of Mars for fifteen weeks. It was surprising to a lot of people, including Phil, that Mars was never terraformed, but by the time the technology was available, Mars had been settled for hundreds of years and terraforming would have destroyed everything that was there and it was decided that the historical value, as well as forced relocation of the residents of Mars, was too great of a sacrifice. Still, with cool air, a fresh breeze and beautiful trees, it could easily be argued that terraforming Mars should still be done regardless on the historical impact and convenience of the residents.

"Can you believe it? We made it, Dave," Phil said as he looked around.

"Yeah, I know. It's incredible."

Sergeant Pachenko walked over to them. "Okay, you two are going to be assigned to first squad. That's my squad. On Monday, we're going to do a squad versus squad exercise. Pay attention so you don't get yourselves hurt."

"Yes, sergeant," the two men replied.

"I wonder how Max is doing," Phil sad as Sergeant Pachenko walked away.

"I'm sure he's fine. Probably settled in by now," Dave replied.

* * * * *

ESS London (SCV-7)
Near Kylar
May 25, 2487, 0814 UT

Captain Barney Novak, Commanding Officer of *ESS London* was not a happy man. A former fighter pilot during the War at Masic Point, he had worked had to earn his position as Commanding Officer of a carrier, especially the lead ship of the current class. While the embarked spacecraft performed in an outstanding manner during the training exercise, he saw a lot of deficiencies with his inexperienced crew, especially in damage control drills. Because of this, he had requested permission to keep the ship out for an extra 36 hours for additional training time for his crew. Assembled in the wardroom were the officers of *London*. He read the evaluation he had received from the Commander of Carrier Squadron One. "So why was our performance so bad?" he asked.

"Sir, I think it's a lack of time underway. We can't expect the crew to perform well when the ship is always in dock. For much of the crew, this was the first time they were out in space.," the First Lieutenant suggested.

"True," the XO said. "But, another problem was not having people assigned to positions properly. This was an oversight by us officers. Being in dock for such an extended period led us to become complacent and not worry about the underway watches. Some of the crew were not sure where their Battle Station was. Some watches were not properly staffed. But, I think for the most part, those problems are resolved. Now we just need practice."

"Good, I just got us approved for an extra 36 hours. Let's put the hours to good use Set up a training schedule and let's get busy," the Captain said.

* * * * *

ESS Argentina (D-868)
Entering Kylar System
May 25, 2487, 0827 UT

ESS Argentina entered the Kylar system with additional watches set as the Captain had ordered. The Port Lookout was posted in a clear dome structure on the port side of the superstructure allowing the lookout to clearly observe the entire port side of *Argentina* as well as above and below the lookout. The unobstructed view made the lookout feel like they were floating in space. Boatswain's Mate Apprentice John Bennett was stationed as the Port Lookout as the ship entered the Kylar System. John had enlisted in the Navy just six months ago and had reported to *Argentina* in March. This was the first time he had been underway on any ship and the first time he had been stationed as a lookout. With the extra watches set throughout the ship, his Chief had posted him here. He looked around amazed at the sight of the stars all around him. *Talk about an office with a view*, he thought.

While John had enjoyed the naval service for the most part, to him it was a means to an end. His ambition was college and then owning his own business. His time in the service would help finance that. But even he had to admit, being in space was a far different experience than being in dock, one that was much more exciting. While he still planned on getting out, he knew he would never forget what it was like at this moment.

On the bridge, the First Lieutenant had the main engines secured and engaged the main thrusters as the ship began the journey to the docks of Kylar II. Albert Singleton watched the sensor display with the Chief Sensor Technician. They had the sensors tuned to one of the most sensitive settings and while the computer was able to filter out most of the debris floating around in the system, the chief and Al had to filter out some manually. Still, if a stealth ship was out there, they wanted to find it and that meant using a high sensitivity setting even if it was a little more inconvenient.

"Report," the XO said to Al.

"Nothing on the sensors," Al said watching the display carefully. The XO glanced over to the Captain who was seated on the starboard side of the bridge. The tension was high on the bridge, not knowing whether there was a stealth ship out there watching them right now.

John Bennett peered through the scope he was issued as lookout searching for anything.

* * * * *

Batronian Stealth Ship
Kylar System
May 25, 2487, 0834 UT

It was a short circuit in a fan unit. A small problem on a ship, but enough to short out the power system for a mere five seconds and start a small fire. The short tripped a number of systems and interrupted the stealth system briefly.

The Engineering Officer saw what was happening and quickly responded. He isolated the circuit to the fan and reset the remainder of the power systems, including the stealth system, which put the ship back in stealth mode. But, for a mere three seconds, the ship had transitioned from stealth mode and into normal mode.

On the bridge, the Captain also reacted immediately, changing course and engaging the main engines to accelerate to a dangerous 2 AMU while in a system. But, he knew his ship had have been detected by the destroyer that they had been observing. Now he knew they were the ones being observed.

* * * * *

ESS Argentina (D-868)
Kylar System
May 25, 2487, 0834 UT

John Bennett was looking at just the right spot at the right time. Suddenly, a ship appeared out of nowhere. He stared for a full second, his mind shocked by the sight. *What the hell?* he thought to himself, with such surprise that he almost said it aloud. Then he reached for the comm unit.

On the bridge, the sensor display showed the ship, the computer seeming confused and like John took a full second before labeling the ship "UNK" on the display.

"Sir, we have an unknown ship, bearing 081 by 017, distance 621! Course 040 by 038, speed 1650!" Al shouted to the Officer of the Deck. "It appeared out of nowhere!"

"Bridge, Port Lookout! Ship bearing 290 by 350 relative, distance 600!" John Bennett was heard shouting on the comm unit. The relative bearings indicated the ship was slightly above and to the left of *Argentina.*

"I lost contact!" Ensign Singleton shouted.

"He disappeared again!" John Bennett reported over the comm.

"I have the deck," Captain McCollum said as he stood. He felt a rush of adrenaline and had quickly came to the correct conclusion that for some reason a Batronian stealth ship had revealed itself in the Kylar system. There was no reasonable explanation why it was here and why it entered normal mode, however briefly. But, remembering the orders they had just received, he pressed a button on the comm unit beside his chair. "Fire Control, Bridge. Fire missiles one and two along last known track."

"Aye, sir," the Fire Control Officer replied. Two seconds later, he said, "Sir, missiles one and two away, thrusters only."

"Very well," the Captain replied calmly despite the fact he had just fired on another ship. It was the first time since Masic Point that he had fired a weapon at a real target. "Helm, come to course 080 by 015."

"Come to 080 by 015, aye, sir," the helm answered, fingers moving over the console to carry out the orders. Thirty seconds later, the helm announced "Steady course 080 by 015."

Another minute passed. Every person on the bridge seemed to be holding their breath in anticipation of what would happen next. Al and the Chief Sensor Technician watched the display carefully. Al just knew that missiles would be fired from the Batronian ship and was waiting to issue the warning. "Sir missiles one and two detonated, no hits," the Fire Control Officer reported.

"Target last known position and fire missiles three and four," the Captain ordered. He knew it was unlikely, knew that the ship had moved on, but he was desperate.

"Missiles three and four away," the Fire Control Officer said. The two missiles exploded a few minutes later, Captain McCollum knowing they missed even before the Fire Control Officer confirmed it.

"Okay, I'll prepare an Action Report. XO, you have the deck. Search the area Ensign Singleton, keep a close eye on the sensor display. XO if you find it, take the shot," the Captain said as he exited the bridge.

"I have the deck," the XO said. Like the Captain, he had served at Masic Point, but as an enlisted crewmember. He had gotten out of the Navy, received his degree and then accepted his commission as an officer and reentered the service.

Boatswains Mate Apprentice John Bennett looked at the spot where the last two missiles exploded. His heart was pounding and his hands trembling from the adrenaline rush. Suddenly, he could think of no job he wanted more than this one. And that quickly, all thoughts of college left his mind.

CHAPTER FOUR

Apartment Building 14
Naval Base Oscar, Kylar II
May 25, 2487, 0445 Local, 1125 UT

Andrew's alarm clock went off at 0445 waking Kaitlyn and him. He reached over and shut off the alarm.

"Already?' a tired Kaitlyn asked.

"You can sleep in," Andrew said giving her a kiss.

"And miss my last day of sending you off to work? I don't think so," she teased. Andrew and Kaitlyn both had the weekend off and she would return to duty on Monday. "Get ready. I'll start the coffee," she told Andrew.

Andrew admired Kaitlyn's naked body as she slid out of bed and put on a robe. By the time Andrew went to the head and got dressed, Kaitlyn had the coffee poured and English muffins ready since neither of them were big breakfast eaters. *I could get used to this,* thought Andrew.

"Do you need the vehicle today?" Andrew asked as he bit into a muffin.

"No. I am going to relax and enjoy my last day off. I'll make you dinner though," she replied.

"We could eat out," Andrew offered.

"No. This is the first week I have ever got to do the domestic thing and I kinda like it."

"I'm glad you do. I can't wait until you are my wife," Andrew said sipping his coffee.

"Me neither," Kaitlyn said glancing down at her ring.

"Well, I better head in," Andrew said, smiling and pleased that Kaitlyn was so happy. He loved watching her look at her ring. She thought he didn't notice, but he did. He didn't want to say anything because he was afraid it would embarrass her and she would stop doing it. Kaitlyn walked him to the door and gave him a kiss goodbye.

Andrew arrived at Fourth Fleet Headquarters at 0530. He retrieved the dispatches and began reading. The third message he read stunned him.

```
250524870841U

From: Commanding Officer, ESS Argentina
(D-868)
To: Commander, Fourth Fleet
Subj: Action Report

1. On May 25, 2487 at 0834 UT, lookouts and
   sensors noted a ship exiting Stealth Mode
   for a period of approximately three
   seconds and then return to stealth mode
   inside the Kylar system.
2. ESS Argentina, on my authority and in
   accordance with message 220524871402U,
   fired four missiles at said ship with
   negative impact.
3. ESS Argentina is remaining in the area in
   an attempt to relocate the stealth ship.
```

Why wasn't I notified? Didn't we just address this with the message about Mexico *hitting the stealth ship. The Admiral himself had told the clerks that we should be alerted to anything of this nature. So why?* Andrew asked himself as he checked the time. The message was almost four hours old! He connected to Admiral Morris' home on the comm unit.

"Yes, Wilson?" the Admiral said.

"Admiral, you are needed here, sir," Andrew said using a phrase that would relay the urgency to the Admiral and allowing Admiral Morris to know it wasn't something to be discussed on an open comm unit.

"On my way," the Admiral replied understanding that Andrew would not be wasting his time if it wasn't something urgent.

* * * * *

Barracks 2nd Platoon, Company A, 2nd Battalion, 1st Regiment
Naval Base Oscar, Kylar II
May 25, 2487, 0530 Local, 1210 UT

Max Finley was awoken when Sergeant Steve Wesley sounded reveille at 0530. Max was well settled into his platoon after just a few days. Although he wasn't as close to anyone as he was with Dave and Phil, he got along well with the other troopers of his platoon and was considered a good trooper. The routine was still military, but far less high paced and stressful than bootcamp. He found himself enjoying the life of a trooper as much as he had anticipated.

"Everyone, outside and ready for chow in fifteen minutes," Sergeant Wesley said.

Max made his way to the head, relieved himself and then splashed water on his face.

"Early mornings suck," a trooper beside at the sink said.

"Yeah, but it's better than bootcamp," Max replied. It was common on Mars, during training to be woke up at 0300 or 0330.

"True," the trooper said.

Max made his way out of the head, dress in his fatigues and put on his boots, then he headed outside. A few minutes later, the platoon was in formation and marching to breakfast.

* * * * *

Headquarters Fourth Fleet
Naval Base Oscar, Kylar II
May 25, 2487, 0550 Local, 1230 UT

Admiral Morris arrived at the office and Andrew handed him the Action Report from *Argentina*. Then, Andrew poured the Admiral a cup of coffee as Admiral Morris read the message. The concern on his face as he read was apparent to Andrew.

"This is four hours old. Why wasn't I notified when it came in?" the Admiral asked, face red with anger.

"I don't know, sir. I contacted you as soon as I received it," Andrew said.

"Have we heard anything else from *Argentina*?"

"No, sir. I just checked."

"Well, if there was a stealth ship, it is long gone by now. Send a message ordering her to dock. And have someone from Intelligence and check her sensor data and see what they think," Morris ordered.

"Aye, sir," Andrew replied as he sat down to prepare the message.

* * * *

ESS Argentina (D-868)
Kylar System
May 25, 2487, 1241 UT

Argentina received the message to break off and dock at 1241 UT. Ensign Singleton was relieved to hear this. Long after the adrenaline rush wore off, the realization hit that his ship had fired upon another ship. That ship could have fired back and that was a sobering thought. *We could have started a war,* he realized.

At 1318, *Argentina* approached Dock 4B orbiting over Kylar II. The ship was now under the steady hand of her Captain.

"Port thrusters to half," Captain McCollum ordered.

"Port thrusters to half, aye, sir," the helm responded. The helmsman was a 26-year-old female crewmember who was qualified as a Master Helmsman, allowing her to perform difficult maneuvers, such as docking or underway replenishing.

"Main thrusters stop," the Captain called out.

"Main thrusters stop, aye, sir," the helmsman replied, her fingers dancing expertly over the controls.

"Secure port thrusters."

"Secure port thrusters, aye, sir."

"Extend docking clamps one and four," Captain McCollum ordered the First Lieutenant who pressed a button on a separate console.

"Docking clamps one and four extended and locked onto the dock," the First Lieutenant announced.

"Very well. Extend docking clamps two and three," the Captain said.

"Docked," the Boatswain Mate of the Watch announced over the intercom as he flipped switches that changed the pattern of *Argentina*'s running lights to indicate to surrounding ships and spacecraft that she was docked and therefore unable to maneuver.

"Connect the tubes," the Captain ordered the First Lieutenant once docking clamps two and three were secure. The tubes were extended to create tunnels to permit movement of people and material between the ship and the dock.

"Ensign Singleton, set your watch on the quarterdeck," the Captain ordered.

"Aye, sir," Al said. He led the Petty Officer of the Watch and the Messenger of the Watch off the bridge. It took four minutes for them to make their way to the quarterdeck adjacent to the forward tube. Once they were in position and ready, Al had the Petty Officer of the Watch announce over the intercom, "The Officer of the Deck has shifted the watch from the bridge to the starboard quarterdeck."

The Petty Officer of the Watch opened the door to the tube. Two First Class Operation's Specialists stepped from the tube to the quarterdeck and saluted Al. "Request permission to come aboard," they said in unison.

"Permission granted," Al said returning their salute.

"I'm from Fourth Fleet Intelligence and I need to speak with the Captain," the taller of the two men said. Al contracted the Captain who met the two and took them to the bridge. Twenty minutes later, they left with copies of *Argentina*'s sensor data. Al was slightly nervous knowing that they would be reviewing the data. *Was there any indication of a stealth ship prior to it appearing? If so, are they going to question my ability on the sensor display since I didn't catch it?* Al wondered. He knew that if they found anything that he should have seen, the least he would receive would be a Letter of Reprimand. *That would be a fine start to my career.*

* * * * *

Fourth Fleet Headquarters
Naval Base Oscar, Kylar II
May 25, 2487, 0656 Local, 1336 UT

Admiral Morris was smoking a cigar in his office when his comm unit chimed. "Yes, Wilson?"

"Sir, Fleet Intelligence confirmed *Argentina*'s findings. There was indeed a stealth ship and none of ours were in the Kylar system at the time," Andrew said.

"Very well. Send Rear Admiral Kilgallon in," Morris replied as he puffed on the cigar.

"Aye, sir," Andrew replied. He turned to Kilgallon and nodded, then Kilgallon got up and headed for the door.

"Frank, come in and have a seat. I assume you've heard about *Argentina*'s encounter this morning?" Admiral Morris asked as Kilgallon sat down.

"Yes, sir. I found out after I got in. Someone should have notified me immediately," Kilgallon said.

"That makes two of us," the Admiral replied. He pressed a button on the comm. "Bring us coffee, Wilson."

"Aye, sir," came the reply.

"So, two things. First, we need to find out why neither of us were notified when this message came in. We can't allow this to happen again. This is the second time it has happened this week," Admiral Morris said.

"I agree, sir," Kilgallon said as the coffee arrived. Andrew poured two cups and left the room.

"Secondly, I think we need to deploy a couple of destroyers in the system to watch for any additional stealth ships. It is obvious that Batron is operating them both here and in the Omar system."

"I have been considering that myself and am concerned. A stealth ship operating inside a system will be incredibly hard to find. Inside a system, they would be on thrusters only and operating at that slow of a speed…hell, I don't know. It would be tough," Kilgallon said.

"How did *Argentina* spot it?" Admiral Morris asked sipping his coffee.

"I hate to say this, but mostly luck. We're not sure why the ship went into normal mode briefly, and I do mean briefly. Apparently just three seconds. Fortunately, *Argentina*'s Captain had set extra watches and had his forward missile launchers ready. A sharp lookout and a new Ensign on the sensor spotted it when it appeared. They fired two missiles in seconds, but apparently the stealth ship reacted quickly as well," Frank said.

"The carriers are returning tomorrow afternoon. I want some destroyers watching as they enter the system. Our carriers would make a beautiful target for a stealth ship. Let's get two destroyers underway first thing in the morning. And we'll send out a few more as the carriers arrive. We're going to have to come in to make sure that we don't miss anything. Let's meet up here at 0800," Admiral Morris said.

"Aye, sir," Kilgallon replied formally.

"And tell Evelyn that I'm sorry for pulling you in on a Saturday," Morris added.

"I will. No reason for me to be the target of her rage," Frank replied with a laugh.

* * * * *

System Monitoring Center
Naval Base Oscar, Kylar II
May 25, 2487, 0714 Local, 1354 UT

The System Monitoring Center was a non-descript, white, single-story building located in the north western corner of Naval Base Oscar. It was connected to a huge sensor array located on the highest mountain on Kylar II, over 750 miles from the Monitoring Center. The entire Kylar System was monitored from here.

Sensor Technician Apprentice Frank Wieman had just graduated from Sensor Technician School at Naval Base Bravo on Mas two weeks ago. At school, Frank had learned to operate, and if necessary, repair sensor arrays and equipment. But as anyone could tell you, theory was one thing, experience was another. To resolve this dilemma, the Navy had new personnel stand watches "under instruction" of someone more experienced. So, Frank was standing watch under the instruction of a Third Class Sensor Technician, who himself only had a year and a half of experience. For the most part, monitoring the Kylar system was boring. Today, they had watched several ships returning to dock from the fleet exercises, including *Argentina*. But, unlike *Argentina*, they didn't catch the stealth ship on their sensors. The long-range sensors used by the Monitoring Center needed time to detect and plot the position of objects and three seconds just wasn't enough time.

"That can't be right," the Third Class Sensor Technician said as a large group of small dots appeared on the display at the edge of the system.

"That looks like over a hundred spacecraft," Frank said watching the dots moving into the system rapidly.

"Yeah. It has to be an error in the array," the technician said as he began adjusting the display to try to correct the problem. "It's probably just some of the spacecraft returning from the carriers and the array is messing up and plotting them repeatedly."

Frank thought about this. He had never heard of such a problem and based on his knowledge, while admittedly limited, he could see no way that could happen. Still, he was the one being trained and felt the Third Class Technician may have encountered a similar problem before. Unfortunately, Frank was wrong. "What do we do?" he asked.

"I'll call it into Intel anyhow just to cover my ass," the technician said. "Intel, this is the Monitoring Center. We have multiple spacecraft inbound," he said over the comm.

"Very well," the Intelligence Officer replied. "It's probably spacecraft returning from the carriers," he added confirming the Technician's thought. The Intelligence Officer was busy reviewing the sensor data from *Argentina*. His distraction may have been the reason he never thought to ask how many spacecraft had been detected.

* * * * *

ESS Argentina (D-868)
In Orbit, Kylar II
May 25, 2487, 1404 UT

Ensign Singleton was on the quarterdeck thinking about how much work he would have during the next week. For such a short deployment, the ship had gone through a lot of supplies, mainly food, and that meant a lot to replenish. *These ships used to deploy for six or even nine months,* Al thought, shivering at the idea of trying to keep the ship supplied for such a long deployment. Even though it had been almost an hour since she had docked, *Argentina* still had not shut down her engines and switched to dock power. Al wondered why it was taking so long. In the end, it was a miracle that she hadn't.

Outside of the ship, forty spacecraft had broken off from a group of 108 and turned toward the ships docked in orbit above Kylar II. Of the 78 ships assigned to Fourth Fleet, 47 were docked at Kylar II at 1404 UT on May 25, 2487, including six battleships, eight cruiser and all eight assault ships. As the Batronian spacecraft approached the dock, they broke into smaller groups and began to fire their missiles. Al was knocked off his feet when one of those missiles hit *Argentina* on the port side. He rose slowly, trying to figure out what had happened.

"Quarterdeck, CIC," a voice from the ship's Combat Information Center said over the comm. "We are under attack! Multiple spacecraft! This is not a drill!"

"Sound General Quarters!" Ensign Singleton ordered the Petty Officer of the Watch whose eyes were wide in surprise. The petty officer moved to the comm unit and selected the intercom.

"General Quarters! General Quarters! All hands man your battle stations! This is not a drill!" he announced, then, pressed a button sounding the klaxon. He then repeated the announcement. Al waited anxiously for the bridge to be manned so that he could move to his own battle station.

"The Officer of the Deck has shifted the watch to the bridge," Al heard over the intercom after what seemed to be an eternity. He dismissed the Petty Officer and Messenger of the Watch and, heart pounding, began making his way to his Battle Station, which was the sensor display on the bridge. Another explosion rocked the ship as Al arrived on the bridge.

"We need to get underway!" the Captain yelled. "Retract the tubes!"

Al checked the sensor display and was shocked at what he saw. There were spacecraft and missiles everywhere! He glanced out of the bridge windows. Two of the forward 75-mm twin gun mounts were already returning fire. He watched in stunned silence as a Batronian spacecraft exploded from one of their bolts.

"Tubes retracted," the First Lieutenant reported.

"Unhook all docking clamps!" Captain McCollum ordered crossing the bridge. He approached Al and said, "Report, Ensign."

"Sir, we have approximately forty spacecraft attacking the fleet. Numerous missiles are still being fired," Al said as he checked the display. His mind was racing as he attempted to sort through the data and determine if any of the missiles were heading toward *Argentina*.

"I need a safe course. Find me one," McCollum ordered.

"Aye, sir," Al replied automatically. The Chief Sensor Technician assisted Al whose hands were visibly shaking.

"Docking clamps clear," Al heard someone say.

"Sir, recommend course 216 by 318 when able," Al said trying to sound confident.

"Very well. Helm come to 216 by 318, main thrusters to full," the Captain said. He pushed a button on his comm unit. "Damage Control Central, Bridge, I need a damage report."

"Sir, we have been hit by two missiles. The first missile hit the port side forward. We have fires in the forward crew berthing and the machine shop is venting to space. The second missile hit port side aft. The aft lookout tower sustained heavy damage and is open to space. There are several fires in adjoining compartments," the Damage Control Assistant reported. "We have numerous injuries and at least twelve crewmembers are missing."

"Very well," the Captain replied.

"Captain, two missiles inbound, starboard side," Al said as he watched the missiles approaching on the sensor display.

* * * * *

Naval Assault Force's Obstacle Course
Naval Base Oscar, Kylar II
May 25, 2487, 0728 Local, 1408 UT

The obstacle course on Kylar II was located in a secluded area on the eastern side of the Third Division's compound and was approximately seven miles from the Space Center. Three ground transports had brought Second Platoon of Company A out to the course, each transport carrying one squad. Max was assigned to Second Squad with Corporal Joseph Hanks as Squad Leader. Corporal Hanks was a 22-year-old from Baltimore who had just signed up for his second tour. A fit 165 pounds and sporting a flat top cut, Hanks would be a perfect trooper for a recruiting poster.

Second Squad had just started its run on the course. Although Kylar's gravity was less than at the Recruit Trainng Command on Mars, even a little less than Earth's gravity, the course was testing Max's endurance. Max had just climbed on top of a 15' wall and holding the rope, he swung his leg over the top when he heard the roar of fast moving spacecraft overhead. He looked up and saw dozens of spacecraft flying over the course.

"Hey, those aren't ours," he heard someone say as the spacecraft headed for the Space Center. As he watched, Max saw something fall from the spacecraft and then there were several explosions.

"Oh, shit!" Corporal Hanks shouted. "Get off the course and into the transport!"

Max quickly climbed down from the wall, dropping the last five feet. He took off in a dead run for the transport, heart pounding as he heard more explosions in the distance. *Batron!* he thought as he ran.

* * * * *

Kaitlyn was chopping onions when she heard the Batronian spacecraft pass overhead, followed almost immediately by a huge explosion, shaking the four-story apartment building and rattling the windows. Kaitlyn hurried over and looked out of the window thinking that a spacecraft had crashed nearby. As she watched in horror, a missile hit the control tower at the Space Center. She saw bombs falling from other craft as more explosions shook the building.

Sirens began to wail as Kaitlyn ran for the door. Kaitlyn stepped into the hall and saw several people in the hall, mostly spouses of service members and their children. Everyone looked confused and several of the younger children were crying.

"Everyone, get to the ground floor. Use the stairs," Kaitlyn said leading the group to the stairwell.

* * * * *

At the sound of the first explosions, Admiral Morris ran out of his office into the reception area where both Andrew and he ran to the window. He saw the spacecraft, the missiles flying and the bombs dropping and his heart fell. *They caught us with our pants down*, the Admiral thought.

"Oh, God," Admiral Morris said as the sirens on the base sounded warning of the attack. He regained his composure. "We need to evacuate the building," he said to Andrew. The Admiral went over and set off the fire alarm knowing that would be the quickest way to get the building evacuated.

Andrew led Admiral Morris to the stairwell and rushed down the steps. Exiting the building, Andrew saw the devastation first hand as the bombs and missiles landed around the base. Fires burned, buildings collapsed and screams could be heard. He looked up and saw two Batronian spacecraft descending toward him. He watched as each of them launched two missiles that seem to pass just feet over his head. All four slammed into the Fourth Fleet Headquarters. The explosions knocked Andrew to the ground knocking the wind out of him and slamming his forehead into the ground.

* * * * *

ESS Argentina (D-868)
Kylar System, Near Kylar II
May 25, 2487, 1409 UT

"Launch decoys, starboard side," the Captain ordered. "Right thrusters to full. Bow thruster down full." Captain McCollum was surprised at how it all came back to him. The battles at Masic Point had molded him into a competent officer even in the midst of a battle.

"Decoys away, sir," the XO said after pressing the button to launch decoys, which emitted heat and electrical activity in an attempt to confuse the sensors of incoming missiles.

"Right thrusters to full, bow thrusters down full, aye, sir," the helmsman responded.

Al glanced up from the sensor display and out of the bridge window as the ship turned. As the docks came into view, his eyes widened in shock. Ships were burning and docks were heavily damaged as Batronian spacecraft darted about. Bolts from ships and missiles from spacecraft passed each other in space. As Dock 10 came into view, *ESS Einstein (B-36)*, a battleship still connected to the dock by two clamps suddenly exploded. Debris from the ship shot in all directions and Al could hear pieces of *Einstein* hitting *Argentina*'s hull. The flash from the explosion was bright enough to force Al to turn his head. He looked back down and saw the two missiles heading toward *Argentina* disappear from the display and breathed a sigh of relief.

"Captain, the missiles hit the decoys," Al said. He quickly assessed the information on the display. "Recommend course 221 by 312."

"Very well. Helm come to 221 by 312," the Captain ordered. Al felt more confident as the Captain continued to accept his recommendations with question or hesitation.

"Come to 221 by 312, aye, sir," the helm answered. As the ship turned, the docks passed from Al's view and the empty void of space filled it.

* * * * *

Apartment Building 14
Naval Base Oscar, Kylar II
May 25, 2487, 0730 Local, 1410 UT

When Kaitlyn descended to the third floor of the building, she exited the stairwell and found a woman struggling with a child, who appeared to be around three-years-old, while carrying infant. The child was screaming and crying as the building shook, sirens wailed and power failed. Kaitlyn ran over and picked up the toddler. The child struggled in her arms, but Kaitlyn refused to let go.

"We have to hurry," Kaitlyn told the grateful mother as she led her to the stairwell. The odor of smoke was beginning to fill the air causing Kaitlyn to wonder if the building was on fire. Another nearby explosion shook the building and glass shattered somewhere in the building. The girl in Kaitlyn's arm was trembling and crying, though no longer struggling to get free.

Entering the stairwell, they headed for the ground floor.

* * * * *

Near Fourth Fleet Headquarters
Naval Base Oscar, Kylar II
May 25, 2487, 032 Local, 1412 UT

Andrew slowly made his way back to his feet. Wiping his forehead with the back of his hand, he discovered he had been cut. Without thought, he wiped the blood on his white trousers. Admiral Morris steadied him and asked, "Are you okay, Wilson?"

"Yes, sir," Andrew said, although he was dizzy and confused. He looked around watching as a pair of Batronian spacecraft fired missiles into the Headquarters for Carrier Squadron One and the building disappeared into a cloud of smoke and fire. The ground shook as Andrew watched two bombs fall hitting the lot near the base's commissary.

"How did this happen?" Admiral Morris wondered aloud appearing completely shaken by the attack. This was his command, his responsibility. *Yet, I didn't see it coming. Not today at least.*

"I don't know, sir," Andrew replied. He was scared as more explosions occurred. He felt like crying. He had been trained and knew that combat was a real possibility in his career, but somehow, he felt overwhelmed and completely unready for the real thing.

Admiral Morris seemed to snap out of his shock and took charge. "I need you to get over to communications and ensure that a message went out broadcasting the attack," he ordered, confidence returning to his voice.

"Aye, sir," Andrew said. He ran to his personal vehicle, which, to his surprise, it was undamaged. He began making his way to the Communications Center. At first, he was excited that he could check on Kaitlyn, but then he realized she wasn't at the center. She was still at the apartment.

* * * * *

The transport came to a sudden stop and Corporal Hanks ordered everyone out. Max jumped out and looked around. Just minutes into the attack and the Space Center was already heavily damaged. Obviously, the Batronians were trying to prevent any spacecraft from being launched by Earth. The control tower and several hangars were destroyed and burning. A Batronian spacecraft dropped down and released several bombs striking the tarmac and exploding sending debris high in the sky and destroying two of Earth's spacecraft on the ground.

Inside the Space Center Complex was Earth's anti-spacecraft missiles and BA-75 anti-spacecraft guns. In theory, they were always on the ready with charge packs standing by.

"Finley, Sabastian, over there," Corporal Hanks ordered pointing to a BA-75 gun. Max ran toward the gun placement, trailed by Carlos Sebastian, an 18-year-old Private from Houston. As they ran, another spacecraft exploded on the ground, destroyed by a Batronian bomb and adding to the sense of urgency for the two men. They arrived at the large gun. The gun consisted of a gunner's seat in front of a long barrel. The gun fired a 75-mm bolt up to 5000 yards. Each round was fired by a separate charge so a loader was needed to continuously feed charges into the gun. A good team could fire 40-45 rounds a minute.

"You load," Max yelled as he slid into the gunner's seat. He removed the safety guard that covered the trigger and flipped the switch that provided power to the motor that allowed him to rotate and elevate the gun. Carlos opened the case containing the charges for the gun. By the time Carlos loaded the first charge, Max was tracking a Batronian spacecraft. Max fired a round, missing the craft. *Not leading it enough*, Max thought. He fired again, this time leading it too much. Max fired once again, missing the spacecraft as it climbed out of Max's range.

Carlos slammed another charge into the gun. He was sweating profusely as he loaded the gun. "Just relax," Carlos said trying to encourage Max.

Max turned the gun to the left and firing at a spacecraft just as it released its bomb. Max watched as the bolt struck the spacecraft. It turned had right, the pilot trying to recover, then turned over and tumbled out of the sky, crashing near a burning hanger.

"Yeah!" Carlos shouted as the rumble from the bomb rattled the ground around them.

* * * * *

ESS Argentina (D-868)
Near Kylar II
May 2, 2487, 1415 UT

Laser fire shot from *Argentina*'s gun occasionally hitting one of the Batronian spacecraft. More ships were managing to get underway and Al was trying to keep *Argentina* clear from both enemy spacecraft and friendly ships. The sensor display was cluttered with dots indicating ships, spacecraft and missiles so that both Al and the Chief Sensor Tech had their hands full.

Out the bridge Window, Commander Pete Williams could see most of Earth's ships had been hit at least once and most were badly damaged. Several were adrift, some burning and some launching escape pods as the crews abandoned ship.

"Captain, a second wave of Batronian spacecraft is inbound for Kylar II. I count 112 craft," Al reported.

"Shit!" Captain McCollum shouted as he pressed a button on the comm unit. "Communications Shack, Bridge. Send a flash message to all stations. Second wave of 112 spacecraft inbound."

Commander Williams came over and studied the sensor display. "Captain, I recommend we move the ship between Kylar II and the incoming craft," the XO said. "We can't stop them all, but maybe we can disrupt their formations and throw off their timing."

"Very well. Give me a heading, Ensign," the Captain said.

"112 by 290, sir," Al replied.

* * * * *

ESS London (SCV-7)
Near Kylar System
May 25, 2487, 1417 UT

Lieutenant Commander Christ Davenport sat in the cockpit of his SF-112. He had been the alert fighter along with Don Franklin since 1200 and had watched the flight bay crew run several drills, including a fire drill. He took the time to watch them since he only had one chapter left in the book that he was reading and was trying to save it until just before he was relieved at 1600.

"Launch the alert fighters," came the command over the comm. *Funny*, Chris thought as he toggled the switch to close the canopy, *I didn't think they were launching spacecraft for these drills*. A twirling finger came from a crewmember and Chris started his LX-15 engines. Minutes later, Chris was racing out of the bay and taking up station above *London*.

"Charlie Leader, Flight Control. The Batronians are attacking Kylar II. We need you to set up a combat patrol. The rest of your flight will be joining you shortly. This is not a drill. This is not an exercise," the Flight Controller said.

Oh shit, Chris thought as he responded, "Flight Control, Charlie Leader, copy all," He switched to the Flight's comm frequency. "Dreamer, let's spread out a little until the rest of the flight joins us."

"Okay, C-Dog," Don replied, banking left while Chris banked right. Each took up a position ½ AMU from *London* both shocked at the sudden change in the circumstances. Chris, like all the pilots his age, had no combat experience and while always being trained to prepare for combat, it never really occurred to him until just now that there could be a war. Suddenly, all the jokes about who would get more kills didn't seem so funny.

"Ensure your weapons are live," Chris told Don as he toggled his own weapons switch.

"Aye," Don replied as he flipped several switches. "Weapons are hot."

CHAPTER FIVE

Office of the Secretary General
United Nations Headquarters, Earth
May 25, 2487, 1417 UT

Vincente Colón sat at his desk preparing for his weekly lunch with members of the General Assembly. One of his favorite parts of the job, this involved meeting with his colleagues informally, without the pressure of politics and discuss Earth's real needs. He found that many times, the best work was done during these lunches. And, of course, the food served at these lunches was top notch. As he was preparing to leave, his comm unit chimed.

"Yes?" the Secretary General asked his Administrative Assistant.

"Defense Minister Weber is asking to see you. He says it's urgent," came the reply.

"Send him in," Colón said. Alex entered the room briskly closing the door before he spoke.

"Mr. Secretary General, Kylar II is under attack by Batronian spacecraft. Damage to Naval Base Oscar and the fleet appears to be severe," Alex said, the stress clear in his voice.

"They what?" Colón exclaimed running his hand through his thinning gray hair.

"Sir, we have confirmation through multiple sources."

Colón press the button on the comm unit. "Cancel all of my appointments," he ordered his Administrative Assistant. He turned to Alex. "Have the Batronian Embassy secured. No one is permitted to leave the Embassy. I will arrange for the Batronians to be transported back to Batron at my earliest opportunity."

"Already working on securing it, sir," Alex replied having known this attack would require those measure as a first response. He was still in shock at the news. The fleet appeared to be caught completely off guard and Alex knew the casualties would be high.

"Get the First Fleet underway just outside of our system to protect Earth." The first fleet was headquartered at Naval Base Alpha in Houston, TX with the fleet in docks above Earth. Like the rest of the navy, unfortunately there hadn't been the funds to keep training up. However, with a direct attack against one of Earth's systems, precautions had to be made. "All available ships," he added.

"Yes, sir," Alex replied.

"Recall all military personnel and active all reserve units," Secretary General Colón said. "God help us."

* * * * *

Near Fourth Fleet Headquarters
Naval Base Oscar, Kylar II
May 25, 2487, 0738 Local, 1418 UT

The intensity of the attack seemed to be subsiding as Andrew made his way back to Admiral Morris. As Andrew told him that the message had been broadcast to the fleet as well as to the Minister of Defense, the Admiral pulled out a cigar and lit it. A Third Class Master-at-Arms, equivalent to a civilian police officer, arrived and saluted Admiral Morris.

"Sir, headquarters for both Carrier Squadron One and Battleship Squadron Three have been destroyed. Destroyer Squadron Ten's headquarters have been damage, but should remain standing," the Master-at-Arms reported.

"Survivors?" the Admiral asked.

"At least a few from Carrier Squadron One. I imagine the same with Battleship Squadron Three. Destroyer Squadron Ten should be better," The attack had practically seemed to stop, although a few Batronian spacecraft were descending and strafing personnel with lasers.

"Very well, dismissed," Admiral Morris said. The master-at-arms saluted and left quickly. "Wilson, go over to the Space Center and get me a damage report."

Aye, sir," Andrew replied as he turned toward his vehicle.

* * * * *

ESS Argentina (D-868)
Near Kylar II
May 25, 2486, 1418 UT

"Here they come!" the XO exclaimed as the 75-mm guns began firing at the incoming spacecraft. Several were hit by *Argentina*'s guns and many more were forced to break formation to avoid being hit as they passed by. The spacecraft zipped over, under and around *Argentina*. As the XO observed, he noticed that the gunners seemed to be missing more than they should. During the War at Masic Point, he was on the 75-mm guns and the accuracy of the gunners appeared much better than now. *But had it been at the beginning of the war?* he asked himself.

"Bring her about!" the Captain ordered.

"Aye, sir," Commander Williams said. "Helm, come to 243 by 170."

"Captain, the first wave of spacecraft is leaving Kylar II. I show their heading 110 by 290," Ensign Singleton said as he watched both waves carefully on the sensor display.

"Very well. XO, make sure we are concentrating on the second wave. Ensign Singleton, track the spacecraft from the first wave. Maybe we can figure out where their carriers are." It was obvious to all that the spacecraft had to have come from carriers since there were no bases close enough to Kylar II to launch the spacecraft from.

"Aye, sir," Al replied.

Captain McCollum watched as *Argentina* came around and was shocked at the condition of the rest of the fleet. Most of the ships were severely damaged, many now drifting in space. *ESS Peru (D-860)* was entering Kylar II's atmosphere and quickly became engulfed in flame as the heat of reentry enveloped the ship. Ships were never intended to enter a planet's atmosphere and the result was catastrophic. Flames surrounded the ship and pieces broke off as the ship began tumbling. It would be too late to use escape pods, so all Captain McCollum could do was pray that they abandoned ship before the ship hit Kylar II's atmosphere. The Captain watched as half of the Batronian spacecraft from the second wave began firing on the tattered fleet.

"Missiles inbound forward!" Al shouted studying the sensor display.

"Decoys," the Captain replied. "Left thrusters to full. Bow thrusters up full."

The ship began to turn slowly. The gunners adjusted their laser fire, bolts steaking out from the 680-foot long ship's six 75-mm twin gun mounts. An explosion from a missile that hit one of the decoys shook the ship. The second missile struck the forward part of the ship. A blast of bright light filled the bridge window. The explosion rocked the ship, knocking most of the bridge crew off their feet. Power failed leaving the ship dark for a few seconds before emergency lighting came on.

* * * * *

Apartment Building 14
Naval Base Oscar, Kylar II
May 25, 2487, 0740 Local, 1420 UT

When she had first started dating Andrew, Kaitlyn had noticed a door labeled "Emergency Shelter". It had never occurred to her that she would one day need it. Now, she led the others through the door and into the basement of the building. As they emerged from the stairs, they found a large room with emergency supplies including water and first aid kits.

"What happened?" a woman asked Kaitlyn.

"I think Batron is attacking us," Kaitlyn replied.

"Why?" the woman asked as she began to cry.

"I don't know," Kaitlyn said. She placed the toddler on the floor near her mother. Like most of the servicemembers on the base, Kaitlyn noticed that the attack had slowed. "I am going to see if anyone else is in the building," she told the young mother, then headed to the stairs. She looked down at her engagement ring as she began to climb the stairs. *Please God, let him be okay,* she prayed silently.

* * * * *

Enroute to Naval Space Center
Naval Base Oscar, Kylar II
May 25, 2487, 07411 Local, 1421 UT

Andrew was racing as fast as he could toward the Naval Space Center. He could see from a distance that the control tower was gone. Smoke was rising from several areas of the Space Center, thick and black. Like everyone else, Andrew noticed that the attack had stopped, but he also knew that there was no all-clear signal and that meant the attack wasn't necessarily over.

His hands were shaking. *How could this happen with no clear warning?* he asked himself. He couldn't help but wonder *how many people died today? And what about Kaitlyn?*

Andrew never looked up, so he didn't see the second wave of Batronian spacecraft descending as they approached the Space Center. Hell, he didn't even know that there was a second wave. And he didn't see the lead craft release the bomb that exploded directly in front of his vehicle. The explosion blinded him as the vehicle rolled three times before coming to a stop as blackness overtook Andrew.

* * * * *

Near Fourth Fleet Headquarters
Naval Base Oscar, Kylar II
May 25,2487, 0742 Local, 1422 UT

Admiral Morris, cigar in mouth, walked in the open as the second wave hit, in what appeared to be as an open defiance; almost as if he was daring the Batronians to shoot at him. Missiles and bombs poured down around the heart of the naval base. Explosions near and far roared as the attack began in earnest again. *How did I miss this?* Admiral Morris asked himself.

"Admiral!" a familiar voice called out from behind him. Turning around, Morris saw Rear Admiral Kilgallon, his uniform covered with dust and debris.

"Frank, you are a sight for sore eyes. Are you okay?"

"Yes, sir," Frank answered looking around. "They got us good, didn't they?"

"Yeah," Admiral Morris said watching as another missile struck a building in the distance. "Now we'll have to make the bastards pay."

"I agree," Frank said. "But, we are being hurt badly. He looked up and saw a ship burning as it streaked across the sky, a ship that was never built to enter a planet's atmosphere. It burned bright looking like a meteor. Most of the ship would burn up during reentry and what remained would hopefully hit the ocean. If it did crash into land, it would mean even more casualties and most likely, civilians at that.

"God help us," Admiral Morris said as he too, watched the falling ship.

* * * * *

Naval Space Center
Naval Base Oscar, Kylar II
May 25, 2487, 0743 Local, 1423 UT

Max Finley opened fire on two spacecraft that descended on the space center as part of the second wave. The BA-75 spit out bolt after bolt, chasing after the spacecraft. Carlos was drenched in sweat as he continued to load charges for Max. The charges were heavy and after firing scores of shots, Carlos was wearing down. Only fear and adrenaline kept the young man going. Two additional spacecraft appeared on the horizon heading toward Max's position. *Damn, these things are fast*, Max thought as continued to fire. He saw a bomb drop from one of the spacecraft as it passed over him.

"Incoming!" Max shouted as the bomb dropped toward him. He leapt from the gunner's seat and dove to his left with Carlos landing right beside him. A flash of light, a deafening explosion and an intense heat surrounded him seeming to fill the entire world. Max closed his eyes and covered his head, curling into a ball in an attempt to make himself smaller as debris fell on and around him. Then, Max felt someone shaking his shoulder and saw Carlos, his mouth moving but producing no sound. *I can't hear*, Max realized as he began to panic. Max struggled to his feet, shaking his head. Slowly, sound started returning as he looked at the destroyed gun.

* * * * *

Batronian Attack Spacecraft 1842
Over Naval Base Oscar, Kylar II
May 25,2487, 0743 Local, 1423 UT

The Batronian pilot watched his bomb explode, taking out the gun, then banked his spacecraft to the right, lining up for a run on his primary target, the control tower. Coming out of the turn, he realized that the control tower had been destroyed in the first wave. He reached for his targeting computer and selected his secondary target, a large hanger to the right of the control tower. He brought his craft to the appropriate heading and quickly determined the secondary target had also been destroyed. Apparently, the attack was more successful than anticipated. A stream of laser fire forced him to bring his spacecraft to the left.

With both the primary and secondary targets destroyed, the pilot's orders were to find a "target of opportunity". He scanned the Space Center looking for a target. Other than some 75-mm guns that were firing at the spacecraft, which wasn't large enough to bother wasting his two missiles on, he saw nothing else at the center. He brought his spacecraft to the left searching beyond the center. He saw a four-story building that appeared undamaged. He locked his missiles onto the building and fired both of them, then brought the nose up and banked left. He saw both missiles slam into the base of the building and watched it collapse.

Thrilled by his success, but out of weapons, the Batronian put his spacecraft into a steep climb and headed back into space.

* * * * *

Naval Space Center
Naval Base Oscar, Kylar II
May 25, 2487, 0744 Local, 1424 UT

Max had just gotten back to his feet when he saw the missiles in the building in the distance and watched it collapse.

"Here!" he barely heard Carlos say although it was obvious that Carlos was yelling as he handed Max his L-29. As Max loaded a charge pack into his weapon, he could once again begin to hear the rumbles of bombs and missiles exploding and the noise of lasers being fired, though just a dull roar compared to what it should be. *I hope I haven't lost my hearing forever*, he prayed.

"Corporal Hanks wants us to help over there!" Carlos shouted, pointing to where the building had collapsed.

"Okay," Max said. Carlos and Max began to make their way to where a pile of debris was standing where Apartment Building 14 had stood.

* * * * *

Barracks Third Regiment, First Battalion, Company C, First Platoon
Naval Base Quebec, Omar IV
May 25, 2487, 1725 Local, 1425 UT

On Omar IV, the working day had ended and First Platoon was getting ready for liberty. Phil and Dave were planning on heading over to the enlisted club with a few other members of the platoon to shoot pool and drink a few beers. Since arriving at Omar IV, the two had quickly befriended several other members of the platoon, many of which were amazed with Dave's skill with the L-29. Dave and Phil had already showered and were dressed in their civilian clothes, ready to leave as soon as the others were ready. It was a hot day on Omar IV, with temperatures reaching the low 90s, so a cold beer sounded perfect.

"You ready?" one of the other troopers asked.

"Yeah," Dave replied. As he stood, he saw Sergeant Pachenko jump up from his desk and dart from the office into the barracks.

"We just got put on alert level delta," the Sergeant said. Delta was the highest alert level for naval bases. It required that all personnel be recalled to the base. The base was placed on lockdown so that no one left the base and all ships that were able to were to get underway were to do so.

"What? On a Friday evening they want to run a drill like this?" Phil asked. He had looked forward to getting to know the other troopers better.

"It's not a drill. Batron has attacked Kylar II. We're going to war," Sergeant Pachinko said.

"Shit!" several people said. Everyone quickly started to change back to their uniforms. Minutes later, a Private showed up with cases of extra charge packs for the L-29s.

* * * * *

ESS Argentina (D-868)
Near Kylar II
May 25, 2487, 1426 UT

Boatswain Mate Apprentice John Bennett was assigned to Repair Locker Two during General Quarters. Repair Two was responsible for damage control for the forward part of the ship. John was in a pressurized suit making his way forward to where the last missile had hit. Electrical power was still out and the emergency lighting cast strange shadows hindering the already reduced field of vision offered by the damage control suit. John was a hoseman on the #1 firehose team. This was hard work since the hose was heavy and hard to maneuver through the narrow passageways of the ship. Thankfully, John hadn't been out of bootcamp long enough to lose the extra strength you gained during it like most naval personnel did as they served on ships.

The team arrived at a door leading to a storage locker. As the Team Leader opened the door, flame shot from the room passing over the head of the Number One Hose Team. John instinctively ducked his head as the Number Two team turned on a low velocity stream creating a mist to shield the Number One Team from the flames. The Number One Nozzleman turned on the hose on high velocity and aimed at the base of the fire, sweeping left and right. The team moved forward into the compartment advancing on the fire and dousing the flames. John was sweating as he helped drag the hose into the space.

"I need a reflash watch," the team leader said. A crewmember advanced with a portable fire extinguisher, her job to be sure the fire didn't reignite when the remainder of the team exited the storage locker and moved to the next space.

On the bridge, Commander Williams was on the comm unit with the Chief Engineer.

"Power will be restored shortly," the Chief Engineer reported.

"Thrusters?" the XO asked

"Working on it. That last missile interrupted the fuel flow somewhere. As soon as we determine where, we'll know more," the Chief Engineer said.

Commander Williams looked out the bridge windows. The Batronians were well outside range now, so her guns were silent, although they could fire at any time since each gun mount had its own backup power system. Every time Pete saw the destruction surrounding Kylar II, he felt like he just took a punch to the gut. *They really caught us with our pants down*, Pete thought as he watched the explosions where missiles struck more of Earth's ships. As he stared at the destruction surrounding Kylar II, the lights came back on.

Down below, John Bennett felt blinded by the lights when they suddenly returned. The hose team had arrived at the Forward Thruster Control room, a compartment that was not normally manned. It was located at the forwardmost part of *Argentina* on the second deck. The team leader opened the door to the space and air was immediately sucked from the passageway, an indication of a hull breach in the Thruster Control Room. John's suit increased pressure automatically to protect John in response to the change of air pressure caused by the hull breach.

Looking into the compartment, a liquid was flowing from a broken pipe and through a hole that was approximately four feet around in the hull of the ship. Damage to the deck, bulkheads and overhead, as well as to the pumps in the room, indicated that this was where the missile had hit.

"Secure that leak," the team leader ordered a crewmember pointing at the ruptured pipe. The crewmember came forward and followed the pipe back to a cutoff valve and shut the valve stopping the flow of fuel.

"Okay, let's get a patch on that hole," the team leader said. The hose handling team laid the hose down as a large 5' by 5' piece of metal was brought forward. The damage control team wrestled the patch into position. Once the patch was in position, a Second Class Hull Technician came forward with a welding torch and tacked the patch to the hull.

John looked at the sensor on his wrist and watched as air pressure began to rise. Looking around the room, John could see that the damage to the forward thruster controls was severe and even without much mechanical knowledge, knew that it would not be easily fixed. Another fire team showed up to relief John's team who were running low on oxygen and need to return to the repair locker to get new canisters.

On the bridge, Commander Williams got word from the Chief Engineer that the forward thrusters were out of commission. *Argentina* would need a tow home.

* * * * *

Remains of Apartment Building 14
Naval Base Oscar, Kylar II
May 25, 2487, 0750 Local, 1430 UT

Carlos and Max approached the collapsed apartment building, sweating heavily by both the stress and the run. As they approached the building, it seemed unlikely that there would be any survivors. Corporal Hanks was directing people in the effort.

"I hear someone!" a trooper shouted. Three other troopers joined him. "There's a shelter below," he said noticing that there were stairs leading down, buried by debris. As the troopers began digging, Max heard a Batronian spacecraft fly by. He looked up and watched as a missile struck the spacecraft. The spacecraft pitched forward and Max saw the pilot eject as flames engulfed the craft.

"Corporal!" Max yelled as he pointed at the pilot who was descending slowly by parachute.

"Grab your weapons!" Corporal Hanks ordered Max, Carlos and two other troopers. Max grabbed his L-29, checked his power cell and flipped of the safety. Corporal Hanks led the four troopers toward the descending pilot.

* * * * *

ESS Argentina (D-868)
Near Kylar II
May 25, 2487, 1437 UT

Argentina drifted in space no longer able to maneuver with her thrusters frustrating everyone aboard. Albert Singleton watched the Batronian spacecraft regrouping on the sensor display and then turning away from Kylar II.

"Captain, the Batronian spacecraft appear to be departing. Same heading as the first wave 110 by 290," Al reported.

"Very well," the Captain said looking out of the angled bridge windows at the destruction left behind by the Batronians. He was angry at the Batronians for attacking and at the fleet commanders for not warning them. *How could something like this happen*? the Captain asked himself like everyone else was doing that dark day.

"I don't know what to expect next. If they want to invade, there's not enough left to stop it," Captain McCollum replied. "But let's prepare in case. Load M-4 missiles in launcher 1 through 3 and 5 through 7 and M-7 missiles in launchers 4 and 8 in case there are stealth ships around. Make sure all guns are ready to fire and electrical power has been fully restored throughout the ship."

"Aye, sir," the XO said as he turned and left the bridge.

* * * * *

Home of Admiral Morris
Naval Base Oscar, Kylar II
May 25, 2487, 0800 Local, 1440 UT

Rose Morris looked out over the base from the porch that Bill and her had sat almost every evening since arriving her for duty. She looked in shock at the smoke rising above the base and the debris streaking through the sky as pieces of ship plummeted from space. Rose knew the death toll would be beyond terrible. And she knew that the war her husband, as well as others, were trying to avoid, had finally come.

A tear ran down her face, not only because of the destruction and the loss of life, but because Rose understood what a war would mean to those serving in uniform. She knew how the War at Masic Point had affected her Bill. He came back a changed man. She still loved him, of course, but the war changed him. And she knew this war would change those who fought it. And this thought, more than anything else brought tears to her eyes.

* * * * *

Near Remains of Apartment Building 14
Naval Base Oscar, Kylar II
May 25, 2487, 0800 Local, 1440 UT

Corporal Hanks led the four men into a wooded area that the Batronian pilot had descended into. The men moving slowly and cautiously, made their way through the palm trees. After several minutes, Corporal Hanks spotted the chute. He held up his fist signaling the others to halt. His eyes darted from tree to tree looking for any movement. He signaled for the others to cover him and moved forward, his L-29 at the ready. Then he saw him. The 6'7" thin build of the Batronian pilot was unmistakable, clearly alien.

"Halt!" Corporal Hanks shouted, stepping out to where the pilot could see him, weapon shouldered and aimed directly at the pilot's chest. Of course, Hanks knew that the Batronian couldn't understand him, but he hoped with the weapon pointed at him, the pilot would get the point. Batronian faces are hard to read and Hanks had no idea how the alien would react. He was relieved when the Batronian raised his hands in an obvious act of surrender.

"One of you, tie his hands," Corporal Hanks ordered. Max and Carlos covered another trooper as he advanced and bound the Batronian's hands. Max's hands trembled as he aimed at the pilot. Partially because of adrenaline and partially because of the natural repulsion that human beings felt about killing another being.

"Piece of shit!" the trooper, a Private shouted, shoving the alien to the ground and kicking him twice.

"That's enough!" Hanks shouted. "No one will harm the prisoner unless he attacks or tries to escape. You two", he said indicating Max and Carlos., "head back to help with the rescue efforts. We'll escort the prisoner to the brig."

* * * * *

Near Headquarters Fourth Fleet
Naval Base Oscar, Kylar II
May 25, 2487, 0804 Local, 1444 UT

With the attack apparently over for now, Admiral Morris ordered search and rescue operations to begin. He also began to think about defenses if Batron decided to invade. If they did, he wasn't sure how much of a resistance Earth could put up. Both the fleet and the base were in shambles. There wasn't much in the way of spacecraft or anti-spacecraft weapons. Still, they had to try.

"I want the base secured. What is the status of the System Monitoring Center?" he asked a Lieutenant, a member of his staff.

"The System Monitoring Center has been destroyed. The Communications Center has been heavily damaged, but we are still receiving messages. *ESS Argentina* has been monitoring the system, but she is adrift, so she probably won't be available for long. We do know that the Batronian spacecraft have left the system and there are no reports of any of their ships in the system," the Lieutenant reported.

"Okay, get a message to the carriers. I want them in the system ASAP. How bad did they hit the fleet?"

"Bad, sir. Very bad. I don't have the numbers, but most of the ships have been damaged and many destroyed," The Lieutenant said. Admiral Morris could hear the shock in his voice.

"We need some protection. Get the carriers back here. Have them send half of their spacecraft to us now to give us something to defend ourselves with," Admiral Morris ordered.

"Aye, sir," the Lieutenant responded. He saluted the Admiral, then he walked away to carry out the orders.

Where's Wilson? The Admiral wondered.

* * * * *

Remains of Apartment Building 14
Naval Base Oscar, Kylar II
May 25, 2487, 0835 Local, 1215 UT

Max and Carlos helped remove the last of the rubble allowing the survivors huddled in the basement to be freed just after 0830. As a woman with an infant and a toddler was freed, she pulled Max aside. "Did you find the girl who save us?" she asked hysterically. Max looked at her blankly. "She went to check and see if anyone else was in the building," she said tears filling her eyes.

Max told relayed what the lady had said to Corporal Hanks. The troopers responded and began to dig desperately, searching for the missing woman. An hour later, the body of Kaitlyn Ryder was pulled from the rubble.

CHAPTER SIX

Naval Space Center
Naval Base Oscar, Kylar II
May 25, 2487, 1007 Local, 1447 UT

Max Finley had spent the past hour helping clear the tarmac of the Space Center as spacecraft from both *Dallas* and *London* arrived at Kylar II. A temporary control tower had been erected using scaffolding. A fuel transport was being used to refuel the spacecraft since the underground tanks had been destroyed in the attack. The fuel tanks were still burning, filling the air with thick, black smoke. Fortunately, the carriers were sending back the craft fully armed. There was little left in the way of missiles at the Space Center in the wake of the attack.

All around Max, hundreds of naval personnel and Assault Forces troopers worked side by side. As the tarmac was cleared, construction men began repairs, pouring concrete and attempting to get as much of the center operational as possible. Heavy equipment had been brought in an hour ago and was removing the destroyed spacecraft. It seemed impossible to Max that not one of

Earth's spacecraft had left the ground during the attack, but that was exactly what had happened. *They caught us that off guard*, Max thought.

Max drew a deep breath. The sky was perfectly clear, only clouded by the smoke from the fires still burning. If it wasn't for the devastation around him, it would have been a beautiful day. As he looked up, twelve spacecraft approached the Space Center. Every time spacecraft approached, Max felt tense. But once again, these were Earth's craft. They circled the base, then landed on a portion of the tarmac that had been cleared. A ground controller directed the craft to the area where they would be refueled.

* * * * *

ESS Argentina (D-868)
In Orbit, Kylar II
May 25, 2487, 1930 UT

Just over five hours after the attack on Kylar II, *Argentina* was towed alongside *ESS Appalachian Mountains (RS-3)*, one of the two repair ships at Kylar II. Since *Argentina*'s damage was limited to hull damage and damage to her thrusters, it was determined that she would be one of the first ships to be repaired. Docked on the other side of *Appalachian Mountains* was *ESS Lake Erie (C-96)*, a 940-foot long cruiser that also managed to avoid serious damage during the attack.

Ensign Singleton walked with Commander Williams as the XO toured the ship. The mood on the ship was somber. The wounded and dead were being moved to *Appalachian Mountains* to be transferred to the surface. As they moved forward, there were signs of damage everywhere: scorch marks from fires, water on the deck from firefighting efforts and doors that were sealed leading to compartments that were open to space with holes that couldn't quickly be patched.

Despite the damage, activity on the ship was picking up as Hull Technicians from the repair ship joined *Argentina*'s Hull Technicians in assessing the damage to *Argentina*'s hull and beginning repairs. Thruster Technicians were disconnecting equipment in the Forward Thruster Control room preparing to receive new machinery to replace what had been destroyed. Hull Technicians were also in the Forward Thruster Control room, beginning to make permanent repairs to the damage that Repair Two's fire team had patched earlier.

"I can't believe this," Al told the XO as he surveyed the scene.

"Yeah, I know." Commander Williams replied. "Let's get the crew busy. If we give them something to do, they can focus on their job rather than thinking about what happened. Let's get people in here to get the water off the decks and paint the bulkheads. We need to ensure the ship is combat ready as quickly as possible."

"Aye, sir," Al replied. He turned and headed out to carry out the XO's orders. After he had left, the Captain approached the XO.

"Attention on Deck!" someone shouted as soon as the Captain was sighted.

"Carry on," the Captain replied. He turned to Command Williams. "What do you think, XO?"

"*Appalachian Mountains*' technicians said they will have us ready in 72 hours. We lost 18 crewmembers with 19 others wounded. Still, we are in far better shape than most of the fleet. Only eight ships were undamaged."

"I know," Captain McCollum replied. Although they were both the same age and both served at Masic Point, Williams had served there as an enlisted crewmember. He received his commission after mustering out and completing college. "We need to pay the bastards back."

* * * * *

Naval Hospital
Naval Base Oscar, Kylar II
May 25, 2487, 1350 Local, 2020 UT

Andrew Wilson awoke to a pounding head. The lights seemed too bright, forcing him to close his eyes once more. His body ached all over. He heard people crying out in pain while other people were shouting orders. Confusion seemed to be everywhere. He was having trouble sorting out his thoughts. It took him several minutes to realize that he was in a hospital. *What happened?* he asked himself.

"Do you know your name?" a voice asked him.

"Andrew Wilson, Yeoman Second Class," Andrew answered. His lips felt dry and cracked.

"Do you know where you are?" the voice asked. A woman, but not Kaitlyn.

"Yeah, a hospital," Andrew said.

"You took a good bump to the head and have some bruised ribs, but otherwise, just lacerations," the woman said. Andrew struggled to open his eyes again. The woman standing over him was shining a light into his eyes. "You suffered a concussion. What is the last thing you remember?"

Andrew struggled. *What did happen?* He remembered being with Admiral Wilson in the office. *How did I get hurt in the office?* he asked himself. *There was a message from ESS Argentina,* he recalled. *Then what…wait, we were attacked,* Andrew remembered. Images began flashing through his mind. The shock, the devastation. *How could I forget?*

"Batron attacked us!" Andrew exclaimed.

"Very good, what else?"

"I was driving…I'm not sure. Who are you?"

"I'm Lieutenant Alice Goodwin, your doctor. You were discovered about three hours ago after a bomb or missile exploded near your vehicle. You are going to be okay," she said. Andrew closed his eyes. He heard a loud scream from somewhere nearby. He also heard moans coming from somewhere further away.

Suddenly, Andrew was filled with panic. His eyes opened wide. "What about Kaitlyn?" he cried out.

"Who?" Alice asked.

"My fiancé," Andrew said. "Kaitlyn Ryder."

"Was she in the vehicle with you?" the doctor asked.

"No, she was at my apartment," Andrew said, his heart pounding. "Is there a comm unit I can use?"

"Yes, right there," Alice replied. Andrew started to sit up, but quickly became dizzy. "Slow down. You suffered a rather bad concussion."

"Maybe I can help," a booming voice said. Andrew looked over and saw Admiral Morris standing in the doorway. His cigar was in his lips, though unlit per hospital protocol.

"Sir," the doctor said upon seeing the Admiral. Admiral's weren't a real common sight in the hospital. As a matter of fact, this was the first time Alice had seen one.

"Can you give us a few minutes?" the Admiral asked the doctor.

"Of course, sir. I'll be right outside," Alice replied. She walked out the door, closing it behind her.

"Admiral, I am trying to find out about Kaitlyn," Andrew said.

"I know," Admiral Morris said sitting down on the edge of the bed beside Andrew. The Admiral drew a deep breath looking down at the floor. "There is no easy way to tell you. Your building took a direct hit and collapsed. I am sorry, Wilson, but Kaitlyn didn't make it."

Andrew stared at the Admiral. He felt like he was dreaming. *Kaitlyn can't be gone*, he thought. *There can't be a war. This has to be a dream*, his mind screamed.

"I'm truly sorry. I can only imagine what you are going through," the Admiral said. Andrews body shook as he began to cry.

How can I possibly go on? Andrew asked himself as he cried.

* * * * *

Naval Space Center
Naval Base Oscar, Kylar II
May 25, 2487, 1930 Local, May 26, 2487, 0010 UT

Max and Carlos were once again manning a BA-75. The gun was ready to fire with a charge loaded and the safety guard removed. Two other privates from their squad were nearby each with a SL-21 shoulder launched anti-spacecraft missile launcher. The other four members of the squad were similarly equipped fifty yards away.

Both men were exhausted. Since the attack began, twelve hours ago, they had been on the move. And there seemed to be no end to this day. Max wondered how much longer he could keep going. *We're supposed to be on liberty, drinking at a bar, not on alert because Batron attacked us,* Max thought. He looked up and saw Corporal Hanks approaching.

"Here," Corporal Hanks said handing each man two energy bars. "I know it's not the best, but at least I can give you some coffee to go with it."

"Thanks, Corporal," Max said taking the energy bars as well as the coffee.

"Call me Joe," Hanks replied.

"Thanks, Joe," Max said.

"Listen, they have Company A assigned to the Space Center. First Platoon is on the perimeter, we have the gun placements and Third Platoon is on cleanup. Companies B and C are deployed outside of the base to defend the area in case Batron attempts a ground assault. So, we're going to be here for a long time. You two will have to alternate sleeping. One of you is to be on the gun and awake at all times," Joe said.

"Understood," Max and Carlos replied in unison.

"If one of you need to relieve yourself, the other one stays on the gun. No bullshit. This gun is to be manned at all times."

"Aye," Max and Carlos replied.

"If those bastards come back, I want to see them falling from the sky," Corporal Hanks said.

"We want the same thing," Carlos ensured the Corporal.

"Good. I'll check back on you two in a little while," Hanks said as turned and walked off toward the two men with the SL-21.

"The coffee tastes good," Max said to Carlos as he took a sip.

"Yeah," Carlos replied. The two men sat quietly as they ate the energy bars and sipped the coffee each in their own thoughts. With the sun going down, the men could see red glows around the base where fires still burned. Debris blazed across the sky as pieces from spacecraft and ships destroyed or damaged in the battle continued to fall to the surface.

Occasionally, a group of spacecraft would land at the Center to refuel. An hour earlier, a trooper had fired at a friendly spacecraft with a BA-75. Fortunately, he missed. Now, a beacon was used when friendly spacecraft approached to avoid a second, potentially more serious, mistake.

"I wonder if they are going to invade," Carlos said after a half an hour of silence.

"I don't know," Max replied.

"I hate to admit it, but I'm afraid," Carlos said softly.

"Me, too," Max admitted.

* * * * *

Office of the Secretary General
United Nations Headquarters, Earth
May 26, 2487, 0915 UT

The mood in the conference room was somber to say the least. At 0700 a special session of the General Assembly was called and the members voted unanimously to declare war on Baton. That was expected of course. Earth could not stand by and do nothing after such a brazen attack on its territory. Members of the Secretary General's cabinet were gathered in the conference room adjoining to his office. Normally, there would be conversations and even some laughter from the members of the cabinet while they waited for the Secretary General to arrive, but today there was silence.

The Secretary General entered the room and the cabinet rose as one. Vincente Colón moved to the head of the table. "Be seated," he told everyone.

"As you know, we are now at war. I never wanted that and I know each of you have worked hard to try to avoid it. I thank each of you for your efforts to avoid this conflict. Unfortunately, the enemy has made the choice for war.

"Now, that the choice has been made, it is my goal to fully engage the enemy and to emerge victorious. I know that each of you will be as valuable in this endeavor as you were when we were trying to avoid it.

"The General Assembly has allocated emergency funding for our war effort. Open contracts will be posted for manufacturers here on Earth and in our territories to provide the products we need for war.

"SDK shipping is already preparing their ships to move equipment and personnel for us. Other shipping companies are expected to provide ships for similar purposes," Vincent said.

"Sir, how much did we lose at Kylar?" the Minister of Treasury, a 52-year-old woman asked. Colón looked over to Alex Weber.

"I won't have official number until later today. The Fourth Fleet has been heavily damaged and many ships were lost. Naval Base Oscar has significant damage as well. The Space Center there was practically leveled, although they have got the Center partially operational now. Fleet Headquarters was destroyed. It is going to take time to recover," the Minister of Earth Defense said.

"Have the Batronians invaded?" another cabinet member asked.

"No. And we don't know why because, bluntly, we couldn't stop them if they did. Our theory is they are not sure how badly they hurt us and don't want to reveal the location of their fleet," Alex answered.

"Could they be heading toward Earth?" Carol Anderson asked. She was not actually a member of the cabinet, but Vincent Colón valued her opinion in dealing with Batron, so highly, that she was included in any cabinet meeting involving Batron.

"It's possible. To protect Earth, we have mobilized First Fleet and positioned those ships between here and Masic Point."

Alex Weber looked around to see if anyone else had a question. When none came, Vincent Colón spoke again. "I'm going to the Batronian Embassy and personally serve the Ambassador a copy of the Declaration of War and then arrange for a ship to take his ass back to Batron."

"Do you want me to join you?" Carol asked, assuming he would. She had always been asked to attend every meeting between the Secretary General and the Ambassador from Batron.

"No, I am putting you on a transport," the Secretary General said.

"Going where?" Carol asked surprised.

"I need you on Kylar II," Colón said, rising to his feet. Less than a day later, Carol found herself on a T-5 heading for Kylar II.

* * * * *

ESS London (SCV-7)
Near the Kylar System
May 26, 2487, 1438 UT

Charlie Flight of the 18th Fighter Wing was once again flying combat patrol, while the remainder of the flights were prepped and ready to launch to cover attack craft if any enemy ships were detected.

When Charlie Flight had been relieved from patrol duty the day before, they met in the ready room watching the news feed. Images from Kylar II were blacked out and information was fuzzy, but the basic truth was evident—Batron had attacked Kylar II and Earth was now at war.

Now, back on patrol, Chris was trying to keep his flight of six alert and ready. It was frustrating and boring being on patrol with nothing happening. Chris was well aware of the fact that he, and probably every member of the wing would know people lost in the attack. The flight was currently operating in three groups of two: Chris and Don were flying just ahead of *London*, Charlie 2 and Charlie 4 to the port side with Charlie 5 and Charlie 6 to the starboard side of the carrier. Delta Flight was on alert and Echo Flight on five minutes standby. An AWC-2 advanced warning spacecraft, with its advanced sensor array was 4 AMU in front of Chris feeding its sensor data back to the carrier.

London's current mission was purely defensive. The ship was to monitor and challenge any ship or spacecraft approaching the Kylar system. Charlie Flight was to respond to any spacecraft approaching. If ships were detected, SA-18s would be launched, escorted by Delta and Echo Flights.

"Dreamer, let's turn to 014 by 217," Chris said over the flight comm.

"Roger, C-Dog," Don replied and they banked into the turn. Just as they came out of the turn, the general comm came to life.

"Charlie Flight, Flight Control. Eagle eyes has four inbound spacecraft bearing 079 by 021, distance 30 AMU, speed 90," the Flight Controller announced, Eagle Eyes referring to the AWC-2.

"Flight Control, Charlie Leader, roger," Chris replied. Then he switched back to the Flight comm. "Charlie 2 and 5, form up on me Charlie 3 and 6, maintain your position and cover the nest." Each member of the flight acknowledged their orders, though disappointment was obvious in the voices of Charlie 4 and Charlie 6. Forty-five seconds later, Charlies 2 and 5 formed up with Chris and Don.

"Let's go, speed 105," Chris said and the flight turned to intercept. Chris throttled up smoothly and the LX-15 engines pushed the spacecraft to a speed of 105 AMU with a satisfying roar.

Each of the SF-112s were currently armed with ten AM-2 short-range anti-spacecraft missiles and two AM-6 long-range missiles. With the enemy only 30 AMU away, using long-range missiles would be a waste since Charlie Flight would have the enemy fighters in range of the AM-2s in less than eight minutes. Besides the AM-2s were more accurate.

"Charlie Leader, Flight Control. Eagle Eyes reports your incoming spacecraft are Batronian Model Four fighters," the voice on the comm unit reported.

"Flight Control, Charlie Leader, roger that," Chris said. The Model Four fighters were Batron's latest models. They were both faster and more maneuverable than the SF-112s, but fortunately for the flight, they were the spacecraft that the Earth's fighter pilots had been training to engage for the past three years. Chris toggled the Flight comm. "You heard that people. Let's be careful. Weapons free. Fire when in range."

Chris selected one of the Batronian spacecraft with his targeting computer. The computer quickly locked on and Chris release an AM-2. His spacecraft shuddered as the missile was released. The AM-2s engine started and it quickly accelerated to a speed of 180 AMU, its internal sensors guiding it toward its target. Chris banked and dove quickly trying to ensure the enemy didn't target him after he fired his weapon.

The AM-2s sensors guided it perfectly. At the last instant, multiple targets appeared around the spacecraft the missile was locked onto, created by decoys launched by the Batronian pilot. Unfortunately, for the pilot, the missile was not fooled. Twelve seconds after launch, the missile struck the Batronian spacecraft. The missile exploded upon impact, engulfing the spacecraft in a fireball. The pilot had no chance to eject before the spacecraft disintegrated.

"Vape one," Chris said over the flight comm. His heart was pounding as, for the first time, he killed another being. That thought weighed heavily on him for a few seconds before he refocused. He brought his SF-112 back around, heading toward the Batronians again. As he prepared to target another one of the enemy craft, a warning alarm sounded in his cockpit. One of the enemy had locked onto him! Again, he turned his spacecraft, this time to the right. His thumb toggled a button on the control stick releasing several decoys. He reversed his turn and pulled up. On his HUD, he saw another Batronian disappear.

"Got one!" he heard a female voice say. Charlie 5 he realized, the only female in Charlie Flight.

The missile exploded behind him, fooled by one of his decoys, but still shaking his spacecraft violently. He turned back to the enemy, quickly targeting another Batronian and releasing a second AM-2. An explosion off to his left caught his eye.

"Damn, they got Snake," Don said over the comm. *Shit*, thought Chris. Snake was Charlie 2 and, although he had never lost a pilot in combat, he had lost one in a training accident. It was his responsibility to notify the next of kin. It was hard and, to Chris, an admission on his part that he had failed to protect the family's loved one. Chris' own missile destroyed another Model Four and Don took out the last one thirty seconds later.

"Flight Control, Charlie Leader. Vape four enemy fighters, but we lost Charlie 2," Chris announced in shock.

"Roger. Return to patrol area," came the seemingly heartless reply. Despite having just lost a member of their Flight, Charlie Flight had a duty to perform. Chris was just beginning to understand the cost of war.

* * * * *

Naval Space Center
Naval Base Quebec, Omar IV
May 26, 2487, 1912 Local, 1612 UT

Naval Base Quebec remained at Condition Delta. There were four ships docked in orbit above Omar IV when the attack on Kylar II occurred, led by *ESS Nile River (C-94)*, the last of the

Mississippi class of cruisers. In addition to the cruiser, there were three destroyers. Shortly after the attack on Kylar II, the ships except for *ESS Mexico (D-866)* which was damaged in a collision with a Batronian stealth ship near Omar VII on May 21, got underway and were now operating just outside of the Omar system watching for approaching Batronian ships and spacecraft. *Mexico* remained docked orbiting Omar IV.

Civilian ships had also been moved to interstellar space. Many were waiting for orders from various shipping companies knowing that it was likely that they would be transferred to military control. Only SDK Shipping had announced that their fleet of cargo ships were being placed under naval control so far, with the cargo ship *Alexander* already enroute to Earth to pick up supplies and personnel to transfer to Kylar II both to reinforce the base and for making repairs to the damage that was incurred during the attack.

At Naval Base Qubec, all military personnel were restricted to the base to ensure a maximum state of readiness. But, it was apparent to all who were present, that Omar IV was in worse shape than Kylar II was when the attack occurred. Defense cuts had badly hurt Naval Base Quebec which was operating with far less ships and fewer personnel than it had just ten years ago. Dave Roberts and Phil Moore were armed with SL-21 shoulder launched missile systems and prepared to shoot down any enemy spacecraft. Behind them, twenty M-4G missiles were ready to fire if any enemy ships entered the system. The M-4G missiles were modified M-4 missiles designed to fire missiles at ships from ground positions instead of other ships.

Since going on Condition Delta, all personnel were on 12 hours on/12 hours off watch rotation. Dave and Phil were tired. News came in slowly from Kylar II, but rumors came much faster. Rumors had been passed around that the entire fleet had been destroyed and that Naval Base Oscar was just as devastated. Every few hours, a rumor would go around that Kylar II had fallen to Batron. This provoke fear among the troopers since the loss of Kylar II would leave no way for

ships from Earth to get to Omar IV to deliver supplies and Batron could simply choose to outwait

the humans on Omar IV. News reports would reveal that the rumor was not true, but just over 24

hours after the attack, everyone was waiting to see if Batron would invade Kylar. And everyone

was waiting to see if Omar IV would be next.

"It only makes sense," Phil told Dave. "Omar is halfway between Batron and Kylar. The

way I figure it, Batron attacked Kylar to destroy the fleet. Now, they can take their time and take

over the whole sector one system at a time."

"Maybe," Dave replied. He looked at the 5'11" African American man. Despite his humble

beginnings, Phil was a well-educated man. It was a logical idea, but it was just overwhelming to

imagine that Batron would attack here. The whole concept of a war hadn't sunk it, even though

there were rumors that several systems between here and Batron were now occupied by Batronian

forces. And at least some of those rumors had proven true.

Forty minutes later, Dave and Phil were relieved of their watch. They ate quickly at the

chow hall, showered and headed for the bunks to get some shuteye. This would become their

routine for almost two weeks.

* * * * *

Naval Space Center
Naval Base Oscar, Kylar II
May 26, 2487, 2250 Local, May 27, 2487, 0430 UT

Carol Anderson arrived at Kylar II under tight security. Fighters from the 14th Fighter Wing,

which had arrived from *ESS Dallas* earlier in the day, escorted her TP-5 from the time they entered

the Kylar System until they landed at the Space Center. The fighters warned the pilot of the TP-5 to follow all instructions or they would shoot it down. Carol had traveled to many military outposts during the time she served in the Embassy on Batron and never saw security quite this tight.

A ground transport quickly took Carol from the Space Center to the Naval Brig where a guard checked her ID before allowing her to enter. Once she was inside, she was met by the Duty Officer, a young Lieutenant who led her into a small conference room that had been transformed into an interrogation room. There was a rectangular table in the center of the room with two chairs on one side and a single chair on the other. The room was brightly lit with white walls and old-style fluorescent lighting. Carol and the duty officer sat on one side of the table. The captured Batronian pilot was led into the room in chains. Two guards forced him into the chair on the other side of the table as he stared intently at Carol and the duty officer.

"Ugly, aren't they?" the duty officer said. Carol turned and stared at him silently. Uncomfortable now, the duty officer continued. "He was shot down during the attack, the only one captured although they lost fifteen spacecraft. Looks pretty damned pleased with himself, doesn't he?"

"He probably is," Carol said studying the Batronian. "Killed over three thousand plus destroyed over half of the Fourth Fleet. At a cost of fifteen spacecraft. I'd say he was involved in a pretty successful operation, wouldn't you?"

"Yeah, I reckon he was, ma'am," he admitted. The duty officer wasn't sure exactly who she was, but she was obviously important and you didn't argue with a VIP.

"Now, listen up," Carol told the Lieutenant. "As of this minute, you are not to speak unless I ask something of you. Understood, Lieutenant?"

"Yes, ma'am," he replied just wondering who she thought she was giving him orders.

Carol looked at the alien who was studying the two humans. <<Hello. My name is Carol Anderson and I represent Earth>> Carol said in Batronian. She wasn't sure who was shocked more the Batronian pilot or the duty officer. <<Let's start with your name.>>

The pilot stared at her for several seconds before answering. <<You can call me Shonze. I am a member of Batron's Defense Force.>>

<<It didn't seem like defense to me.>>

The alien snorted. <<Those decisions are made by others. I just follow orders.>>

<<That's interesting. Let's talk about your orders.>> Carol said thoughtfully. <<Not so much your orders here, we already know about that. But what would be next? If you hadn't been captured of course.>>

<<Do you think Batronians are that stupid. Our leaders just run around and tell us pilots what the plan is. They tell us what to destroy and we destroy it. Then, they give us the next order.>>

<<Normally, I would agree with you. But, in your case I think you know exactly what the plan is. Do you think I'm dumb? I spent my entire adult life studying Batron. I know your language, your history and your traditions. I even know your famous heroes. Did you think I would recognize you Captain Shonze of Gablin, Commander of the Strikers?>> Carol asked. Normally, Batronian facial expressions are hard to read. But this time, the shock on Shonze's face was clear even to the duty officer.

"Have him returned to his cell. Ensure he has absolutely no contact with anyone for the next 72 hours. Then, I will talk to him again," Carol told the duty officer.

"Yes, ma'am," the duty officer replied, suddenly and completely impressed by this woman.

CHAPTER SEVEN

Headquarters Destroyer Squadron Ten
Naval Base Oscar, Kylar II
May 27, 2487, 0730 Local, 1410 UT

A thunderstorm rolled over Naval Base Oscar in the early morning hours of the 27th. Thunderstorms were common on Kylar II due to its tropical environment, but this storm was particularly strong. Lightening flashed almost continuously followed by the roar of thunder. Rain came down torrentially, with water puddling in debris and muddying the ground where the attack had bared it.

Admiral Morris sat in his temporary office at the Headquarters of Destroyer Squadron Ten, one of only two squadron headquarters that weren't destroyed during the attack. Stealth Squadron Three managed to avoid any damage, but the building was too small to handle even the decimated staff of Fourth Fleet. Admiral Morris stared out of the window and watched the storm as he reflected upon the disaster. The numbers were mind-numbing. Over 3100 dead. Another 2800 wounded. The Space Center practically destroyed. Although spacecraft could land and refuel there, no maintenance on the craft could be performed. Hangers were gone, so spacecraft were sitting on the tarmac, even in this weather. Almost 60% of the buildings at Naval Base Oscar had been damaged or destroyed. The Commanders of both Carrier Squadron One and Battleship Squadron Three were dead. Many Commanding Officers of smaller units were also dead, including the Commanding Officer of the Communications Center where Kaitlyn had worked. And finally, the fleet. Of the 47 ships on Kylar II on May 25, only eight (the two supply ships, the two repair ships and four of the assault ships) were undamaged. 27 ships were destroyed and the remaining eleven were damaged, some very severely.

As the storm continued outside, Admiral Morris began to note the positives. The four carriers had not been at Kylar II. *London* and *Dallas* were out of the system finishing training exercises. *Beirut* was in the lunar shipyards for maintenance and *Tokyo* was at Masic Point when the attack occurred. In addition to *Beirut* and *Tokyo*, 25 other Fourth Fleet ships were not at Kylar II during the attack. Many of these were at Masic Point. Since First Fleet was moving ships toward Masic Point, Morris would be able to bring at least some of his ships from there to reinforce Kylar II.

In addition, Admiral Morris had ordered that the Fourth Division of the Naval Assault Forces be moved from Masic Point to Kylar II. The Fifth Division would remain at Masic Point.

But then what? Even with all the ships he was recalling, he would have less than 30 at Kylar II. And at Omar IV, he had only a cruiser and three destroyers, one of which was already damaged. He didn't have enough available to begin a counter attack. Hell, he really didn't have enough to prevent Batron from occupying Kylar II if they chose to do so.

As the storm continued to rage outside, Morris moved to the outer office where Wilson would normally be. With Wilson in the hospital, Admiral Morris had to handle his own schedule.

He could, of course, have another Yeoman temporarily assigned, but that seemed to be disloyal to Wilson, who not only was injured in the attack, but lost his fiancé.

The Admiral noted that Carol Anderson was due at 0900. Hopefully, the representative of the Secretary General had luck questioning the Batronian prisoner. But even if she did, how could he fight a war with only 29 ships?

* * * * *

Naval Hospital
Naval Base Oscar, Kylar II
May 27, 2487, 0750 Local, 1430 UT

Andrew awoke with a jump after watching the apartment building fall on top of Kaitlyn in his dream with tears rolling down his cheek. Admiral Morris had told him that Kaitlyn had saved the lives of many by leading civilians and children to the basement shelter before the building was struck. She was a hero; the Admiral had said. *But, how am I supposed to go on without her?* Andrew asked himself for the hundredth time since he learned of her death.

Andrews injuries, other than the concussion, were not serious and he was expecting to be discharged from the hospital today. Overnight, the activity in the hospital was intense. Only now were things slowing down to the point that medical staff were able to check on patients that were stabilized. Andrew wiped his eyes as a doctor entered his room not wanting the doctor to see him crying. It wasn't Doctor Goodwin this time, but a new male doctor.

"How are you feeling?" the doctor asked.

"I'm fine," Andrew replied

"Problems with your vision?" the doctor asked flashing a light in Andrew's eyes.

"No."

"Let's try sitting up," the doctor said, helping Andrew into a sitting position. "Now take your time. When you are ready try standing." Andrew slowly rose to his feet. His head still hurt and he felt a little light headed, but he was certainly not going to let the doctor know that. If he did, the doctor may want to keep him here and Andrew needed desperately go get out of the hospital.

The doctor had Andrew stand on one foot, and then the other, as well as sit down and stand back up. Andrew felt embarrassed doing these things over and over again, feeling almost like a child. "I think we'll go ahead and release you. Give me a few minutes to prepare your discharge orders."

A few minutes, in accordance with the long-established military tradition, turned out to be forty-five minutes. A nurse finally came in and gave Andrew a prescription and an order for three days of no duty. A new set of dress whites had been provided, probably by Admiral Morris, and Andrew changed. As Andrew left the hospital, he threw both the prescription and no duty order away.

He sat at a bench watching the thunderstorm as he waited for a ground transport. Thank God, the stop was sheltered as Andrew sat thinking of Kaitlyn again. She had become his everything in such a short time. He remembered her smiling on the beach, her saying yes and the love for him in her eyes. He knew he would have a good cry when he got home. It was then that he realized he no longer even had a home. *No home, no Kaitlyn*, he thought as he began to cry once more.

Ten minutes later, he boarded a transport with red eyes. He found out that Fourth Fleet Headquarters had been relocated to Destroyer Squadron Ten's headquarters and took the ground transport there.

Headquarters of Destroyer Squadron Ten was a large, plain concrete structure standing three stories tall with a two-level basement. Part of the third floor on the west wing had collapsed, but the rest of the west wing had been stabilized allowing the entire east wing, basement levels and part of the west wing to continue to be used. The storm had finally ended, although the sky remained overcast and the humidity was high indicating the rain may begin again later that afternoon. Most of the fires on the base appeared to be out as search and rescue operations continued. Just over an hour ago, three more people were rescued from the debris that had been Headquarters of Battleship Squadron Three. They were in bad shape, but they were still alive. Still, as time continued to pass by, fewer and fewer people were being rescued and more bodies were being found.

Andrew entered the building and after showing his ID to a guard asked for directions to Admiral Morris' office. The Admiral was not in the outer office, so Andrew knocked on the inner office door.

"Enter," the Admiral ordered. Andrew entered the office and saluted Admiral Morris.

"Reporting for duty, sir," Andrew said formally.

"The hospital cleared you for duty?" the Admiral asked.

"Yes, sir," Andrew lied.

"Wilson, if I comm the hospital and they tell me that you are not cleared for duty…" the Admiral said looking Andrew in the eyes.

"Sir, I need to work. I have nothing. Kaitlyn is gone. My apartment is gone. Don't take work away from me too, sir," Andrew pled, brown eyes becoming filled with tears.

"Okay, Wilson," the Admiral said after a thoughtful pause. "Set yourself up. I have an appointment in a few minutes."

"Aye, sir," Andrew said and returned to the outer office. Admiral Morris lit a cigar as he watched Andrew leave. *I'm going to have to keep an eye on him as tightly wound as he is*, the Admiral thought as he puffed on the cigar. Still, the Admiral had a great deal of sympathy for the young Yeoman. He would probably be in worse shape himself if it had been Rose.

At 0857, Carol Anderson arrived. Andrew escorted her into the Admiral's office, shutting the door as he exited the room.

Admiral Morris stepped from behind the desk and introduced himself. At 31, Carol was younger than Morris expected. While not a beautiful woman, she was attractive in a hard to describe way. She was professionally dressed with short, brown hair.

"So, Miss Anderson, I assume you have met our guest," the Admiral said as he returned to his seat, puffing on his cigar.

"Yes, I did. Late last night," Carol replied as she settled into the chair she was offered.

"Did you learn anything?" Morris asked.

"Nothing yet, but I didn't expect to learn anything from him, at least, not yet. I did confirm his identity. He is indeed Commandant Shonze. That is one hell of a prize you got there," Carol said.

"So now what?" the Admiral asked.

"I have him completely isolated. He is to have no contact with anyone. Even his meals are being passed through a slot in silence," Carol replied.

"Why?"

"Batronians are very social beings, far more so than humans. They need contact with others. On Batron, few Batronians live alone. Unattached Batronians generally live with four to six roommates. Even couples live with other couples. Being totally isolated is torturous for them. So, as of now, I will be the only social contact he has."

"But, the question, Miss Anderson, is will he tell you anything?" the Admiral asked.

"Yes," Carol said after reflecting for a moment. "Not as soon as we would like, but hopefully soon enough.'

"Good," Admiral Morris said standing. "If there is anything I can do to assist you, let me know."

"I will Admiral," Carol said, shaking the Admiral's hand. Admiral Morris summoned Andrew who escorted Carol out of the office. Five minutes later, he called Andrew on the comm.

"Get me Fleet Intelligence on the comm," Morris ordered.

"Aye, sir," Andrew said. Andrew go the Commander of Fleet Intelligence Services on the comm and patched him through to Admiral Morris.

"We need to get a better track on Batronian ships," Admiral Morris said.

"Yes, sir," the Intelligence Officer replied. "We are getting reports that the Batronians have occupied a number of systems beyond Omar, but we need to get more details on what ships they are using for those operations and which ships of theirs we cannot account for."

"Let's set up a Hawkeye network and get some more information," the Admiral said.

"Aye, sir," the Intelligence Officer replied.

* * * * *

ESS Armstrong (SS-16)
Near Kylar System
May 27, 2487, 1930 UT

ESS Armstrong, a stealth ship was traveling at 16 AMU, well below its maximum speed of 21 AMU that she could achieve in normal mode. In accordance with her latest orders, *Armstrong* was actively searching for Batronian ships. Now that war had been declared, she had the authority to attack any enemy ship.

Commander Carl Adams, the 36-year-old Commanding Officer of *Armstrong* had just assumed command of the ship on March 24th, was watching his bridge team at work. The stealth ship had a crew of only eight officers and 112 crewmembers. Stealth ships, unlike other ships prior to the attack on Kylar II, spent much time in space. That resulted in Carl's officers and crew being comfortable underway and prepared for the mission at hand.

"Officer of the Deck, I have a Batronian cargo ship and a Destroyer bearing 005 by 008. Distance 45 AMU," the Chief Sensor Technician reported. Unlike other ships, stealth ships with their smaller crews used senior enlisted men in positions occupied by officers on other ships. So, the Sensor Officer was the leading Chief Sensor Technician.

"Very well," the Officer of the Deck replied, glancing over to Commander Adams who simply nodded. "Prepare the ship for stealth mode. Helm come up and left to 020 by 006 and reduce speed to 3 AMU.", the OOD ordered.

"Come left and up to 020 by 006 and reduce speed to 3 AMU, aye, sir," the helm responded. Getting the ship under 5 AMU before the ship entered stealth mode was essential. A stealth ship moving faster could easily be detected due to distortions in the stealth field which given the thin armor of a stealth ship, was a death sentence.

The Boatswain Mate of the Watch keyed the intercom on the comm unit. "All hands prepare the ship for stealth mode. Secure all nonessential equipment and minimize power usage." Throughout the ship, the crew flipped switches, opened or closed breakers and pushed buttons to reduce power usage. Lights dimmed and ventilation slowed to a minimum.

"Steady course 020 by 006, speed 3 AMU, sir," the helm reported a minute later.

"Ship prepared for stealth mode," the Chief of the Watch reported as he checked the display that showed power usage levels throughout the ship.

"Chief of the Watch, engage stealth mode," the Officer of the Deck ordered.

"Aye, sir," the Chief of the Watch replied. He pressed a button on the panel in front of him and a light changed from red to yellow. After thirty seconds, it changed to green. "The ship is in stealth mode."

"Very well. Boatswain Mate sound general quarters," the OOD ordered.

"General Quarters! General Quarters! All hands man your battle stations!" the Boatswain Mate of the Watch called over the intercom followed by the sound of the klaxon.

"Captain, the ship is in stealth mode and all battle stations are manned and ready," the OOD informed Commander Adams four minutes later.

"Very well," Carl replied, "carry on." It was Carl's policy that every officer on the ship was prepared for and qualified to take the ship into battle, even the young Lieutenant who was currently the Officer of the Deck. He would take the conn only if the ship was in imminent danger.

The Officer of the Deck went over to the sensor displayed and after discussing it with the chief made a small course correction. "Sir, estimate enemy in range in twenty minutes."

"Very well," the Captain replied as he looked at his display, double-checking all the calculations with his expert eye.

"Weapons Chief, load forward missile launchers with M-4s. Load aft launchers 5 and 6 with M-4s and launchers 7 and 8 with M-7s," the OOD ordered over the comm. The Captain nodded his approval. Never could tell if another stealth ship was out there, so it was best to have some M-7s ready just in case. Twenty minutes later, the Chief Sensor Technician announced that the enemy ships were in range.

The Officer of the Deck decided to move closer. "Weapons, lock missiles one through four onto the cargo ship," the OOD ordered. Taking out supplies was more important than a single destroyer. After all, without supplies, the enemy could not fight. "Captain, I don't think she detected us."

Commander Adams once again looked at his display. *Armstrong* was now only 20 AMU from the cargo ship and 17 AMU from the destroyer, well within the range of 30 AMU for the M-4 missiles. The Captain waited for the OOD to make the call.

"Fire missiles one through four," the OOD ordered.

"Missiles one through four away," the Weapons Chief, a Master Chief Missile Technician announced over the comm.

"Reload one through four with M-4s," the OOD ordered as he move to the sensor display. "Helm, come up and right to 180 by 316. Increase speed to 5 AMU."

"Come right and up to 180 by 316, increase speed to 5, aye, sir," the helm quickly responded, fingers moving over the panel.

"The destroyer fired four missiles!" the Sensor Chief shouted.

"Launch decoys!" the OOD ordered.

"Steady course 180 by 316, speed 5," the helm announced.

"Target missiles 5 and 6 on the destroyer," the OOD said looking at the sensor display. "Bow thrusters down full!"

"Shit! I think they got us!" the Chief Sensor Technician shouted as he watched the missiles pass through the decoys on the sensor display.

We're dead, thought the OOD.

"Missile hit, port side," Commander Adams announced.

"Damn!" the Officer of the Deck swore.

"What went wrong?" the Captain asked ending the simulation.

"I was too close when I fired," the OOD replied

"Yes. And you should have maneuvered to the other side of the cargo ship. That way you could use the cargo ship as an obstacle. The destroyer would have to come around it but that would have bought you some time to move away. Finally, once the destroyer fired, you should have immediately returned fire. If we are going to get destroyed, take him with us," Commander Adams coached. Sticking with his training methods, he ended with a positive. "However, you handled to the transition to stealth mode expertly and got the ship to battle stations quickly. And you did destroy the cargo ship."

"Yes, sir," the young Lieutenant said looking disappointed.

"You did well. Learn from the mistakes you did make," Carl said.

* * * * *

Enlisted Bachelor Quarters
Naval Base Oscar, Kylar II
May 27, 2487, 2130 Local, May 28, 2487, 0410 UT

The Enlisted Bachelor Quarters at Naval Base Oscar was within walking distance of the major commands, including Headquarters of Destroyer Squadron Ten. The quarters were used by single naval personnel who chose not to pay for their own housing. The lower level housed women and the upper four, men. Each room in the quarters contained three beds with lockers arranged to give each bed some privacy. Each room also held a desk, a refrigerator and a comm unit. The head was adjacent to each room. The walls were painted a dull green and the floors were white tile, waxed to a shiny finish.

Andrew Wilson was relieved to find out his new roommates were pulling duty. This allowed him to be alone in his thoughts without the need to meet strangers and to explain to them why he was so down. As he sat alone in the room, he cried and then got angry. He got up and left the quarters to take a walk and found a few men who had come up with a couple of bottles of whiskey. With the base exchange and club closed, it was a seller's market and Andrew ended up spending four times what the bottle would have normally cost. After buying the whiskey, he made his way back to his quarters.

Andrew sat at the desk, the bottle in front of him. He hadn't drunk in almost three years since being picked up at the base club by the base's master-at-arms when he was drunk and involved in a brawl. After a night in a cell, he swore off drinking. He remembered telling that to Kaitlyn early in their relationship. He still went to the base club on occasion, but no alcohol, he had told her. The memory brought up a fresh wave of grief.

He opened the bottle and took a long drink, feeling the warmth of the liquor filling his stomach. As he drank, Andrew thought about how good it would feel to kill one of the skinny aliens. The more he drank, the more pleasure he got by imagining what it would be like to kill Batronians. By the time Andrew passed out, it was after 0100 and he had killed hundreds of Batronians in his mind. His new roommates were not impressed to find him passed out at the desk with an empty bottle in front of him.

*****

ESS Newton (B-39)
In Orbit, Masic Point
May 28, 2487, 1450 UT

ESS Newton was an *Einstein* class Battleship, a ship that contained the navy's largest guns: three triple mounted 400-mm guns. The nine large barrels dominated the view of the ship from just about every angle. The huge guns were meant to tear other ships apart or bombard a planet with constant and heavy fire power. In addition, the 1200-foot long ship was covered with twelve additional 125-mm guns and sixteen 35-mm anti-spacecraft guns. *Newton* was the first of the battleships to have received the new BX-17 engines during her last overhaul two years ago. These engines gave her an additional 2 AMU of speed, making her top speed 32 AMU.

Commanding this monster of a ship was Captain Kendra Allgood. The 44-year-old stood on the bridge as the ship pulled away from the dock. Captain Allgood had served during the War at Masic Point, but in the Supply Corps and had regretted not getting the opportunity to get any combat experience which she felt was the reason she had not been promoted to Rear Admiral. But, with a new war came new opportunity, one that Kendra desperately wanted.

"Thrusters ahead full," Captain Allgood ordered as the ship broke orbit. Masic Point was both the name of the system and of the large single planet circling an exceptionally bright star in it. Around the system, pieces of destroyed ships continued to orbit Masic Point's sun, over twenty years since the war here had ended, almost acting as a reminder what the war had cost both sides.

"Thrusters ahead full, aye, ma'am," the Quarter Master First Class at the helm replied as the ship moved away from the planet. Kendra ran a tight ship, as she felt any battleship Captain should. Sharp and obedient response to orders and good, safe watch standing were demanded of every one of the 51 officer and 691 crewmembers onboard *Newton*. She looked around the bridge, pleased by the nearly complete silence.

Once outside the system, *Newton* met up with eight other ships that would be moving with her to Kylar II; another battleship, six destroyers and a cruiser.

"Captain, all ships have reported in, ma'am," the comm unit announced. As the senior officer in the group, Captain Allgood would be in overall command of the group as they moved the 479 AMU to Kylar II.

"Very well, signal the group: course 095 by 020, speed 25 AMU," Kendra ordered the Communications Shack. "Helm, come to course 095 by 020. All engines ahead standard, make your speed 25 AMU."

"Come to course 095 by 020, engines ahead standard, make my speed 25 AMU, aye, ma'am," the helm responded as fingers tapped the control pad executing the orders.

Here we go, Kendra thought, excited by the prospect of combat. And of showing the navy what she so rightfully deserved.

* * * * *

ESS Argentina (D-868)
In Orbit, Kylar II
My 28, 2487, 1630 UT

"Underway," the announcement came over the intercom as *Argentina* pulled away from *Appalachian Mountains*. Repairs to the ship were complete, although in several areas, painting and other cosmetic work was needed.

"Captain recommend course 212 by 187," Ensign Singleton said from the sensor display. The confidence in his voice was incredible considering that he had just got underway for the first time less than two weeks ago.

"Very well, come to 212 by 187, thrusters ahead full," Captain McCollum ordered.

Al watched ten TP-5s inbound for Kylar II, transporting the first troops from Naval Assault Forces Fourth Division to Kylar II. Al was still unsure why the Batronians had not followed up on the attack. But with ships being repaired, ships being transferred, spacecraft being redeployed and reinforcements being brought in, an invasion of Kylar II was becoming much more difficult, which gave Earth hope. As the ship settled on the new course that would take her out of the Kylar system, the Captain walked over to the comm box and activated the intercom.

"Onboard *Argentina*, this is the Captain. Listen up," the Captain began. "We are going to take up position just outside of the system and monitor inbound ships and spacecraft. This is exactly the same mission we had during the training exercise we just finished. Remember what we have learned. We are at Condition Three which means extra watches. Stay sharp. Any problems or concerns, talk to your chiefs. That's all."

"Well done, sir," the XO said.

"Thank you, XO. Ensign Singleton keep a close watch for stealth ships as we exit the system," Captain McCollum said.

"Aye, sir," Al replied.

"You have the first watch once we are clear of the system. Set a good example," the Captain told Al.

"I will, sir."

Boatswain Mate Apprentice John Bennett needed no encouragement to keep a sharp lookout, clearly recalling what happened last time he was on lookout watch. He looked through his scope scanning the space along the port side of the ship as *ESS Argentina* headed out for war.

CHAPTER EIGHT

Headquarters Destroyer Squadron Ten
Naval Base Oscar, Kylar II
May 28, 2487, 1410 Local, 2030 UT

Admiral Morris sat in the temporary office reviewing the intelligence reports. Batron continued to occupy systems between Omar and Batron. Antron seemed to be holding her own, but just barely. And with Earth going to be unable to send aid for a while, Morris couldn't help but wonder how long Antron could hold out on her own. As he studied, the comm unit chimed.

"Yes, Wilson?" the Admiral asked pressing a button on the comm.

"Sir, *Argentina* reports that she is on station," Andrew said. Admiral Morris had noticed how rough his Administrative Assistant looked this morning, correctly diagnosing it as a hangover. That was very unlike Wilson and Morris vowed to continue to watch the Yeoman.

"Very well. Rear Admiral Kilgallon is on his way. Send him straight in," the Admiral said.

"Aye, sir," Andrew replied. Andrew leaned back in his chair. God, his head hurt. But, at least he got some sleep. Without the whiskey, he had no doubt, he wouldn't have gotten any. When we woke up, his roommates got on his case about drinking in the quarters. Sure, it was technically against regulations to drink in quarters, but who was going to bust him with a war going on and that he just lost his fiancé.

"Hey, Wilson," Rear Admiral Kilgallon said as he entered the office. "You up and about already?"

"Yes, sir," Andrew replied. "The Admiral said you can go right in, sir."

"Thank you," Kilgallon said. He walked over, tapped on the door and entered the Admiral's office.

"Have a seat, Frank," Admiral Morris said. He pressed a button on the comm unit. "Wilson, get us some coffee."

"Aye, sir," Wilson said.

"Have you heard what the Batronians are up to?" Morris asked.

"Yes, sir. Seems that they are taking advantage of the situation and grabbing some systems."

"Seems to me that it could be the entire reason for the attack. We can't do anything. They grab a bunch of systems, then offer some sort of peace treaty before we can counter attack," the Admiral said.

"And when they gain control of huge part of the sector they will isolate Antron even further," Kilgallon said as Andrew entered the room with the coffee. *Boy, he looks rough*, Kilgallon thought as Andrew set the coffee down and left the room.

"I have Intelligence activating a Hawkeye network. I need to be able to track their ships and get an idea of which systems they have," Admiral Morris said. A Hawkeye Network would be a set of agents chosen from the indigenous population from various planets in the sector. Each Hawkeye agent would be provided a concealable sensor array and track Batronian from otherwise neutral, or even occupied planets, and provide that information to Fourth Fleet Intelligence via a secure comm system. This would extend Earth's ability to track Batronian movements and give it a clearer picture of what they were up to. The agents would be well compensated for their service.

"That's great, but how do we take advantage of that information?" Frank asked, sipping his coffee as the Admiral considered his response.

"Why don't we move the eight stealth ships out?" Admiral Morris asked. He brought up a map display of the Young-Wise sector. "Maybe have them operate in pairs. Place four on our side of Omar and the other four here on the Batron side of Omar. We would allow them to operate on their own unless we get something from the Hawkeye Network that we want them to look at."

Frank studied the display. "Actually, just to be safe, I would move two of the stealth ships on the Kylar side of Omar and keep two closer to us just in case. Otherwise, I agree, keeping all eight of the stealth ships here serves no purpose."

"Okay, then, I'll have the orders cut to Stealth Squadron Three," Admiral Morris said. "You know you are the senior squadron commander left, so I will be relying on you for advice. Never hesitate to point something out that you don't agree with me about."

"Have you ever known me to blindly agree with people, Bill?" Frank asked with a laugh.

"That's true," Admiral Morris said laughing himself for the first time since the attack. "Thanks, Frank. I needed that."

* * * * *

ESS Newton (B-39)
Approaching Kylar System
May 29, 2487, 1100 UT

"All engines stop. Thrusters ahead full," the Officer of the Deck ordered as *Newton* entered the Kylar system. Captain Allgood checked the sensors. Several spacecraft had approached the group that *Newton* had led into the system, no doubt verifying the identities of the new arrivals.

Kendra had been hoping to take her ship directly into action. However, she had been ordered to Kylar II first and take on supplies. *Relax, it's going to be a long war and I'll have plenty of time to show my skills,* she told herself. *They can't keep me out of the action again.*

An hour later, the ship approached the docks. In the bridge window, damaged ships still adrift came into view. Not one or two, but maybe fifteen ships adrift and worthless. Eight of the docks were destroyed and most of the remaining sixteen were damaged. Fortunately, most of the damaged docks could still handle at least one small or midsized ship, leaving the few undamaged docks to handle the larger ships, like *Newton* which would dock at 20B.

As the devastation came fully into view, a murmur ran through the bridge as crewmembers were shocked at what they were seeing.

"Silence on the bridge!" Kendra ordered with a raised voice, not quite a shout, but ensuring the order was heard and obeyed. She could not stand an unruly bridge. She waited until the murmuring stopped. "That is better. We will keep order on my bridge."

The ship slipped passed the other docks and the hulls of dead ships. Kendra noticed that some of the ships were still being worked on. Naval personnel in pressurized suits were cutting through the twisted hulls of the destroyed vessels.

They're trying to get in, the XO realized. *Could there be people in there?* The thought sent a chill down his spine.

"XO, I want you to have the Damage Control Assistant assemble a Rescue and Assistance Detail, fully equipped and have them report to the dock and assist in rescue operations. Tell him to bring extra Hull Technicians with cutting torches," Captain Allgood ordered, seeing an opportunity to show her worth.

"Aye, ma'am," the Executive Officer said, moving toward the comm unit to carry out his orders.

* * * * *

Naval Brig
Naval Base Oscar, Kylar II
May 29, 2487, 1820 Local, May 30, 2487, 0100 UT

The brig's Duty Officer personally met Carol Anderson and, once again, led her into the interview room.

"Once the prisoner enters the room, you are to say nothing. It is imperative that I remain his only contact," Carol instructed the Duty Officer.

"Understood, ma'am," he replied. Even though he didn't understand, this woman had earned his respect by shocking the prisoner with whatever she had said last time. As the guards brought the Batronian in, the duty Officer said absolutely nothing. He merely signaled the guards to leave once the alien was secured in the chair.

Carol studied Shonze carefully. Already the isolation was showing physical effects on the Batronian. He appeared to be too pale and his shoulders seemed to slump slightly. His eyes seemed dull and unfocused. *This is going to work. Maybe not today, but soon*, Carol thought.

<<How are you feeling today, Commandant?>>

<<Does it matter?>> the alien replied

<<We don't want you ever saying we tortured you. We want to make sure you are not being beat by guards. Nothing like that has happened has it?>>

<<You know it hasn't. But again, what does it matter?>>

<<We just want to be sure that when you are returned to Batron, whenever that may be, you can tell your government how we treat our prisoners and that your people don't treat any humans you capture any worse,>> Carol said. That, of course, was not the point of this conversation, but for now allowing him to debate would further Carol's goals.

<<You have no idea how to handle prisoners. Your way is inefficient. If the situation was revers, I would already know everything you know>> the alien replied with a smile.

<<Trust me, we are already aware of your techniques. The Antronians have told us all about it. What we are trying to figure out is the purpose of the attack on Kylar II. We haven't been invaded. Was it just to prevent our fleets from stopping Batron taking systems?>> Carol asked.

<<You still don't know, do you?>> Shonze asked, laughing at her. <<I hope you are not what Earth is counting on. That they are hoping you will break me with your pathetic mind games. Surely, Earth is smarter than this or else this is going to be a very short war.>>

Carol looked at him, her face clearly showing the sting of his words. She knew that while humans struggle to read Batronian facial expression, Batronians could certainly read human faces. Shonze watched her closely, then sat back obviously pleased that he hurt her. In truth, she was excited because he told her exactly what she wanted to know.

"Put the prisoner back in isolation. He is to see no one. I will return in a week," she told the Duty Officer, acting as if she were angry.

* * * * *

Headquarters Destroyer Squadron Ten
Naval Base Oscar, Kylar II
May 30, 2487, 0910 Local, 1530 UT

"Did you read Miss Anderson's report on her interview with Shonze?" Admiral Morris asked Rear Admiral Kilgallon.

"Yes. She indicated that the invasion of other planets is not the objective. It is indeed an attack on Earth's territories. She believes that an invasion is imminent.," Frank replied.

"What impressed me is that she led him into revealing the information without him realizing it," Morris said pausing to sip his coffee. "She used his arrogance to her advantage."

"She is smart," Frank agreed.

"I wish the fleet's intelligence officers were half as good as her. Anyhow, now that we know that Earth's territories are their goal, how can we use that information? Without knowing a target, of course."

"I assume that you have an idea," Frank said as he continued to sip his coffee.

"I think I do," Morris said. He pulled out a cigar, lit it and took a puff, exhaling a cloud of smoke. Then he took another sip of coffee. "I'm under a lot of pressure to make some sort of counter attack, but with what I have available at this point, I would have no way of launching a direct assault. But, what if we put together a small task force to conduct quick strikes against small targets. We might not be able to hurt the enemy like they did us, but we can harass them, disrupt their supply lines and generally, just be a pain in the ass."

"At least show them that we're not just laying down and licking our wounds," Frank replied, obviously in favor of the idea.

"Exactly," Admiral Morris said sticking the cigar in his mouth. He stood up and began to pace as he thought. "Maybe I could send a carrier and a battleship. Maybe even a cruiser. Add maybe four destroyers and give the task force a couple of the stealth ships. It isn't much, but it has some bite," Admiral Morris said, a cloud of smoke following him as he paced.

"It sounds like the best plan possible for now," Frank said as he poured himself a second cup. Admiral Morris watched as he added cream and sugar and stirred it in.

"Yeah, unfortunately, the plan has one aspect that I don't like," Morris said sitting down again. He took a puff on the cigar. "Frank, I have to put you in command of the task force. You'll be expected to report aboard *London* tomorrow. I don't want to send you, but, you are the senior surviving squadron leader."

"You, of all people, should know that I would have volunteered if you hadn't asked," Frank said. "I would never duck such a responsibility."

"Yeah, but if something happens, Frank…"

"We can't live in a world of ifs. I appreciate the thought, Bill, but this is our job," Frank said addressing the Admiral as his friend and touched by his concern. The friends looked at each other for a moment, before Admiral Morris broke the silence.

"Yeah, well if anything happens to you, you won't be the one who has to explain to your wife why I sent you," Morris said with a chuckle.

Admiral Morris crushed out the cigar and the two men began to discuss which ships to send. The list was quickly put together: *ESS London (SCV-7), ESS Newton (B-39), ESS Lake Erie (C-96)* a cruiser, *ESS Argentina (D-868), ESS France (D-874), ESS Ukraine (D-877)* and *ESS Norway (D-883)*, the newest destroyer and first in her class. The stealth ships *ESS Armstrong (SS-16)* and *ESS Glenn* (SS-17) were added.

"One more thing, Admiral," Frank said, back in professional mode. "I want an assault ship."

"An assault ship? Ground forces aren't what I would call a quick strike," the Admiral said.

"No, sir, they aren't. But I would prefer to have one just in case."

"Okay, Frank, I'll give you one," Morris said adding *ESS Iwo Jima (AS-38)* to the list.

"That will do just fine," Kilgallon said.

"As far as an assault force, I can give you a Battalion. Do you want one from Fourth Division? They just arrived."

"I'd prefer one from Third Division. They have been under fire. It's not much experience, I know, but it's a start," Frank replied after thinking it over for a moment.

"Okay, I'll give you Second Battalion from the First Regiment," Morris said.

"Thank you, sir," Frank said finishing his coffee.

"Well, you better get home and explain this to Evelyn. Good luck and good hunting, Frank," Admiral Morris said. He stood and shook his friend's hand.

"Thank you, sir," Frank said. He turned and left the room.

After Kilgallon left, Admiral Morris buzzed Wilson. "I have something for you."

"Yes, sir?" Andrew asked entering the room.

"I need a message drawn up assigning each of these ships and Second Battalion of the Third Regiment to Task Force One under the command of Rear Admiral Kilgallon," Admiral Morris said.

"Aye, sir," Andrew responded. *A task force? To go on the offensive maybe?* Andrew went to his desk, prepared the message and then comm'd the Communications Center to have a Yeoman from there sent over to pick up the message.

Andrew sat back, staring at the messages. In the past two nights, since he was released from the hospital, he had gotten drunk. He was hung over right now. Everything reminded him of Kaitlyn. The only thing that brought him any pleasure was imagining what it would be like to kill some Batronians. Once the Yeoman from the Communications Center picked up the message, Andrew knocked on the Admiral's door.

"Enter," the Admiral ordered in his booming voice. Andrew walked into the room and looked directly at Admiral Morris.

"Sir, I have a request," Andrew said.

"What is it?" asked Admiral Morris.

"Sir I would like to be assigned to one of the ships that is part of Task Force One" Andrew said.

Admiral Morris studies his Yeoman's face. It was obvious that the young man had been drinking. His eyes were bloodshot. *Probably not sleeping either,* the Admiral thought, *but if it was Rose, what would I do?* "Is that what you want?" the Admiral asked.

"Yes, sir. I qualified on the 75-mm guns when I served aboard *ESS Mississippi River*. I know I could be of some use," Andrew said.

"Wilson, you know that killing Batronians won't make you feel any better and it won't bring her back," Morris said sympathetically.

"I know, sir," Andrew replied, though clearly not believing it.

"Sit down," the Admiral ordered. Andrew sat stiffly. "You aren't the first man who wants a little revenge. Hell, I want to pay them back for what they've done, too. But, Wilson, it won't bring you peace. I know, I've been there."

"I understand, sir," Andrew said, his dark face showing the pain he felt. "But, sir, I can't stay here. Everything on Kylar II reminds me of her. I can't sleep. I've started drinking again and drinking too much. Other than work, my life has no meaning. I need this. I need to go somewhere and do something. I won't deny that I want to kill the bastards, but it is more than just that. I need to go, sir."

Morris stared at the young man. "Okay, Wilson. *Argentina* lost her leading Yeoman. I'll assign you to her. But remember, you'll always be welcome to return here. Don't become a bitter old man. Kaitlyn wouldn't have wanted that."

"Thank you, sir," Andrew said, his brown eyes filling with tears.

"Write up your orders. I'll sign them and then you are relieved so that you can go and pack your things," Admiral Morris said. When Andrew returned to have his orders signed, Admiral Morris handed him paperwork promoting him to Yeoman First Class.

* * * * *

ESS London (SCV-7)
Near Kylar System
May 31, 2487, 1130 UT

The TP-5 transport arrived at *London* and landed in the Flight Bay without problems. Onboard the transport were 65 personnel who were being assigned to the ships of Task Force One, including Andrew Wilson and Rear Admiral Frank Kilgallon, who would be the last one off the transport. The TP-5 vibrated as the Flight Bay was repressurized, then the transport's rear door was lowered allowing the passengers to disembark.

Andrew and the others stepped off the transport and were pointed to a door that would lead them out of the Flight Bay. As Andrew headed toward the door, six bells rang out.

"Ding…ding, ding…ding, ding…ding, Task Force One arriving," a voice called over the intercom using Kilgallon's new title to announce his arrival. A single bell rang as his foot hit the deck of the Flight Bay.

"Sir, if you come with me, I'll show you to your quarters," a Lieutenant told the Rear Admiral. The Lieutenant led him through the maze of passageways common to all ships, to the Flag Quarters on the second deck of the carrier. The quarters were large and included a private head (a huge prize on a warship), a large sleeping quarters, an office with an oversized desk and a small wardroom where the Rear Admiral could dine with his staff. Just forward of his quarters was he flag bridge, where the Rear Admiral could observe operations and monitor the task force.

A Third Class Boatswains Mate let Andrew to an airlock which led to a shuttle. The shuttle would stop at several of the ships in Task Force One to distribute personnel to their new homes. All the ships of Task Force One were nearby, just outside the Kylar System, with the exception of *Iwo Jima* which was in orbit above Kylar II awaiting to receive Second Battalion and the two stealth ships which were halfway between Kylar and Omar.

* * * * *

Open Field Near Third Division Headquarters
Naval Base Oscar, Kylar II
May 31, 2487, 0520 Local, 1140 UT

Assault Craft Units (ACUs) were used to transport ground troops from assault ships to planets and vice versa. They were not winged, so their powerful engines had to control the craft when in the atmosphere, reducing their maneuverability, but allowing them to carry loads that would be far beyond what spacecraft like fighters or attack craft could carry. They were boxy and clumsy looking, but their heavy armor made them ideal for transporting troopers and their equipment. A single ACU could carry two armored vehicles and a company of 72 troopers with their equipment.

Max Finley boarded ACU-14 with the rest of Company A. Moments after being loaded, the Assault Craft lifted off in the predawn hours from an open field, arriving at *Iwo Jima* twenty minutes later.

"Move out," a Captain (equivalent to a Lieutenant in the regular Navy) ordered as the rear ramp of the ACU dropped. The troopers made their way into the Assault Bay of *Iwo Jima*. The bay was an open space two decks high on the ship, with an space to store the ACUs. There was also a partial open upper deck used to store vehicles unloaded from the ACUs so that maintenance could be performed on them. Unlike the flight bay of a carrier, the assault bay was open to space only aft. The bay was also smaller, barely large enough to accommodate the three ACUs.

The Captain led the men of Company A out of the Assault Bay, through a door, through several confusing passageways, up two decks and into a berthing area. The berthing had 80 bunks arranged four high, two large tables and rows of locker, but little else. Max Finley and the others grabbed a bunk in what was now their temporary new home.

* * * * *

ESS Argentina(D-868)
Near Kylar System
May 31, 2487, 1215 UT

The shuttle from *London*, docked near *Argentina*'s quarterdeck and Andrew Wilson, along with another man and a woman, both Engineman Apprentices, came aboard. The Chief Engineer met the two Engineman Apprentices and pulled them aside to talk to them. A commander approached Andrew.

"I'm Commander Williams, the XO," a short man to Andrew. "We lost the Personnel Officer in the attack, so I'll get you to where you are going."

"Sir, Yeoman First Class Andrew Wilson reporting for duty sir," Andrew said formally while saluting.

"You came from Admiral Morris highly recommended," Commander Williams said, returning the salute. "Let me show you to the Administrative Office. You'll be the Leading Petty Officer for X-Division." X-Division on ships referred to the Administrative Department responsible for all administrative functions on the ship.

"Aye, sir. And where is my battle station?"

"Eager, are we?" the XO asked. "You're qualified on the 75-mm, so you'll be on Mount 54, second gun mount on the port side."

"Aye, sir," Andrew replied as they entered the Administrative Office. Andrew barely looked around the office, instead thinking about the gun mount.

* * * * *

ESS London (SCV-7)
Near Kylar System
May 31, 2487, 1357 UT

Rear Admiral Kilgallon sat on the flag bridge staring out into space. It had been a long time Frank had been on a carrier. As Commander of Destroyer Squadron Ten, his flagship was normally one of the cruisers assigned to the squadron. The carrier was large and allowed the entire fifteenth deck (decks were numbered from the bottom up, so the fifteenth deck was the second deck from the top of the ship), unlike a cruiser where he would have had only a few compartments for him and his staff.

"Sir, all ships report ready for deployment," a messenger reported.

"Very well, signal the task force, standard formation Juliet. Heading 102 by 048, speed 29 AMU," Admiral Kilgallon said. Formation Juliet would place the four destroyers around the other four ships, shielding the others from spacecraft or stealth ships. The combat patrol fighters would deploy further out and to the sides of the task force further protecting the task force.

"Aye, sir," the messenger said. Three minutes later, Kilgallon observed the turn from the Flag Bridge and noted the increase in speed.

"Signal the task force. I want the Commanding Officers of all ships and of the Second Battalion to report to *London* for a briefing at 1800."

"Aye, sir," the messenger replied.

Rear Admiral Kilgallon sat back and felt the weight of command. Last night, Evelyn had been supportive when he told her what he had been assigned to do. They had been through this before. Of course, when it came time to leave this morning, there had been tears and promises to return home safely.

Three hours later, Frank briefed the Commanding Officers on his plans for Task Force One.

* * * * *

ESS Armstrong (SS-16)
Between Omar and Kylar, 500 AMU from Omar
June 2, 2487, 0708 UT

The ship was in stealth mode and at General Quarters. Out of the bridge window, just 29 AMUs away were two Batronian cargo ships escorted by a single destroyer. All missile launchers were loaded and ready. The young Lieutenant who had failed the training exercise just a week ago, once again had the deck. Commander Adams checked the sensors. *Armstrong* was now stopped, waiting like a predator stalking prey, hiding in the shadows. The Lieutenant was sweating as he paced between the sensor display and his normal position on the forward part of the bridge.

"Relax Lieutenant. Timing is the key here," Commander Adams said.

"Aye, sir," the Lieutenant replied, but a minute later, nervous energy required him to do something. "Weapons Chief, status of forward missiles?"

"Missiles one and two are targeted on the destroyer, Missile three on the lead cargo ship and missile four on the trailing one. Missiles are ready to fire," the Master Chief Missile Technician reported.

"Distance to targets?" the Lieutenant asked.

"28 AMU, sir," the Sensor Chief said. "Wait a minute! Missiles fired on the cargo ships, sir!"

"Very well," the Officer of the Deck said looking at the Captain. To his credit, the Lieutenant continued to wait.

"Two missiles are heading to each of the cargo ships," the Sensor Chief reported. The Lieutenant nodded his acknowledgement. "The destroyer is moving to intercept the *Glenn*." *ESS Glenn* had fired the missiles and now the Batronian destroyer was moving to fire back at her. But, in doing so, the destroyer moved into perfect position.

"Fire missiles one and two!" the Lieutenant ordered. The two missiles were jettisoned from the launchers. Once clear of the ship, they fired their engines and accelerated to 180 AMU heading for the destroyer. Explosions flashed outside of the bridge windows as both cargo ships were hit by *Glenn*'s missiles.

"Helm come to course 312 by 216, speed 5," the OOD ordered, voice shaking as he watched the sensor display.

"Come to 312 by 216, speed 5, aye, sir" the helm replied. As *Armstrong* began making its turn, the cargo ships were hit by additional missiles and both ships began coming apart. Cargo and debris poured from the hulls of the dying ships.

"Both missiles hit!" the Weapons Chief reported. The OOD saw the on the sensor display that the destroyer had reduced speed drastically. It was no longer a threat and it was time to move away.

"Course 312 by 216, speed 5 AMU, sir," the helm reported.

"Nicely done, Lieutenant," the Captain said. He reached over and pressed a button on the comm unit. "Communications, Bridge. Signal *Glenn* that we are heading away on 312 by 216 at 5. We will remain in stealth mode for a few hours to ensure that the area is clear."

"Aye, sir," came the reply.

"Officer of the Deck, secure from General Quarters," Commander Adams ordered.

* * * * *

Naval Brig
Naval Station Oscar, Kylar II
June 5, 2487, 0850 Local, 1430 UT

<<So, how are we today, Commandant?>> Carol Anderson asked as she studied the alien. He looked tired and pale. It was obvious that he was not sleeping. The Duty Officer had noted the change in appearance as well, but of course said nothing.

<<You seem awful arrogant this morning>> the alien replied. <<You would think humans would see how desperate their position is. We destroyed your fleet and your base, and yet you put on this fake attitude. You are so weak.>>

<<Now, Shonze, it doesn't have to be like this. Do you think I can't see how this is affecting you? You are the weak one and getting weaker everyday.>>

<<What is the date?>> Shonze asked.

<<June 5th.>>

<<Talk to me tomorrow and we will see who is weak.>> the Batronian said.

<<Where? Here on Kylar II? Another attack?>>

<<Tomorrow>> Shonze said giving his best impression of a smile. He would say no more.

Thirty minutes later, Carol sat in front of Admiral Morris.

"Could it be a lie?" Admiral Morris asked.

"I don't think so. He is arrogant and believes that whatever Batron is planning can't be stopped. I think this is one hundred percent true, at least as far as he knows," Carol said.

"No idea where?" the Admiral asked as he puffed on his trademark cigar.

"No, sir. He won't say anything else."

"Okay, I'll send a message to all commands," the Admiral said after a moment of thought.

"Okay, sir. I'll notify the Secretary General," Carol said rising to leave. After Carol left, the Admiral composed a message and buzzed the new yeoman. She entered the room, picked up the message and left. While she sure looked better, she was no Wilson.

CHAPTER NINE

ESS Mexico (D-866)
In Orbit, Omar IV
June 5, 2487, 1602

Captain James Allen was in his cabin when Yeoman Third Class Bruce Tivis buzzed him on his comm. "Yes, Tivis?"

"Sir, I just received flash traffic," Bruce replied.

"Bring it in," Captain Allen ordered. *Mexico* had been docked since it collided with a stealth ship on May 21st. The ship had sustained heavy damage to three decks of the starboard bow section, including the destruction of her forward missile launchers. Although repairs had been started, parts were needed that simply weren't available on Omar IV. So, requisitions had been made for the parts to be shipped from Kylar II, but with the damage to the Naval Base Oscar, who knew if they even had the parts now and when they would arrive, especially with the war on.

The war. I should be out there with the others fighting, but I am stuck here, the Captain, a 26-year veteran, thought.

Bruce Tivis entered the room. Though Bruce was one of the shortest people on the ship at 5'4", he was also one of the strongest. His weight of 165 was high for his height, but it was the pure muscle of a power lifter. The African-American had once had the goal of becoming a professional boxer, but fell in love with being in space and decided to make a career out of the Navy.

"Thank you, Tivis," the Captain said. Although they were in different positions, the Captain and his Yeoman had one thing in common; they were both from Detroit. The Captain looked at the message.

```
050624871547U

From: Commander Fourth Fleet
To: All Fourth Fleet Commands
Subj: Attack Warning

1. On 6/5/2487, information from a reliable
   source indicates a Batronian attack will
   occur within 24 hours. The target of this
   attack is unknown.
2. All commands are to take whatever
   defensive options are available to repel
   this attack.
```

The Captain read the message again, paused to think and then told Tivis, "Have all the Department Heads muster in the wardroom."

"Aye, sir," Bruce replied, leaving the cabin as the Captain reread the message for a third time. A half-hour later, the Captain entered the wardroom.

"Attention on deck!" Lieutenant Commander Rich Collier called out as the Captain entered.

"At ease," the Captain said. He passed out copies of the message to the Departments Heads. "Alright, as you can see, there isn't a lot of detail, but I don't want to be docked if the attack comes here. So, we need to get underway. I know we are in no condition to fight, but I want the ability to get out of the system and give us some room to maneuver. We need to batten down the hatches, so to speak.

"Sir, with the damage we have to the ship, interstellar travel will have to be kept slow. Say 15 AMU or so, or the stress to the hull may be too much for the ship," the Damage Control Assistant said.

"Understood," Captain Allen replied.

"Sir, forward missiles are obviously unavailable, but due to damage, power is out to gun mounts 51 through 54 and turret 1," the Weapons Officer said referring to four of the six 75-mm guns and the 125-mm main gun turret.

"I know, but we're not going to go into battle. We are simply giving ourselves room to maneuver. Anything else?" the Captain asked waiting to make sure there was nothing. "Okay, let's get the ship ready."

At 0207, on June 6, 2487, *ESS Mexico* got underway exiting the system at 0308, just in time it turned out.

* * * * *

System Monitoring Center
Naval Base Quebec, Omar IV
June 6, 2487, 0620 Local, 0320 UT

The Second Class Sensor Technician was alert and saw them as soon as they entered the system, just twelve minutes after *Mexico* had cleared the Omar system. The Batronians entered the system from the opposite side of where *Mexico* had left. He pushed a button on the comm unit.

"Intel, System Monitoring. Thirty-one Batronian ships have entered the system," the Sensor Tech report, calm despite the imminence of the attack.

"System Monitoring, this is Intel. What ship types?" a voice replied over the comm.

"Working on it," the Technician said as he continued to work the controls of the sensor array. One minute later, he was able to provide the information. "Intel, System Monitoring. Ship breakdown as follows: Three carriers, four battleships, six cruisers, twelve destroyers and six assault ships."

"Monitoring, Intel, copy all."

* * * * *

Naval Space Center
Naval Base Quebec, Omar IV
June 6, 2487, 0622 Local, 0322 UT

Warning sirens began to wail on Naval Base Quebec, sending personnel quickly to their battle stations. The base had been on high alert since receiving the attack warning, so battle stations were quickly manned. Dave Roberts and Phil Moore were already on their station, manning their SL-21 missile launchers when the sirens sounded, having just taken the watch at 0600 locally. They scanned the skies, searching for Batronian spacecraft, but could see none.

Less than a mile away, the 24 SA-18s and 48 SF-112s took off. Dave watched as they went into a steep climb, obviously heading into space to meet the enemy. The spacecraft exited Omar IV's atmosphere and accelerated toward the Batronians, engaging them minutes later just inside of Omar VII. The SA-18s operated in pairs, primarily targeting the destroyers that surrounded the rest of the Batronian ships. The 24 attack spacecraft began firing their six-foot long M-4 missiles, dodging laser fire as they did.

While the attack craft were engaging the ships, the fighters engaged the Batronian fighters that came from the carriers to defend the ships. The SF-112s fired missiles and lasers in an attempt to keep the Batronian fighters away from the SA-18s as they attacked the Batronian ships. Two missiles from the SA-18s managed to hit one of the destroyers, both of them exploding at the keel and splitting the destroyer into two. Seeing the soundless explosions from the cockpit, the wingman of the pilot who scored the hits, released two more missiles striking each of the two pieces of the destroyer. The pieces began to breakup as the two pilots banked their spacecraft to the left and began looking for other targets.

The Thirteenth Fighter Wing was similarly having some success destroying six Batronian fighters at the cost of only two SF-112s. An SA-18 was also lost attacking the ships. Unfortunately, with three carriers, the Batronians well outnumbered all the spacecraft Earth had available at Omari IV and could afford the losses.

* * * * *

Naval Space Center
Naval Base Quebec, Omar IV
June 6, 2487, 0628 Local, 0328 UT

Back at the Space Center, Dave and Phil heard a loud roar as the twenty M-4G ground-to-space missiles were fired. They watched them blast off and head toward space.

"You know, if they fired those missiles, Batron has ships in the system, not just spacecraft," Phil told Dave.

"Yeah, you're right," Dave said. *How come I hadn't thought of that*, Dave asked himself, amazed at how quickly Phil realized that the missiles would only be used at ships, not spacecraft. Throughout bootcamp, Phil had consistently demonstrated his intelligence to Max and Dave, starting with the fact that he had looked up and memorized the training schedule and knew exactly what to expect next.

The twenty missiles headed toward the Batronian ships. As the missiles approached, Earth's spacecraft broke off, clearing the way for the missiles. Three missiles hit a Batronian cruiser, which exploded in a tremendous fireball. One missile took out another destroyer. A carrier, a battleship and two other destroyers were also hit and damaged by the M-4Gs.

"Concentrate all remaining fire on the damaged battleship," the Commander of one of the attack flights ordered. Seventeen missiles were fired at the huge Batronian ship, fourteen of them hitting the monster. Fires could soon be seen raging from inside the battleship. Power appeared to have failed and the anti-spacecraft guns fell silent. Minutes later, escape pods were launched from the ship which began to collapse in on itself. Low on weapons and having lost three more SA-18s and three more SF-112s, the spacecraft turned around and headed back to Omar IV to rearm and refuel.

* * * * *

Command Center
Naval Base Quebec, Omar IV
June 6, 2487, 0658 Local, 0358 UT

The Command Center at Naval Base Quebec had been established shortly after the war began to allow the four major elements of the Naval Base (Fifteenth Attack Wing, Thirteenth Fighter Wing, the Third Regiment of the Naval Assault Forces and the Naval Base itself) to coordinate efforts and establish a unified chain of command in the event of an attack on Omar IV. The Command Center was located in a bunker beneath the base's headquarters. The bunker was dominated by a large rectangular table around which sat the major officers assigned to Naval Base Quebec. Along the sides of the room were various service members in communication with various elements around the base. In addition, each of the officers at the table were in direct communication with their command.

"Spacecraft have returned to rearm and refuel," the Commander of the Fifteenth Attack Wing reported.

"I am having 24 fighters launched to provide air support over the base," the Commander of the Thirteenth Fighter Wing announced.

"Very well," Captain Amber Harrington acknowledged. The 42-year-old with bright red hair and piercing green eyes was the Commanding Officer of Naval Base Quebec and had overall command of the defense of Omar.

"Batronian ships are entering orbit," a Senior Chief Sensor Technician reported from one of the sensor displays along the wall of the bunker.

* * * * *

Naval Space Center
Naval Base Quebec, Omar IV
June 6, 2487, 0705 Local, 0405 UT

Dave and Phil watched the fighters circling overhead, a sure sign that the battle would soon be moving here. Both SL-21s were loaded with missiles, their safeties off and targeting computers turned on. Their L-29 assault rifles were beside them, their safeties also off and fresh charge packs loaded. Tension filled the air as the troopers waited. Suddenly, a laser bolt descended from the sky into the Space Center just 1000 yards from where Dave and Phil's position, followed by a large explosion which caused the ground to shake and threw dirt and debris high into the air.

"Shit! That's a 400-mm bolt from a battleship!" Phil shouted.

"Take cover!" a voice shouted behind them. Dave turned and saw Sergeant Pachenko diving behind the barricade protecting their position. Dave and Phil quickly ducked down with him in what was essentially a foxhole surrounded by a concrete barrier reinforced with sand bags. A rapid succession of 400-mm bolts came down on the center. Smoke filled the air as debris and spacecraft were tossed into the sky.

* * * * *

"Battleships are bombarding the Space Center, Zelerod and an area southwest of Zelerod near the village of Lansing, a Sensor Technician reported. Zelerod was the capital of Omar IV and was located approximately 200 miles southwest of the Naval Base.

"Very well," Captain Harrington replied. She hated to hear that the Batronians had targeted the Capital where civilians would be killed, but with the six assault ships that they had brought, it was obvious that they were planning a full-scale invasion. "Colonel Nelson, how big of a force are we looking at on those assault ships?"

Colonel Byron Nelson was Commander of the Third Regiment. The 6'2", 210-pound Texan had been raised on a ranch and never lost his cowboy appearance. "Probably the equivalent of a division, around 2000 or so troops, plus armor. That's about three times more than we have here."

"We need to start thinking about where to position ourselves," Amber said.

"Yes, ma'am. I reckon it depends on where they land," the Texan replied.

* * * * *

The bombardments stopped as suddenly as it began, after just a few minutes, shocking both Dave and Phil. But the sound of fast approaching spacecraft made clear what was happening and brought Dave and Phil to life. They grabbed both their SL-21s and their L-29s and headed out of the safety of their barricade, shouldering their SL-21s and scanning for Batronian spacecraft as they did. Phil locked on to one of the Batronian spacecraft first and as soon as he heard tone

indicating that the missile was locked onto the spacecraft, fired his weapon releasing the missile.

The missile raced toward the spacecraft. At the last instant, the spacecraft bank right in attempt to

avoid it, but it was already too late. The missile slammed into the spacecraft and a fireball quickly

engulfed it. Dave released a missile seconds later, bringing down another spacecraft, but not before

the pilot released several bombs on a group of SA-18s that were being refueled. Several large

explosions left only clouds of smoke and flames where the SA-18s had sat.

As Dave and Phil reloaded their launchers, they saw several SF-112s engaging the enemy.

Missiles dropped from the SF-112s and headed toward the enemy spacecraft which were filling

the air with decoys.

Dave and Phil fired their missiles again, Phil taking down another Batronian, while Dave's

missile was fooled by a decoy as Batronian fighters engaged with the spacecraft from the

Thirteenth Fighter Wing. As the battle began, an SF-112 came crashing down less than 100 yards

from Dave and Phil's position. The impact created another huge explosion, knocking the troopers

off of their feet and showering them with debris.

* * * * *

ESS London (SCV-7)
1450 AMU from Omar System
June 6, 2487, 0410 UT

Rear Admiral Kilgallon was sound asleep when a knock came at the door of his cabin. It

took him a split second to realize what had awoken him. He sat up, stretched and put on his robe.

"Enter," he ordered. A young Boatswain Mate Apprentice entered the cabin.

"Sir, the Captain is requesting your presence on the main bridge," the Messenger of the

Watch said as he saluted the Rear Admiral.

"Very well. Tell him I'll be there in a few minutes," Kilgallon responded. After the Messenger of the Watch left his cabin, Frank made his way to the head and splashed water on his face. He removed the robe and pulled on his khaki working uniform, then grabbed his cover and pulled it on. He exited his cabin, walked aft to a ladder, descended three decks before moving forward and arriving at the main bridge.

"Rear Admiral on the bridge!" the Boatswain Mate of the Watch announced as Kilgallon arrived. Crewmembers did not come to attention on the bridge to avoid interrupting their duties at a critical moment. Instead, senior officers were simply announced when they arrived or departed the bridge. Frank made his way to the Captain who was in his seat on the starboard side of the forward part of the bridge.

"Sir, we just received word that Omar IV is under attack by Batronian ships and spacecraft," Captain Novac reported.

"Where are we?" Frank asked, heading over to the Navigation Station. Barney Novac got up and joined the Admiral.

"Sir, the ship is currently 1440 AMU from Omar," the Quartermaster of the Watch reported.

"What's our speed?" the Frank asked the Captain.

"28 AMU, sir," the Captain replied.

"What's the best speed the task force can make?"

"*Iwo Jima* is the slowest. Top speed for her is 30 AMU," Captain Novac said.

"Signal the task force to increase speed to 30. Tell *Iwo Jima* to give us everything she's got. She'll set the pace," Frank said.

"Aye, sir," the Captain said. Barney turned to the Officer of the Deck and nodded, silently giving the order.

"Next, signal *Armstrong* and *Glenn* and tell them to head for Omar at best speed," Kilgallon ordered.

"Aye, sir," the Captain replied once again nodding to the Officer of the Deck.

"When will we be in range to launch spacecraft?" Frank asked the Quartermaster of the Watch. The Second Class Quartermaster did some quick calculations.

"Sometime very late on the seventh, say around 2300 or so. That will be early morning on Omar IV," the Quartermaster said.

"Let's hope they can hold out until then," Frank said as he studied the navigation display.

* * * * *

Home of the Secretary General
New York, Earth
June 6, 2487, 0414 UT

Secretary General Colón's comm unit buzzed waking him from his sleep. When he noticed the time, he had no doubt that Batron had attacked again.

"Yes?" he asked into the com.

"Sir, Batronian forces are attacking Omar," Alex Weber reported.

"How bad?"

"It's early and it isn't a surprise attack like Kylar was, so it's hard to tell. Unlike Kylar, this appears to be a large-scale invasion and we don't have a lot out there, but we will at least make them work for it. Rear Admiral Kilgallon reports that Task Force One is heading to Omar at best speed, but they are still almost two days away," Alex said.

"I'll head to the office. Keep me informed," Vincente said.

"I will, Mr. Secretary General," Alex replied.

* * * * *

Naval Space Center
Naval Base Quebec, Omar IV
June 6, 2487, 0714 Local, 0414 UT

It took several minutes for Dave and Phil to reposition themselves away from the heavy smoke from the crashed fighter. They found themselves near a BA-75 that was firing at Batronian spacecraft under the direction of Sergeant Pavlo Pachenko.

"Bring your launchers and set them up here," ordered Pachenko. Dave and Phil moved into position and reloaded their launchers. They fired their missiles simultaneously. The missiles streaked outward, but the Batronians were responding faster now and quickly released decoys that fooled both of their missiles. Model Four Batronian fighters swooped down on their position.

"Get down!" Sergeant Pachenko shouted. Dave, Phil and the two men on the BA-75 hit the dirty as the fighters strafed them with 35-mm fire. Dave heard a cry of pain and looked over to where he saw the BA-75 gunner had taken a hit to the leg.

"Medic!" the loader yelled.

* * * * *

Home of Jack Mitchell
Village of Lansing, Omar IV
June 6, 2487, 0716 Local, 0416 UT

The Village of Lansing was located southwest of Zelerod. Unlike the large capital, Lansing was primarily a farming community with a small retail store, a feed store and a few other small businesses located on the single road leading through the heart of the village. It was a quiet, safe place to live, where everyone knew their neighbor and there was literally no crime. The village council consisted of three members who had held office for over a dozen years adding to the stability of the small village.

Jack Michell lived by himself on a small farm at the edge of the village since his wife's death just over a year ago. The 56-year-old had served 32 years in the navy, retiring three years ago as a Master Chief Engineman. After he retired, Jack and his wife, Julia, returned to the Village of Lansing on Omar IV where they were originally from. Retired life was quiet and peaceful. Jack and Julia had saved as much as they could while Jack was in the service to ensure that. But on the morning of June 6th, all of that changed.

As was his habit, Jack had been up since 0530. Early to rise was an aspect of military life that Jack felt he would always keep. He had been enjoying his morning coffee on the porch (he had long ago given up on smoking), when he saw flashes in the sky followed by a rumble east of the village. Because of his service during the War at Masic Point, he knew he was hearing gun fire from a ship and a large one at that. He ran into the house and grabbed his binoculars. Now, just ten minutes or so after the bombardment began, he watched through his binoculars as assault craft began landing in a field just a couple of miles from the village. After getting a good estimate of the number of troops landing, he went to the comm unit in his house.

* * * * *

Command Center
Naval Base Quebec, Omar IV
June 6, 2487, 0718 Local, 0418 UT

"Ma'am, we have a man on the comm stating that Batronian troops are landing near the Village of Lansing," a Communications Technician reported.

"Patch him into my comm," Captain Harrington ordered. She looked around at the others who huddled around the comm unit in front of her. She toggled the com to broadcast over the speaker instead of her earpiece. "This is Captain Harrington. Are you there, sir?"

"Yes, ma'am," Jack said

"Who am I speaking to?" Amber asked.

"Jack Mitchell. I'm a retired Master Chief," he replied. Everyone around the table was taking notes as he spoke.

"Very well. And what did you see?" she asked.

"Earlier, I observed a bombardment from a large laser from a ship. Probably a 400-mm gun. This was a couple of miles east of here. After several minutes of intense fire, assault craft landed dumping troops and equipment. These are definitely Batronians," Jack said.

"How many?" Colonel Byron Nelson asked.

"Sir it appeared to be an entire division," Jack answered. Byron looked at Amber and nodded indicating that was what he had expected.

"Okay, Master Chief. As long as it is safe for you to do so, I want you to report back if the Batronians move. I need to know what direction they head out for," Captain Harrington said.

"Aye, ma'am," Jack replied.

* * * * *

Naval Space Center
Naval Base Quebec, Omar IV
June 6, 2487, 0718 Local, 0418 UT

A second Batronian fighter descended on Dave's position as a medic began working on the wounded man. Again, the troopers were strafed by 35-mm fire as they flattened themselves on their bellies.

"You two! Man that gun!" Sergeant Pachenko ordered Dave and Phil after the spacecraft passed.

"I'll load!" Phil yelled. "You're a better shot."

Dave and Phil moved to the BA-75 and Dave jumped into the gunner's seat and rotated the gun as Phil slammed a power pack into it. Dave aimed at another descending fighter that was lining up for another run on their position. Dave took careful aim and began firing, Phil reloading the gun faster than he ever had in boot camp. The third bolt ripped through the right wing of the fighter and the two men watched as it spun to the ground. Then, Dave began scanning the air for another target.

* * * * *

Home of Jack Mitchell
Village of Lansing, Omar IV
June 6, 2487 0735 Local, 0435 UT

The invading Batronians appeared to have it all: artillery units, ground transports and plenty of troops. They were highly organized and operated with the clocklike precision of combat veterans, Jack observed. Obviously, the war with Antron, which had been going on for two years, had given the Batronians plenty of combat experience. Jack had retrieved his JV-9 handgun. It fired a 9-mm bolt, but had a very limited range. Still, it was better than nothing.

As he looked through his binoculars, he could see them as they started toward the village. He moved to the comm unit and was connected to Captain Harrington.

"Yes, Master Chief?" she asked.

"Ma'am, they are moving toward the village. I'm moving out," Jack told her.

* * * * *

Command Center
Naval Base Quebec, Omar IV
June 6, 2487, 0735 Local, 0435 UT

"Acknowledged. Be careful Master Chief," Captain Harrington said.

"I will, ma'am," Jack said. Amber heard the comm unit disconnect.

"I want to move the entire Third Regiment here," Colonel Byron Nelson said, indicating a position five miles west of the capital of Zelerod. "We'll have Naval personnel take over defensive positions on the base."

"Okay," Captain Harrington said.

"And I want to lead them, ma'am," the Colonel said.

"I understand," she replied as she watched the Colonel get up and leave.

* * * * *

Naval Space Center
Naval Base Quebec, Omar IV
June 6, 2487, 0740 Local, 0440 UT

"Cease fire!" a voice bellowed.

Dave, surprised at the order, turned and saw Sergeant Pachenko. Behind the Sergeant, sever ground transports were arriving. Two men from the regular Navy were approaching the gun apparently to relieve Phil and himself.

"Let's go. Grab your L-29s and get on the last transport," Sergeant Pachenko ordered. Dave and Phil grabbed their rifles as the two men from the Navy took over the BA-75. They headed for the transports, unsure of what was going on. Less than five minutes later, the transports raced off the Naval Base. Dave and Phil looked around noticing that there were only first platoon troopers onboard, but only 21 troopers. That meant three troopers were gone.

"Okay, listen up," the platoon's Lieutenant said. "Batronian troops are on the ground. We are setting up a defensive position here," he said pointing to a position near Zelerod. "We are going to be on the southern end of the line. We need to hold it. Be ready."

The troopers were handed energy bars which were quickly eaten and water drank as they headed for the line, most of them nervous as they prepared for their first ground combat operations.

CHAPTER TEN

ESS Nile River (C-94)
Omar System
June 6, 2487, 0512 UT

ESS Nile River slowed as she entered the Omar System, flanked by the destroyers *ESS Egypt (D-845)* and *ESS Finland (D-846)*. *Nile River*, commissioned in 2463 and both destroyers, commissioned in 2465, were among the oldest ships in the Navy. All three ships had fought together at Masic Point and it was fitting that all three would once again fight together at Omar. The ships sped past Omar VIII, seemingly undetected by the Batronian ships. *Maybe they just aren't looking*, thought Captain Joseph Clark, Commanding Officer of *Nile River*. *Maybe they are overconfident*. The ship was large compared to the two destroyers. She was 910 feet long with a 225-foot beam. Her primary weapons, two 325-mm gun turrets, were more than capable of punching holes into even the thickest armor of an enemy ship. Like his ship, Captain Clark, a large man at 6'4" and 245 pounds, had served at Masic Point. *Nile River* was at General Quarters as were the two destroyers

"Sir, we will be in range of the 325-mm guns in four minutes," the Quartermaster of the Watch reported.

"Very well," the Captain acknowledged, his heart pounding as he relived the days of combat.

"Sir, *Egypt* and *Finland* report they are within missile range," the Communications Officer reported over the comm unit from the Communications Shack.

"Have them target the closest carrier and hold fire until we open fire with the main gun," the Captain said.

Clark analyzed the Batronian force. Fortunately, for *Nile River* and the destroyers, the Batronians were set up to protect their ships for an attack from Omar IV. The carriers were stationed in a high orbit with the destroyers and cruisers orbiting between the carriers and the planet. This left the carriers open to an attack from *Nile River*'s position. As *Nile River* approached Omar VI, the Batronians appeared to finally notice.

"Captain, firing range in two minutes," the Quartermaster reported

* * * * *

Command Center
Naval Base Quebec, Omar IV
June 6, 2487, 0814 Local, 0514 UT

"Ma'am, *ESS Nile River*, *ESS Egypt* and *ESS Finland* are passing Omar VI enroute to enemy positions," a Third Class Sensor Technician reported. Unlike the commands located on Naval Base Quebec, the ships were not under her direct control. Earth's spaceships always maintained an independent command to allow decisions to made on the ship by its Commanding Officer allowing him to act on his own authority. The ships were notifying her as a courtesy, not seeking her permission. Still, the ships were the best weapons that were available at the time to try to repel the Batronian invasion.

"Very well," Captain Harrington said. Over the last 40 minutes, she had managed to get more naval personnel to man the BA-75s and SL-21s that had been manned by the Third Regiment, who had abandoned them when they moved out for Zelerod. "Can we wend some spacecraft to support them?"

"Yes, ma'am," the Commander of the Fifteenth Attack Wing said as he moved to a comm unit.

* * * * *

ESS Nile River (C-94)
Omar System
June 6, 2487, 0516 UT

Gunner's Mate First Class Bill Phillips was the gun crew leader for Turret One, the forward 325-mm gun aboard *Nile River*. The 34-year-old from Laos Beach, Kylar II led a crew of two other Gunner's Mates in the turret. Unlike smaller gun mounts, turrets required multiple personnel. One person controlled the orientation of the gun, another controlling elevation and a leader who controlled the targeting computer and actually fired the gun.

"Left five," Bill ordered. The Third Class Gunner's Mate handling the orientation controls brought the gun slightly to the left.

On the bridge, Captain Clark watched the sensor display. "In range," the Quartermaster reported.

"Open fire," the Captain ordered. The Officer of the Deck relayed the order to the Combat Information Center. From there, the order was given to the gun turrets.

In Turret One, Phillips heard, "fire at will," over his headset. He checked the targeting computer. "Up two," he ordered the Gunner's Mate Apprentice on the elevation controls. The barrel of the huge gun moved up slowly and Bill pulled the trigger. For the first time in twenty years, *Nile River* fired a shot in anger. The 325-mm bolt slammed into the side of the enemy carrier, rocking the ship, although not causing any significant damage.

Bill waited, listening as the gun recharged. A green light came on indicating the gun was ready and Bill fired the gun again, this time punching a hole in the hanger bay. Bodies and other debris were vented through the hole.

"Right two, up one," Bill ordered as he prepared to fire again.

On the bridge, Captain Clark watched as the enemy destroyers began moving trying to get between his ship and the carrier. Missiles from both of Earth's destroyers streaked out toward the carrier. Only two missiles were fooled by the decoys the Batronian ship released. The other six found their mark. Explosions appeared on the carrier, silently observed from the bridge of *Nile River*.

In Turret One, Bill Phillips fired the gun as quickly as the gun could recharge, while the other two Gunner's Mates performed perfectly, adjusting as soon as Bill ordered them. The gun managed a dozen hits in the first minute of the battle.

The carrier, heavily damaged by missiles and gun fire, pulled out of orbit and began to move away from *Nile River*.

* * * * *

Ground Transport
Enroute to Zelerod
June 6, 2487, 0820 Local, 0520 UT

The ground transport raced along the road, heading from Naval Base Quebec toward Zelerod. The men in the transport were sitting quietly with no knowledge of the battle raging in space above them. Dave Robert's hands were visibly shaking. He was trying to keep anyone else from noticing, but of course, Phil did. He looked down, avoiding eye contact when he realized that Phil had noticed.

"Don't worry, I'm nervous, too," Phil said. But, the black man had his rifle laying on his lap and looked perfectly calm to Dave. His hands were steady and his jaw fixed with a look of determination not fear.

"You don't seem nervous," Dave said.

"Shit, you'd have to be nuts not to be scared. This isn't like training. Everyone in here is scared. But, we all have each other's back and we'll get it done," Phil said.

Dave looked down and thought for a minute. "Did you see that guy's leg?"

"Yeah, I saw it," Phil said looking up. "It was terrible."

"Do you think we'll ever get used to seeing stuff like that?"

Phil thought for a moment, then turned and faced Dave. "I sure hope not," he replied.

* * * * *

ESS Nile River (C-94)
Omar System
June 6, 2487, 0521 UT

As he watched the carrier move away, Captain Clark saw six Batronian destroyers heading toward the three ships from Earth. But, they seemed to be holding back for some reason.

"Come right to 165 by 040," Clark ordered turning the cruiser toward the enemy ships. The Captain keyed the comm unit to CIC. "Target those destroyers" the Captain ordered. Laser bolts shot out of the two turrets, striking two of the destroyers. Incredibly, the destroyers slowed even further. *What are they doing?* Joseph Clark asked himself.

"Captain, missiles inbound from multiple headings! Sir we have at least four stealth ships firing missiles at us!" the Lieutenant monitoring the Sensor Display announced.

Shit, I should have thought about stealth ships, Clark thought heading for the sensor display. Stealth ships hadn't existed during the War at Masic Point and not considering them during the battle may have been the result of the Captain's prior combat experience. The sensor display showed sixteen missiles heading toward the three ships. "Decoys! Bow thrusters down full! Main thrusters ahead full!"

The ship began to move down. Captain Clark saw the two destroyers taking evasive action as well. *Too many*, Clark realized as the first missile hit *Nile River*. The three veteran ships never had a chance. After surviving Masic Point, they were destroyed at Omar by ships they couldn't see.

* * * * *

ESS Mexico (D-866)
Near Omar System
June 6, 2487, 0525 UT

Captain James Allen shared the shock of the loss of *ESS Nile River* and the two destroyers with the rest of the bridge crew. The four ships had been stationed together at Omar IV for almost ten months and the officers and crews of all four ships knew each other and often took liberty together. The mood on the bridge turned somber.

"Captain, I have a message," the Messenger of the Watch announced as he handed the message to Captain Allen.

```
0606248705156

From: Commander Fourth Fleet
To: Commanding Officer, ESS Mexico (D-866)
CC: Commander Task Force One
Subj: Order to ESS Mexico (D-866)

1. Maintain position outside the Omar system.
   Do not enter the system.
2. Monitor all Batronian activity as safety
   permits.
3. Report to Commander of Task Force One upon
   his arrival.
```

Captain Allen found it a hard pill to swallow that he was so close to the battle, and yet, unable to help. Especially when so many people were dying.

* * * * *

Personal Vehicle
Near Malyn, Omar IV
June 6, 2487, 0927 Local, 0627 UT

When the Batronian soldiers first arrived in the Village of Lansing, Jack Mitchell had hidden in the woods near his home and observed them from a distance, using his binoculars. The Batronians had assembled the people living in the village, killing several who did not react as quickly as they wanted. It had taken every ounce of Jack's self-control not to go in firing away with his handgun. After the village's inhabitants were rounded up, the Batronians ransacked the homes, including Jack's own home. *Julie would have rolled over in her grave if she had seen this*, Jack thought.

The main road leading out of Lansing ran almost directly north before splitting to the northeast and the northwest, and each branch linked with the east-west road that connected Zelerod to the east and Malyn to the west. Because of his position, Jack was able to get to his personal

vehicle and follow what appeared to be a regiment of soldiers heading toward Malyn. He had noted

that another regiment was heading toward Zelerod, which left the remain regiment in Lansing.

Now, just an hour and a half later, Jack watched the Batronians as they entered Malyn.

Malyn was one of the four larger cities on Omar IV with a population of about 75,000. Before

entering the city, the Batronians had fired artillery rounds into the city for close to half an hour.

They were joined by Batronian spacecraft which bombed Malyn as well. There seemed to be no

reason for this, since the only military units on Omar IV were stationed at Naval Base Quebec,

which was on the other side of the continent. Following the bombing, the Batronians entered Malyn,

which offered no resistance. Jack watched from the woods and then crawled over to his private

vehicle. He decided to risk using the comm unit in it.

* * * * *

Command Center
Naval Base Quebec, Omar IV
June 6, 2487, 0938 Local, 0638 UT

"Ma'am, Mater Chief Mitchell is back on the comm," the Communications Officer told

Captain Amber Harrington

"Mater Chief, do you have something?" Amber asked with the comm unit on speaker.

"Yes ma'am. A regiment of Batronian soldiers has occupied Malyn," Jack said.

"Okay, what about casualties?"

"There will be many. They bombed the ship and fired artillery for at least a half an hour,

probably to take the fight out of them. It sure worked. I saw absolutely no resistance."

"Okay. Anything else?" Amber asked.

"They have another regiment heading toward Zelerod and one still at Lansing. I would assume they are holding it in reserve for reinforcements because holding Lansing cannot be a priority," the Master Chief said. He paused for a moment while he considered the situation. "I sure hope we have something planned, ma'am."

"We do, Master Chief," Captain Harrington replied.

* * * * *

Naval Space Center
Naval Base Quebec, Omar IV
June 6, 2487, 0948 Local, 0648 UT

The twelve attack craft took off and formed up with the 24 fighter escorts. They turned southwest deliberately choosing a flight path over Zelerod to show the people living in the capital that the Navy was defending the planet and allow them a small measure of comfort. It took the spacecraft just four minutes to reach and pass over Zelerod. Then they flew over the Third Regiment and quickly located the Batronians moving in armored vehicles toward Zelerod.

The twelve attack spacecraft dove at the armored vehicles releasing M-31 missiles used for attacking ground positions. Explosions disrupted the Batronian lines and soldiers poured out of the ground transports. Six armored vehicles and three tanks were destroyed. The spacecraft circled around and dove again on the enemy positions, this time dropping bombs on the enemy. Two more armored vehicles were destroyed and dozens of Batronians were killed as the spacecraft circled around for another pass.

* * * * *

Third Regiment/First Battalion/Company C/First Platoon
Five Miles West of Zelerod, Omar IV
June 6, 2487, 0953 Local, 0653 UT

Sergeant Pachenko watched the attack craft bombing the enemy who were about three miles away. His adrenaline was pumping as he moved from position to position checking on the troops in his platoon. Despite his seniority, this would be his first time in combat and he was just as nervous as the young troopers under his command. The more he looked at his platoon's position, the more he liked it. His platoon was set up 150 yards south of the main road, on an incline of about twenty feet above the road. This gave them the high ground and, with the cover from the trees, it was an excellent position from which to ambush the enemy.

Pavlo Pachenko watched as the attack craft began bombing the enemy again. Three more miles. It wouldn't be long.

* * * * *

Armored Vehicle
Five Miles West of Zelerod, Omar IV
June 6, 2487, 0955 Local, 0655 UT

Colonel Byron Nelson observed the bombing of the Batronian forces from his armored vehicle just a half a mile further to the east than Sergeant Pachenko making Colonel Nelson just a little further from the enemy. Colonel Nelson watched as the spacecraft finished their attack, bank and headed back to the Space Center.

"Let's get some artillery fire on their positions," the Colonel yelled to a Private manning the comm unit.

"Yes, sir," the Private replied. Three minutes later, mortar rounds flew overhead from behind Nelson's position and into the Batronians.

* * * * *

Command Center
Naval Base Quebec, Omar IV
June 6, 2487, 1012 Local, 0712 UT

Captain Harrington was trying to keep track of her available resources so that she could continue to hit the Batronians at multiple locations and in different ways. For the time being, she realized, she would have to leave their ships alone and concentrate on maintaining control of ground positions. When she received a report of Batronian spacecraft inbound for the Third Regiment's position, she immediately ordered all available fighters from the Thirteenth Fighter Wing to get airborne and protect the limited number of ground troops she had. The Third Regiment had consisted of only 648 troopers to try and contain a full division of Batronians, an over three to one advantage for the enemy.

* * * * *

Third Regiment/First Battalion/Company C/First Platoon
Five Miles West of Zelerod, Omar IV
June 6, 2487, 1028 Local, 0728 UT

Sergeant Pachenko made his rounds to each position. "Fire only when order," he told each pair of men. "If anyone fires before I order, I will hang them personally."

As they hunkered down, Dave felt Phil elbow him. Dave looked over at Phil, who was pointing toward the road, his eyes wide. Batronian soldiers were making their way down the road in two columns, carrying their weapons at port arms. Dave shouldered his L-29, taking aim and flipping the fire control switch to full auto. Out of the corner of his eye, he saw Phil taking aim as well. Dave was sweating heavily, nerves rattled as he watched the enemy soldiers. He noticed that he was holding his breath and had to remind himself to take steady breaths.

Dave began silently praying, trying not to move a muscle because he was afraid to make a sound. He saw that Phil had three fresh power packs laying out on the ground beside him rather than in his vest like Dave had. *What a smart idea?* Dave thought as he pulled two packs out and laid them out as Phil had. He again took aim on the Batronian troops. He had the first Batronian in the near column in his sights.

"Open fire!" Sergeant Pachenko yelled.

Dave squeezed his trigger, seeping back and forth at the Batronians. Laser bolts slammed into the Batronian soldiers from several angles. Dave watched several fall from his bolts. The Batronians seemed to be caught completely off guard as bolts flashed from Company B on the other side of the road. Dave heard screams of pain and shouts of orders in a language that he couldn't understand, Dave changed his power pack automatically as soon as he drained the first one. Still on auto, he opened fire again, quickly draining a second power pack.

The enemy fell back, moving west, leaving bodies lying on the road. Dave switched his rifle to single fire mode and loaded a fresh power pack. He fired at any Batronian laying on the road who appeared to move. Fewer bolts were fired as the enemy pulled back out of range.

"Cease fire! Cease fire!" yelled Sergeant Pachenko as he surveyed the area. The enemy was no longer firing. The ones on the road appeared motionless. Still, there were only about three dozen bodies in the road and from his position, it was difficult to see where the Batronians that pulled back went. He looked through his binoculars, thinking for several moments before deciding. "Okay, First Squad with me. Second and Third Squads, cover us."

Dave and Phil grabbed their empty power packs, stashed them and left the safety of their cover joining up with the rest of the squad. The eight men, led by Sergeant Pachenko, began making their way down to the road.

* * * * *

ESS Iwo Jima (AS-38)
1360 AMU from Omar
June 6, 2487, 0735 UT

The forward troop berthing compartment on *Iwo Jima* was eerily quiet as the seventy plus members of Company A of Second Battalion prepared their packs. They cleaned their rifles and packed extra power packs. And, of course, they waited to hear what was happening on Omar IV. Word had reached the ship a few minutes ago that Third Regiment had engaged the enemy on the ground. Max sat praying for Dave and Phil. It was hard to believe that it had been less than three weeks since the three of them had left Mars together.

* * * * *

Third Regiment/First Battalion/Company C/First Platoon
Five Miles West of Zelerod, Omar IV
June 6, 2487, 1038 Local, 0738 UT

At the edge of the woods, Dave, Phil and the others were forced to break cover and move out onto the road. Rifles shouldered, they moved quickly, men pairing off and watching in all directions. There was no one in sight. About three quarters of a mile from their position, the road turned to the left, obstructing their views.

"Start searching the bodies and see if you can find anything useful," Sergeant Pachenko ordered.

Phil knelt by one of the bodies. It was the first time he had seen a Batronian up close. He was surprised at how tall they were. The one he was searching had to be at least 6'10". He had also never touched a dead body before. He found nothing of interest on the first body and moved toward the next one. As he was searching the second body, bolts of incoming laser fire zipped around him.

"Take cover!" Sergeant Pachenko ordered. The squad dove into a ditch that ran along the south side of the road. The remainder of First Platoon fired from their positions above First Squad. Phil opened fire on the enemy troops who were on the northside of the road, west of his positions, using a tree line for cover. The Batronians were near the limit of his L-29's range.

"We need to advance! Stay low!" Sergeant Pachenko ordered. The squad belly crawled along the ditch slowly advancing on the enemy. Getting into position, Phil began firing on the enemy, but the Batronians had great cover and he couldn't tell whether his rounds were hitting anyone.

"We need artillery!" Sergeant Pachenko yelled into the earpiece that served as a comm unit. As he was giving targeting information, a bolt hit his left shoulder driving him to the ground. "Son of a bitch!" he yelled grabbing his shoulder.

Phil was to the right of the Sergeant when he was hit. Immediately, Phil made his way over to the Sergeant, keeping low as the Batronians continued to fire at the men in the ditch. Phil saw that Pachenko's wound wasn't as bad as it could have been. The bolt had passed through his shoulder. The wound was cauterized so there was little blood. Removing a patch from the Sergeant's first aid kit ("Don't use your first aid kit to treat others. Use theirs or you won't have what you need when you get your ass shot!" Sergeant Blake, the Drill Instructor at bootcamp had driven into their heads.), Phil covered the Sergeant's wound the best he could while ducking from incoming fire. As he worked, mortar rounds passed over his head, exploding into the woods across the road.

"Fifty yards left!" the Sergeant yelled into his earpiece.

Dave, was still firing at the enemy and unaware that Sergeant Pachenko had been wounded when mortar fire began pouring down on the Batronians' position. Almost immediately, the rate of incoming fire became significantly less.

"Alright, pull back to our original positions," Sergeant Pachenko ordered.

Dave began to move, keeping his head down, joining the others as they climbed out of the ditch and made their way up the hill. Though the rate of incoming fire was low, suppressed by the artillery fire, some bolts were still being fired at First Squad as they moved toward the tree line. A bolt hit the trooper in front of Dave squarely in the back and the trooper fell silently. Dave moved up to him and rolled him over. The Private's eyes stared blankly ahead. Dave checked for a pulse and found none. He managed to get the dead man over his shoulders and carried him up the hill. Dave left the trooper behind the line and joined Phil back in their position on the line.

* * * * *

Naval Space Center
Naval Base Quebec, Omar IV
June 6, 2487, 1049 Local, 0739 UT

As soon as spacecraft touched down at the Space Center, dozens of personnel descended on it. Pilots were helped out of the spacecraft to allow them to grab food, water and use the head while their spacecraft was serviced. As soon as the pilots were cleared, refueling began. Once the craft was refueled, Ordinance Technicians driving large red vehicles carrying missiles and bombs for the spacecraft moved in to rearm it. Maintenance Technicians checked for damage to the body of the craft, making temporary repairs as needed. An hour after setting down, the spacecraft was refueled, rearmed and ready for the pilot to return for the next mission.

Unfortunately, more and more spacecraft were returning that were too heavily damaged to be repaired or simply not returning at all. The Thirteenth Fighter Wing had lost a number of fighters and a dozen or so were too damaged to fly. They continued to fly cover over the Naval Base, but now a call had come for a new mission. Nearby an AWC-2 Advanced Warning Craft took off escorted by SF-112s.

* * * * *

Command Center
Naval Base Quebec, Omar IV
June 6, 2487, 1056 Local, 0756 UT

"Eagle Eyes is over the ground troops," a Communications Technician Apprentice reported.

"Very well. Tell him to contact Colonel Nelson on 182.6 and give the Colonel whatever he wants," Captain Harrington ordered.

"Aye, ma'am," the technician replied.

* * * * *

Third Regiment/First Battalion/Company C/First Platoon
Five Miles West of Zelerod, Omar IV
June 6, 2487, 1112 Local, 0812 UT

Dave and Phil were in a foxhole waiting for the action to begin again. The body Dave had brought back was no longer where he left it, apparently having been moved off the battlefield. While there was no incoming fire at the position and the road below was clear, they could hear fire north of the road. Company B was obviously engaging the enemy somewhere. The sun was overhead now and despite the shade of the trees, it was becoming hot. And it was becoming humid. Add to that the stress of combat and the troopers of First Platoon were soaked in sweat. Despite everything, First Platoon was in good shape. They had lost only one man while two others, including Sergeant Pachinko, had relatively minor wounds.

Dave took a long drink from his canteen as his eyes scanned for the enemy.

* * * * *

Armored Vehicle
Five Miles West of Zelerod, Omar IV
June 6, 2487, 1128 Local, 0828 UT

"Regiment Commander, Eagle Eyes. The Batronians are making another push both on the north and south sides of the road. Estimated strength is 450 troops," the voice said over the comm unit reporting what was being seen from the AWC-2.

"Very well," acknowledged Colonel Nelson. He turned to the Communication Technician on the Unit comm. "Pass the word along."

"Aye, sir," came the reply.

* * * * *

Third Regiment/First Battalion/Company C/First Platoon
Five Miles West of Zelerod, Omar IV
June 6, 2487, 1135 Local, 0835 UT

Dave Roberts saw the Batronians advancing down the road and opened fire. Several of the Batronians fell while the others ran from the road and into the woods below his position. Bolts hit the sandbags stacked in front of the foxhole that protected him and Phil with a large smack. Dust rose from the bags as the bolts struck them. A cry from somewhere off to his right indicated someone in the platoon had been hit.

"They're on our left flank!" Phil Moore shouted as he turned left and started firing. There wasn't as much protection from incoming fire from that direction and bolts were soon flying over Phil's head. He dropped down on his belly blindly returning fire.

"We're being flanked! I need artillery!" Sergeant Pachenko yelled into the earpiece as he joined Dave and Phil and began firing himself.

Phil changed his charge pack and once again fired to his left. He was still firing blind, but his primary goal for now was suppressing the enemy's fire.

Dave was not firing blindly from his position. He could see the Batronians advancing from the road toward his position. There were so many of them that it seemed he could never stop them all. But then, artillery fire slammed into the Batronians. Many went down, but several continued to advance.

"I need help!" Dave yelled.

Phil repositioned himself closer to Dave. He could now see the Batronians less than fifty yards away, slightly downhill. Phil toggled his L-29 to full auto and fired a long burst into the enemy. More artillery rounds fell as Phil changed his charge pack. Sergeant Pachenko joined Dave and Phil, firing at the Batronians with deadly accuracy. As the Batronians continued to close, Sergeant Pachenko threw two grenades, killing three Batronians and forcing the remaining Batronians to retreat down the hill. As the incoming fire slowed, Dave and Phil switched back to single fire mode to conserve charge packs. Over the next ten minutes, the firefight reduced greatly in intensity and finally ended.

* * * * *

AWC-2
In air, Seven Miles West of Zelerod, Omar IV
June 6, 2487, 1208 Local, 0908 UT

The pilot banked the spacecraft looking down at the battlefield. The AWC-2 had been providing targeting information for artillery fire as well monitoring troop movements for the command units on the ground.

"Looks like their withdrawing," the pilot reported as they watched the enemy continue to pull back from their positions. The pilot could see that the Batronians had lost about a quarter of the regiment that had engaged the humans and it was obvious that the Third Regiment had lost a lot less. "They are out of artillery range. Better call it in."

In the rear of the spacecraft, a team of six Sensor Technicians and four Communications Technicians worked in the dim lighting. One of the Communications Technicians updated Colonel Nelson of the enemy's position.

CHAPTER ELEVEN

ESS Argentina (D-868)
1240 AMU from Omar
June 6, 2487, 1130 UT

Yeoman First Class Andrew Wilson sat alone in the Administrative Office having excused the other Yeoman to lunch. His stomach was knotted as he checked with the Quartermaster of the Watch on the ship's position. They were still so far from Omar. Andrew was anxious, ready to start killing his enemy. He got up from the desk and started pacing.

On the bridge, Ensign Singleton was the Officer of the Deck as Task Force One raced toward Omar. The tension in the air was heavy. The crew knew that Omar IV was under attack and they were hoping that the ship would arrive in time to save the planet. Despite the tension, the watch on the bridge, so far, was uneventful.

Throughout the morning, the ship was engaged in routine work. Maintenance was being done on machinery, cleaning tasks performed, and most recently, the crew had begun to eat lunch.

Suddenly, the Sensor Technician Third Class looked up from the sensor display. "Missiles inbound, port side!" she shouted.

"Sound General Quarters!" Al ordered as he moved to the sensor display. Four missiles were inbound from a distance of 20 AMU. The Boatswain Mate of the Watch called General Quarters over the intercom as Al calculated the trajectory of the missiles. They were headed for *Newton*.

Andrew's heart raced when he heard the call to General Quarters. *Finally*, he thought as he made his way to Mount 54. A single person operated the 75-mm gun mount. Unlike the BA-75, there was no loader, since the gun was charged by the ship's power supply with its own emergency backup supply. Andrew grabbed the headset that connected him to the Combat Information Center (CIC) which would assist him in tracking the enemy.

Back on the bridge, Al went to the comm unit and selected the Weapons Officer. "Fire missiles one through four on a return trajectory," Al ordered. *Argentina* had all missile launches loaded with M-7 missiles.

"Aye, sir," the Weapons Officer replied.

"Come right to 218 by 060, decrease speed to 28," Al ordered as the Captain arrived on the bridge and moved beside him, silently studying the sensor data. He was pleased to see how the young Ensign was handling the situation.

"Missiles one through four away," the Weapons Officer reported over the comm.

"Very well. Reload launchers one through four with M-7s," Al replied. He watched the sensor data as he moved the ship between the inbound missiles and *Newton*. The destroyer's primary mission was to protect the capital ships: the carrier, battleship and cruiser. As the ship settled into position, Al ordered, "Come left to 218 by 048, increase speed to 30," resuming the base course and speed of the task force.

"Nicely done, Ensign," the Captain whispered as the ship settled into position.

Al watched the missiles closing in on the ship on the sensor display. "Launch decoys…now…now…now…now," Al ordered releasing four decoys in an attempt to fool the missiles. The four missiles locked onto a pair of decoys and exploded off *Argentina*'s port side. The ship shook violently from the shock waves generated by the explosions.

"Damage report," Captain McCollum asked after selecting Damage Control Central on the comm unit.

"Damage Control teams are checking now, sir," the Damage Control Assistant replied.

Al continued to track the outbound missiles. Looking out of the bridge window, the explosion of the first missile briefly revealed a stealth ship, which then exploded as two additional missiles struck it. The bridge crew cheered at the sight and Captain McCollum slapped Al on the back and joined in, cheering loudly.

Down below decks, John Bennett was in his pressurized suit, searching an area on the fourth deck, looking for any damage caused by the violent shaking of the ship from the nearby explosions. Even though the ship wasn't hit, the shock wave could cause short circuits which could start a fire or even separate hull plates which could cause air to be vented into space. John found nothing and passed that information on to Repair Two, which once all the crewmembers checking for damage in Repair Two's area reported in, passed that information on to Damage Control Central.

The bridge crew had just settled down from celebrating the destruction of the enemy's ship when the Damage Control Assistant reported, "No apparent damage, sir," to Captain McCollum over the comm unit.

"Very well," the Captain replied. He turned to Al. "Well done, Ensign. Move the ship back to our patrol position and secure from General Quarters."

"Aye, sir," Al replied, the reality of what just happened hitting him. He had just destroyed an enemy ship, the first officer on the ship to be able to make that claim.

Perhaps the only person disappointed by the quick outcome was Andrew Wilson, who powered down his gun, angry that he had not had his chance to kill the Batronians.

* * * * *

Third Regiment/First Battalion/Company C/First Platoon
Five Miles West of Zelerod, Omar IV
June 6, 2487, 1515 Local, 1215 UT

The withdrawal of Batronian troops gave First Platoon the opportunity to repair and reinforce their positions. Over the last three hours foxholes had been dug again and more sandbags were brought in to provide additional protection for the troops. A few small fires were started allowing the troops to heat up some food.

Dave and Phil alternated watch. One would be able to relax and eat while the other one watched for enemy movement. Sergeant Pachenko checked on the men periodically. He brought them charge packs for their L-29s, energy bars and even at one point, coffee. He encouraged his men, boosting morale. "You kicked their Batronian asses right back down the road," he boldly proclaimed. At 1515, the bolts started falling from the sky onto Company C's position.

"Bombardment!" Dave heard someone shout as 400-mm bolts began pouring down on them. Dirt and debris filled the air as tress caught fire and crashed to the ground. The roar of the impacts of the bolts was overwhelming. A bolt hit close to Dave and Phil's foxhole raining debris

down on the two men who had their hands over their heads as they laid face down in their foxhole.

* * * * *

Armored Vehicle
Five Miles West of Zelerod, Omar IV
June 6, 2487, 1516 Local, 1216 UT

Colonel Nelson saw the bolts raining down on the troops. He silently prayed for their safety.

As he watched, the bolts began working their way up toward his position

"Everybody out! Take cover!" he ordered the crew in his command vehicle. He ensured

that every trooper got out of the vehicle and then led them to the ditch that ran alongside the road.

"Get your heads down!" he yelled over the thunder of the falling bolts.

Like Dave and Phil, dirt and other debris quickly covered the men laying in the ditch.

Colonel Nelson peeked out of the ditch and watched as his armored vehicle took a direct hit from

a bolt. Pieces of the vehicle flew like shrapnel, killing four of the men in the ditch.

* * * * *

AWC-2
In Air, Seven Miles West of Zelerod, Omar IV
June, 2487, 1518 Local, 1218 UT

The pilot and copilot watched in silent horror as the 400-mm bolts rained down on the

Third Regiment. The pilot banked the spacecraft trying to move away from the enemy fire.

"Sir, thirty enemy spacecraft inbound!" a Sensor Technician reported

The pilot pulled out of the turn and reduced the throttle slightly.

"Sir, I need you to turn to 215 to allow the sensors to identify the types of spacecraft," the

Sensor Technician requested.

"Very…" the pilot began just before a bolt tore off the right wing of the AWC-2. The spacecraft tipped to the right and began to spin as the nose dropped and pointed to the ground.

"Mayday…mayday!" a Communications Technician shouted into the comm unit as wind screamed through holes in the crat. It rolled over one final time before it plunged into the ground.

* * * * *

Command Center
Naval Base Quebec, Omar IV
June 6, 2487, 1519 Local, 1219 UT

"Eagle Eyes had reported there were thirty enemy spacecraft inbound before we lost comms with them," one of the Communications Technicians reported.

"Very well," Captain Harrington replied looking over to the Commander of the Thirteenth Fighter Wing.

"I'll launch what we have available," the Commander said.

"Ma'am, escorts report that Eagle Eyes is down," another Communications Technician reported.

"Acknowledge it," Amber said with a heavy heart. Even though they were doing damage to the enemy, the casualties were mounting which bothered the 42-year-old mother of two.

"Ma'am, we have launched 18 fighters heading toward Third Regiment," the Commander of the Thirteenth Fighter Wing reported.

"Very well," Amber replied. Eighteen fighters against thirty enemy craft was a reminder of how bad the situation was.

* * * * *

Third Regiment/First Battalion/Company C/First Platoon
Five Miles West of Zelerod, Omar IV
June 6, 2487, 1520 Local, 1220 UT

Debris continued to pour down on Dave as he laid in his foxhole. The noise was deafening. He could feel rocks and debris hitting his helmet as he tried to protect his head. Phil was beside him, similarly positioned. Suddenly, the laser fire ended. Dave raised his head and could hear the roar of incoming spacecraft.

"Incoming!" someone yelled as Dave looked up and saw bombs dropping from the enemy craft. At the same time, he saw SF-121s firing at the enemy. Explosions again rocked the area. A hot, searing pain caused Dave to instinctively pull his hand to his chest. Dave looked at the blood flowing from his hand.

"Shit! I'm hit!" Dave yelled as he began to panic.

"Let me see," Phil said crawling over to Dave. Bombs continued to explode. The sky darkened from smoke and debris forcing Phil to pull a penlight out to check Dave's hand. Phil was relieved to see that while, Dave had a cut on the back of his hand, he still had all his fingers and could move them. "Relax," Phil told his friend, "it's just a cut." As the bombs continued to fall, Phil bandaged Dave's hand. By the time Phil had finished, the bombing had ended. Unfortunately, the battleship or battleships opened up again.

* * * * *

Naval Space Center
Naval Base Quebec, Omar IV
June 6, 2487, 1528 Local, 1228 UT

The Fifteenth Attack Wing was down to just 21 functioning SA-18s. The situation required sending all 21 craft along with ten SF-121s to escort them. The spacecraft pulled up to a 70-degree angle and quickly climbed into orbit. The pilots located the two battleships that were bombarding the Third Regiment. The SA-18s fired dozens of AM-4 missiles at them. Decoys fooled many of them, but several found their targets, striking each ship a half of a dozen times, not enough to destroy the monsters, but enough to get them to cease fire and engage the SA-18s. As the SA-18s attacked, several of the pilots noticed a third battleship near Omar VII, obviously waiting for any ships to try to enter the system.

Model Four Batronian Fighters joined the fight, swarming around the SA-18s and defending the battleships. But, having accomplished their mission, the SA-18s with their fighter escorts, dropped back into Omar IV's atmosphere, but not before the Batronians had destroyed four more SA-18s and three SF-112s.

* * * * *

Third Regiment/First Battalion/Company C/First Platoon
Five Miles West of Zelerod, Omar IV
June 6, 2487, 1535 Local, 1235 UT

The bombardment ended and the screams began. Dave and Phil moved from the foxhole and made their way to a screaming man. Downed trees, smoke and piles of debris made the trek difficult. The trees that had provided cover were now obstacles to overcome.

Dave and Phil found the screaming man lying in a foxhole with a bad wound to his head and his hand a bloody mess from a piece of shrapnel. Two other men laid nearby, clearly dead.

"Get a medic," Phil told Dave as he tore the man's shirt. He applied a tourniquet to the man's lower arm using a branch from one of the fallen trees to tighten the knot. He used another piece of the man's shirt to put pressure on the trooper's head wound. The wounded man reached for is L-29 and tried to rise.

"Stay down,' Phil urged him. In the distance, Phil could hear small arms fire, but for now, First Platoon's position appeared secure.

Several minutes later, Dave showed up with a medic who relieved Phil. The cost of the bombardment was heavy for First Platoon. Four men and a woman were killed and three wounded, two of which had to be evacuated.

* * * * *

Headquarters Destroyer Squadron Ten
Naval Base Oscar, Kylar II
June 6, 2487, 0810 Local, 1430 UT

Admiral William P. Morris studied the reports he was getting from Omar IV. While the planet consisted of a single continent slightly larger than the size of Asia, almost the entire population lived in the northeastern one-eighth of the continent and now the western half of that area, with the exception of the city of Tylan, was under the control of the Batronians. To make matters worse, the Batronians had more ships, spacecraft and ground troops there than Earth had. Even counting Task Force One, which was still over 1000 AMU from Omar, Earth's forces were vastly outnumbered.

The Admiral puffed on his cigar. *It could be worse*, he thought. *We could have computers running everything like at Masic Point.* When war broke out on Masic Point, computers controlled ships and flew spacecraft. It wasn't long before those systems were hacked and Earth's own weapons were used against her. The Navy adapted quickly, removing computer controls from all warships and spacecraft. Now computers were tools to help targeting, processing data from sensors and assisting in navigation. People controlled the ships and spacecraft, not computers. *But*, the Admiral thought as he put out his cigar, *unfortunately people die.*

* * * * *

It was growing dark outside and the curtains were closed in the small two-bedroom farmhouse that Tony and Amy Fillmore lived in. Tony, who nearly everyone called "T", raised corn, beans and tomatoes on the nearly two-hundred-acre farm located on the north side of the village. Since the invasion, Tony and his wife had remained indoors watching the news stream on the wall display. A knock on the door surprised both of them. Tony looked at Amy and raised an eyebrow. Amy shook her head, shrugging her shoulders at the same time silently telling her husband that she didn't know who would be at the door. Tony got up and signaled for his wife to remain out of sight.

At 400 pounds, Tony waddled, more than walked to the door. Tony didn't have a weapon and had never wanted one until now. The invasion by Batron had rattled both him and his wife. They had been born and raised on Omar IV and was used to the simple life that the planet provided. The person on the other side of the door knocked again. Tony took a deep breath, opened the door and saw Jack Mitchell.

"'T', let me come in," Jack said. Tony stepped aside and closed the door once Jack was in.

"Where have you been?" Tony asked. Despite being twelve years Jack's junior and physically being so different, Jack and Tony were the best of friends.

"Checking out the Batronians," Jack said glancing over at the news stream. "What are they saying?"

"The feed out of Malyn shows a Batronian officer telling everyone that Omar is now under Batronian control and it will mean a better life for all of us. He said we should continue to work and go about our lives during the transition. But the feed out of Zelerod says that the Navy is still fighting the Batronians and that the Batronians aren't in control. I don't know what to believe. I know they have control of the village."

"The Navy is still fighting, but I don't think they can hold out. One day, we may have to be the ones to take action," the former Master Chief said.

"But, I don't have any weapons and I wouldn't know how to use one if I did. Hell, look at me. Do I look like a soldier?" the 400-pound man asked.

"Not every action has to be a fight. Sometimes, there are better ways to help," Jack said as Amy brought the men some beers.

* * * * *

Third Regiment/First Battalion/Company C/First Platoon
Five Miles West of Zelerod, Omar IV
June 6, 2487, 1943 Local, 1643 UT

The temperature dropped quickly after nightfall and soon Phil and Dave were drinking coffee for warmth. The two men remained alert despite the lack of activity since the last bombardment ended over four hours ago. Though the adrenaline high was gone, fear of another attack kept the men awake and alert. Sergeant Pachenko approached Dave and Phil.

"Here's the deal. We're going to remain here tonight, but we can't risk lighting fires, so use your bags to stay warm. One sleeps, the other watches. This is no joke. Make sure one of you is awake at all times."

"Yes, Sergeant," both men replied.

"How's the shoulder?" Phil asked the Sergeant.

"Hurts like hell, but thank you for treating it," the Sergeant said.

"You're welcome," Phil replied.

"Early tomorrow, we are going to move out. I'll tell you an hour before we move."

"Where are we moving to?" Phil asked.

"I have no idea, but you'll have an hour to get your gear packed and be ready to move," Sergeant Pachenko replied.

"Aye, Sergeant," the men replied.

"How many troopers do we have left?" Phil asked.

"Sixteen," the Sergeant said solemnly, "including me. Three of those are wounded." Phil quickly realized that First Platoon had lost a third of their troopers.

"Four wounded. Don't forget yourself," Phil told Pachenko.

"Yeah. Keep a sharp lookout," the Sergeant ordered and then moved out.

"You can sleep first. I'm too wound up," Dave said.

"I can't sleep yet either," Phil replied. "When one of us gets tired, we'll start rotating." Thirty minutes later, the two men would be glad they decided to wait for sleep.

* * * * *

Armored Vehicle
Five Miles West of Zelerod, Omar IV
June 6, 2487, 1959 Local, 1659 UT

Colonel Nelson had commandeered another vehicle to use as his command vehicle. He had managed to get a small scanner unit, as well as several comm units which were being operated in the back of the vehicle. He sat in the rear of the vehicle looking over reports from his Company's Commanding Officers. He was losing troopers quickly. They were killing more Batronian soldiers than they were losing, but the Batronians could afford the losses. He couldn't. He brought up a map of the area on a display and studied it carefully. He needed to find a position that was easier to defend. He sat, silently studying the map before him.

* * * * *

Third Regiment/First Battalion/Company C/First Platoon
Five Miles West of Zelerod, Omar IV
June 6, 2487, 2017 Local, 1717 UT

All the troopers in the Naval Assault Forces were issued night vision goggles and both Phil and Dave were wearing them. But, even with the goggles, they didn't see the Batronians until they opened fire.

Once again, the Batronians had managed to flank them, coming from Dave and Phil's left. And they were close! Less than fifty yards away, having somehow managed to move silently into position. This forced Dave and Phil to reposition themselves, bringing their weapons to the left. They began to return fire, trying to keep their heads down as they did. There seemed to be dozens of Batronians converging on them.

"Keep firing!" Phil yelled to Dave as he grabbed four grenades. He pulled the pin on the first one and lobbed it toward the enemy. The explosion flashed in front of them temporarily messing up their night vision goggles. Dave continued to fire blindly as Phil lobbed three more grenades in rapid succession.

"Shit!" Dave yelled as a bolt grazed his cheek. It burned like hell. "I'm hit!"

Phil grabbed his L-29 and began firing. "How bad?" he asked as he took down a Batronian soldier.

"I don't know. It hurts, but I don't think it's bad," Dave said as he continued firing. The grenades had reduced the incoming fire some, but not much as bolts continued to pound their position.

"Can you cover me?" Phil asked as he saw the Batronians moving toward Second Platoon with heavy firepower.

"Yeah," Dave replied changing his charge pack.

"Okay," Phil said. He moved from the foxhole keeping his head down. He was sweating heavily now despite the cool air. He moved behind one of the few trees still standing and looked right toward Second Platoon. Approximately fifteen Batronian soldiers were firing on Second Platoon and appeared to have the platoon pinned down.

"Where are they?" Phil heard Dave ask. Phil looked and saw Dave had moved to a downed tree near him.

"They have Second Platoon pinned down," Phil said. "We have to move closer.

"Okay, I'll cover you," Dave said. He rolled over and watched as Phil advanced thirty yards to another standing tree. Phil turned and signaled for Dave to join him. As Dave prepared to move, a bolt hit the tree he had been laying behind. Dave rolled back and saw a Batronian soldier as two more bolts passed over his head. He watched as, in what seemed like slow motion, the Batronian brought the muzzle of his rifle down slightly toward Dave's head. As Dave braced for the shot that would surely end his life, he saw the Batronian suddenly drop, hit from behind. Dave saw Sergeant Pachenko step from behind a tree and move up kneeling beside him.

"I saw Moore and you move from the foxhole. What did you see?" Sergeant Pachenko asked.

Dave's heart was pounding in his chest and his body was shaking. He felt like he was about to throw up. He took a deep breath and then answered. "Second Platoon is pinned down. We're trying to help."

"You got hit," Sergeant Pachenko said looking at the wound to Dave's face in the glow of his night vision goggles.

"I'm okay," Dave replied. Phil was signaling urgently. "I have to move." Dave made his way to Phil's position, keeping his head down, his legs still shaking from the close call. As Dave took cover, Sergeant Pachenko moved to his side.

"Sergeant," Phil said pointing at where the Batronians had Second Platoon pinned down about one hundred fifty yards from and slightly downhill of their position. However, there were more trees for cover in the Batronian's position. Fortunately, the Batronians were facing away from Dave, Phil and the Sergeant.

"Okay, let's move forward fifty yards and we'll get them," the Sergeant said. It took almost ten minutes for all three men to get into position almost directly behind the Batronians who were firing away at Second Platoon. Sergeant Pachenko signaled for Dave and Phil to take aim and both Privates switched their L-29s to auto. As soon as Sergeant Pachenko fired the first round, Dave and Phil opened fire as well, sweeping their weapons as they were trained to do in boot camps. Some of the Batronians dropped, while others turned toward the three humans. Several returned fire, but none of the Batronians lasted long as Dave and Phil mowed them down before the enemy could get an accurate fix on them. When the last one dropped, both men instinctively changed charge packs and switched their L-29s back to single fire mode.

"Oh shit!" Phil yelled moving quickly away from Dave. Dave looked in the direction that Phil was headed and saw Sergeant Pachenko was lying face down, his weapon on the ground beside him. Dave joined Phil, who was checking the Sergeant for a pulse. Phil looked at Dave and shook his head. The two friends picked up the Sergeant and began to carry him back to the Platoon's position. As they retraced their path, Dave took the earpiece from the Sergeant's ear and placed it in his own.

"This is Private Roberts. Sergeant Pachenko is KIA," Dave said his voice cracking.

"Roger," the Platoon Lieutenant replied.

By the time Dave and Phil made it back to the Platoon, the firefight had died down to a trickle and by 2015, the Batronians had withdrawn once more. Exhausted, Dave slept as soon as Phil had bandaged the wound to his cheek. He was shivering in the cold night air when Phil woke him two hours later to take the watch.

CHAPTER TWELVE

ESS London (SCV-7)
950 AMU from Omar
June 7, 2487, 0130 UT

Rear Admiral Frank Kilgallon could not sleep, so at 0045 he helped himself to some coffee and moved to the flag bridge to watch the stars. Despite all the years in the Navy, he was still captivated staring out in space from a ship. The number of stars appeared to be ten times what you could see from Earth. His thoughts drifted to Evelyn and then to his daughter who was due dot have a baby in just a few weeks. His daughter, Vanessa, was the first member of his family to be born on a planet other than Earth when Evelyn gave birth to her at the Naval Hospital on Kylar II. Now his grandchild would also be a native of Kylar.

The Task Force continued racing toward the Omar System, now at a speed of 30 AMU, *Iwo Jima*'s Chief Engineer somehow getting her to do two more AMUs than her rated speed. *London* would be able to launch spacecraft that could reach Omar IV at approximately 2300 tonight and Rear Admiral Kilgallon, like every other member of Task Force One, prayed that Omar

IV could hold out that long. Waiting, Kilgallon had learned long ago, was the hardest part of serving in the military.

"Sir, I have a message from Fourth Fleet," the Messenger of the Watch said as he came onto the Flag Bridge.

"Thank you," the Rear Admiral said as he took the message.

```
070624870059U

From: Commander, Fourth Fleet
To: Commander, Task Force One
Subj: Enemy Ship Movement

1. Hawkeye One reports a large number of
   enemy ships passing Icor, heading toward
   Omar at 23 AMU.
2. Recommend that Task Force One avoid
   contact with this force due to numeric
   advantage and superior firepower of the
   enemy force.
```

Frank closed his eyes. Icor was 1100 AMU or so from Omar. That meant that Task Force One had less than 24 hours once they arrived to do what they could.

* * * * *

Command Center
Naval Base Quebec, Omar IV
June 7, 2487, 0508 Local, 0208 UT

Amber Harrington returned to the Command Center just after 0500 on June 7th after having left at 0130 for a few hours of sleep. Her red hair, normally perfectly arranged, was a mess. She looked and felt exhausted. Gathered at the Command Center was the Commanders of the Thirteenth Fighter Wing and the Fifteenth Attack Wing, who both looked as tired as Amber, and a new face, a Major representing the Third Regiment who looked fresh and unrattled. His appearance caused a pang of jealousy for Amber, though it certainly wasn't the Major's fault that she had lacked sleep.

"Report, gentlemen," Captain Harrington said as she sat down at the conference table with a steaming cup of black coffee.

"Ma'am, my crews have managed to get two more craft repaired, so we have nineteen SA-18s operational," the Commander of the Fifteenth Attack Wing reported.

"I have only fourteen SF-112s ready, ma'am," the Commander of the Thirteenth Fighter Wing reported. "We're trying to get more up and running, but I'm not hopeful."

"Third Regiment is at 65% strength, ma'am. They will be repositioning themselves shortly to compensate for losses and to better defend Zelerod," the new Major reported.

"It's not much, but we need to hold out. Task Force One is less than 24 hours away. Let's do what we can with what we have," Captain Harrington said.

And so, the Battle for Omar entered its second day.

* * * * *

Third Regiment/First Battalion/Company C/First Platoon
Five Miles West of Zelerod, Omar IV
June 7, 2487, 0536 Local, 0236 UT

A Corporal had shown up in the middle of the night assigned to take Sergeant Pachenko's spot by the Commanding Officer of Company C. The Sergeant's body, along with several others, had been removed hours earlier and transported to Naval Base Quebec. The Corporal had come by again at 0500 and told Phil and Dave to pack up and to be prepared to move out in a half an hour. At 0536, First Platoon rejoined the remainder of Company C and along with the rest of Third Regiment began to redeploy.

Dave and Phil walked along the road to Zelerod in silence. It was a cold morning with clouds covering the stars. Omar IV had no moon, but if it had one, the cloud cover was thick enough that it wouldn't have been seen. The air was damp in a way that suggested that rain was coming.

As they marched, Dave noted a large open field on his right. Such fields were common on Omar IV where agriculture was the primary industry. The field was surrounded by a three-foot high stone wall. Company C was dispatched behind the eastern side of the wall. The company separated into platoons with First Platoon on the southernmost position. They setup defensively behind the wall facing west. Dave couldn't help but be reminded of the wall the fireteam had encountered during bootcamp, when Max directed the fireteam during the exercise. As First Platoon was setting up, Dave noticed that they were down to twelve troopers. His hand and cheek wound hurt, but he didn't complain as he set up his gear beside Phil.

* * * * *

Command Center
Naval Base Quebec, Omar IV
June 7, 2487, 0618 Local, 0318 UT

Captain Harrington sat at the table working on her third cup of coffee already this morning, far exceeding what she normally drank. But coffee and adrenaline were the only two things that was keeping her going.

"Ma'am, we are getting reports that Tylan has been occupied by Batronian Forces," a Communications Technician reported.

"Very well," Amber replied. Running her hand through her long red hair, she studied the map of Omar V on the display on the table. With Tylan in enemy hands, Batron now controlled over half of the inhabited portion of the planet. Earth still held Zelerod and the strategically unimportant city of Akin, plus the Naval Base. Still the Batronians were moving faster than she liked. She knew she needed to find a way to slow them down and that hope would have to rest with the Third Regiment.

* * * * *

Space Center
Naval Base Quebec, Omar IV
June 7, 2487, 0710 Local, 0410 UT

The alert came as soon as the sensors detected the Batronian spacecraft and the Thirteenth Fighter Wing launched the remaining fourteen SF-112s. Bombs started falling on the space center and explosions rang out. A hanger was destroyed in the first minute of the bombing. Naval personnel fired the Batronians, while SF-112s launched their missiles and fired their 35-mm guns at the enemy.

* * * * *

Third Regiment/First Battalion/Company C/First Platoon
Three Miles West of Zelerod, Omar IV
June 7, 2487, 0712 Local, 0412 UT

Batronian attack craft also hit the Third Regiments new position in the early morning hours of June 7th. Dave and Phil pressed against the wall, flat on their bellies with their heads covered by their hands. The bombs were close and loud, pounding the human's positions. 400-mm laser fire from the battleships joined the bombing showering dirt and debris on Dave and Phil once again.

I'm never going to get used to this, Dave thought as he tried to make himself as small as possible. A tremendous explosion came from a bomb hitting the wall just ten yards to the right of him. Searing heat, the sound of shrapnel falling and a concussive blast that rattled his bones followed.

"Damn!" he yelled. He looked over at Phil who was laying perfectly still. Dave reached over to his friend, tapping him on the shoulder. Phil didn't move. Then Dave saw the blood, and a lot of it, coming from Phil's waist. Panicking, Dave tried to pull Phil toward him. His upper body moved, but his lower body remained in position, separating from each other. Blood seeped from Phil's opened eyes and mouth.

"Medic!" Dave yelled as tears began to flow. Bombs continued to fall around him, but all Dave could do was hold his friend's body and weep almost unaware of the chaos occurring around him.

* * * * *

Home of Tony Fillmore
Village of Lansing, Omar IV
June 7, 2487, 0814 Local, 0514 UT

"You're right," the 400-pound man said as he looked out the window using Jack Mitchell's binoculars. "Most of them are gone."

"All of the armored vehicles, too," Jack said.

"Yeah," Tony said after searching for a few minutes. "All of the vehicles are gone. I wonder where they went."

"I'd guess they left only 20 or so soldiers here to hold the village. The rest are gone," Jack said as he took the binoculars back and looked again. He studied the village carefully. "Listen, Tony, I have to call this in."

"You know where the comm unit is," Tony said.

"But, 'T' there's a chance the Batronians could pick it up."

"I know. Let's just hope they don't," Tony replied looking over at Amy who nodded her head in agreement of her husband's decision.

* * * * *

"Yes, Master Chief Mitchell?" Captain Harrington asked after being informed that Jack was back on the comm.

"I have to be quick Ma'am. The Batronian regiment that was here last night is gone except for twenty or so soldiers that they left here for security. I have no idea where they went," Jack said.

"Thank you, Master Chief. Keep safe," Amber replied.

"Aye, ma'am," Jack said and the comm disconnected.

Amber looked at all the information that they had available. The Batronians were bombing the Space Center which kept the fighters busy there, while battleships and spacecraft bombed Third Regiment. And now, another regiment of Batronians was on the move. Amber knew what was happening. "Warn Colonel Nelson that the Batronians he engaged yesterday are about to be reinforced by at least one more regiment," Amber ordered.

* * * * *

The bombardment ended at just a little after noon. By then, the wall that Company C was using for protection was practically destroyed and the field was scorched earth. Company C retreated into a wooded area, once again giving Batron a little more territory. Dave knew that Batron didn't have to move quickly. Gaining one inch at a time still meant that they would eventually control the planet.

A medic had arrived and removed Phil in a body bag fifteen minutes after he died. Despite being shell-shocked, Dave somehow pushed on. First Platoon was down to just seven troopers with four of those wounded. Yet the fight would have to continue.

Dave was now in the northernmost position of First Platoon and near Second Platoon which had suffered nearly as badly as First Platoon had. Dave looked up and saw the Corporal approaching.

"We are going to hold the line here. We have artillery support and we have barricaded the main road, so the Batronians will have to cross that field. With cover here, we'll have an advantage," the Corporal said as he handed Dave a bowl of chili and a bottle of water. Dave wished he had the Corporal's confidence. *Every time we push the enemy back, they come again*, he thought.

"Okay," Dave said. He was tired, dirty and sweating. He felt as if he couldn't go on any further. Although the sky was overcast, the humidity was extremely high. Dave knew there was a storm coming.

* * * * *

Armored Vehicle
Three Miles West of Zelerod, Omar IV
June 7, 2487, 1229 Local, 0929 UT

The rain started to fall as Colonel Nelson verified that he had another AWC-2 in the air. The news that another regiment of Batronian soldier on its way to reinforce the enemy troops filled the 44-year-old Colonel with dread. The problem was that he was low on everything: artillery, troops and even air support. He had armored vehicles, but only enough to move approximately half of his troopers. Lightning flashes followed by a rumble of thunder hit as the Colonel considered his options. There weren't many.

* * * * *

Third Regiment/First Battalion/Company C/First Platoon
Three Miles West of Zelerod, Omar IV
June 7, 2487, 1315 Local, 1015 UT

Dave was soaked despite the covering from the trees and having his poncho on. With the temperature dropping quickly into the mid-50s, the rain was bitterly cold. He looked across the field, the scorched earth now muddy with puddles of water. He thought he saw movement but he couldn't be sure because of the pouring rain. Plus, his eyes stung from the smoke that managed to hang in the air from this morning's bombing.

Dave raised his binoculars to his eyes. His L-29 was leaning against a tree beside him. Sure enough, he could see the Batronian soldiers approaching from the other side of the field. As he watched, he heard artillery rounds passing high over his head and seconds later exploding in front of the Batronians. Dave heard the enemy yell and then watched in shock as the Batronians ran full speed across the field screaming as they did. Batronian soldiers were stretched out as far as he could see, their shout being heard above the pouring rain. Mud splashed as the enemy advanced across the field. Dave reached over and grabbed his weapon. He pulled out four extra charge packs, set them on the ground beside him and knelt on the soft, wet ground as he brought his rifle to his shoulder using the tree for cover.

More artillery shells fell on the enemy, yet they continued to scream and run toward the humans. The rain seemed to pick up as the Batronians, still screaming reached the stone wall where Phil had died the previous evening. As they began to climb over the rubble, Dave opened fire. With his weapon on auto, he swept back and forth watching in pleasure as they enemy fell to his rounds. He changed his charge pack as the Batronians returned fire. Several rounds hit the tree and others flew past Dave as he finished loading the charge pack and brought his rifle back up. Bolts were flying in both directions as Dave emptied a second and then a third charge pack, rain running down his face. Artillery continued to be fired into enemy lines, but the Batronians continued to advance as they yelled and were now only fifty yards from First Platoon's position.

Dave grabbed the remaining two charge packs, put one in his pocket and loaded the other. He moved, keeping his head low, retreating twenty yards to another tree and turned to fire. He saw that the Batronians had slowed as they approached the woods. Their yell was briefly drowned out when thunder roared after a bright flash of lightening. Dave knew that he needed to conserve his charge, so he switched his L-29 into single fire mode. He pulled out a grenade, pulled the pin and lobbed it toward the enemy. When the grenade went off, he moved again, this time fifty yards toward the main road.

Lightning and thunder increased adding to the confusion of the battle. For the rest of his life, he would never forget the sounds of the battle. The ground was muddy causing Dave to slip as he moved behind another tree. Dave knelt, rifle shouldered and scanned the woods for the enemy in the pouring rain. Four Batronians appeared from the woods just thirty yards from Dave's position. They were moving quietly now, no longer screaming, as they searched for humans. Dave fired putting two rounds each into two of the four soldiers before the remaining two ducked behind a tree and returned fire. The rounds struck the tree that he was behind using for cover. He flinched and ducked instinctively. He recovered and brought his rifle up and fired six rounds blindly toward the enemy. A sudden explosion at the enemy's position surprised him. He looked to his right and saw another private behind a tree just two feet from him. He recognized her, although he didn't know her name. Apparently, she had just thrown a grenade at the Batronians who had pinned Dave down.

"Cover left! I'll cover right!" she shouted over the pouring rain. Another bolt of lightening struck as Dave moved into position.

* * * * *

ESS London (SCV-7)
680 AMU from Omar
June 7, 2487, 1030 UT

Lieutenant Command Chris "C-Dog" Davenport and the rest of Charlie Flight, along with Alpha and Beta flights, sat in the Ready Room for the briefing of flight operations that would commence at approximately 2300.

"The plan is this," the Commander of the Air Group (CAG) began. The CAG was overall command of the spacecraft on the carrier. "We have divided the fighters into four groups. Group One will include your flights. Alpha Flight Leader will have overall command of the group. You will escort and defend the SA-18s that will engage the enemy. Group Two will engage planet base targets. Groups Three and Four will be relieving you, launching as soon as you begin your return flight. We expect continuous operations for at least the next 24 hours, so get some sleep."

While all the pilots tried to sleep, few actually did.

* * * * *

Third Regiment/First Battalion/Company C/First Platoon
Two Miles West of Zelerod, Omar IV
June 7, 2487, 1335 Local, 1035 UT

The advance by the Batronians seemed to be slowing down as they apparently consolidated their position in the newly gained territory. Firefights were becoming sporadic and it had been several minutes since Dave had seen the enemy. Even the rain, though still heavy, seemed to be slowing down. Dave looked up and saw the female trooper making her way over to him.

"I'm Karen Baker," the trooper said as she took cover behind the tree she now shared with Dave.

"Dave Roberts," Dave replied, eyes still scanning the woods for the slightest movement. After several minutes, Karen sat with her back to the tree and drank from her canteen. Like Dave, she was drenched. She closed her eyes and appeared to rest for a couple of minutes.

"Get yourself a drink,' Karen said as she picked up her L-29 and aimed into the woods, like Dave, scanning for movement. Dave did. As he sat and drank, Dave looked at her for the first time and noticed how attractive she was. Her blond hair was cut short, but still was feminine. She was in great physical shape from her training. She was shorter than Dave at 5'7". As he looked at her, she turned towards him and he noticed her blue eyes. *What the hell am I doing*? Dave asked himself. *We're in a combat zone, not the base club*. He took another drink to cover his staring at her and then moved back into position.

"How bad of shape is your platoon in?" Dave asked.

"Bad. Last I heard, we only had twelve troopers left."

"We're down to seven. We even lost our Sergeant."

"Damn," Karen said. Suddenly, she held a finger to her lips. Dave froze, watching her as the rain dripped down her face. She moved her finger, pointing into the woods. Dave looked where she was pointing and saw four Batronians approaching. Silently, Dave and Karen took aim. Dave shot the two on the left and Karen the two on the right before the Batronians even knew they were there.

"Nice shooting," a voice behind them said. Dave spun around ready to fire, but hesitating just enough to not shoot the Sergeant.

"Damn it, Sergeant!" Dave said, his heart pounding. Adrenaline pumped through his body.

"Relax, Private. We're moving back to the edge of the city," the Sergeant said. Dave recognized him finally as the Sergeant from Second Platoon.

"I have to report to the First Platoon's Corporal," Dave said.

"He's dead," the Sergeant said. He was chewing tobacco and spat on the wet ground. Rain poured down on the spot he spit, breaking it up. "I've been given both First and Second Platoons, not that it's much. Together, there are only fourteen of us left."

Dave was shocked. Just fourteen troopers left out of the two platoons. That meant at least thirty-four dead between them.

"Wow," Karen said, the shock evident on her face.

"Where are we forming up?" Dave asked.

"We're not. I want you two to move north and east. When you see other troopers, link up and continue to move. I'll catch up after I round up the rest. Breaks on the hour, no more often than that," the Sergeant said, spitting again.

Dave and Karen moved out together just two minutes later.

* * * * *

Governor's Office
Zelerod, Omar IV
June 7, 2487, 1412 Local, 1112 UT

Colonel Nelson was sitting in the brightly painted Governor's Office on the third floor of the capitol building in Zelerod, briefing the Governor of Omar IV about the operations to the west of Zelerod. The Governor had been in office only six months and was shocked by the invasion. Omar IV hadn't ever been directly involved in a war, and the concept seemed foreign to the Governor. And from what the Colonel was telling him, he needed to start preparing for the worst.

"I sent an alert on the video stream warning the people here to move to emergency shelters," the Governor said.

"Good. We're trying to keep the fighting outside of the city, but if it does move into the city, I want to keep civilians as safe as possible," Colonel Nelson said. He looked out of the window at the light rain that was falling.

"I want that, too," the Governor said. "Are we going to win?"

'I don't know," Colonel Nelson admitted as he rose from his seat. "I'm doing everything I can."

The Governor watched the Colonel leave the office, he took a deep breath and wondered what his next step should be. He didn't have a clue, but the fear of being in Batron's hands overwhelmed him.

* * * * *

Third Regiment/First Battalion/Company C/Combined Platoons
One-half Mile West of Zelerod, Omar IV
June 7, 2487, 1702 Local, 1402 UT

The rain had slowed to a drizzle, though the ground was saturated and muddy when they stopped and set up for a break. So far, they had linked up with ten of the twelve other surviving members from First and Second Platoons. Dave and Karen sat together eating cold beans and drinking water.

"Where are you from?" Karen asked Dave.

"North Dakota, you?"

"Newport News, Virginia," Karen said eating a spoonful of beans.

"That's near the old American Naval Base, isn't it?" Dave sked.

"Norfolk? Yeah, it is. Back then Newport News had a shipyard and built and serviced the Navy's ships," Karen said as Dave finished his beans. It turned out that Karen was Dave's age and that she finished boot camp in April. Somehow, to Dave, she appeared more experienced than that.

As they talked, Dave saw movement out of the corner of his eye. Eight Batronians rushed into the clearing where the troopers were eating, firing as they did. Karen turned toward the sound of the rifle fire instinctively to see what was happening. Dave grabbed her, pushing her down, as a bolt struck her arm. Dave grabbed his weapon, fired blindly and then drug Karen with him behind a tree.

"How bad?"" he asked as he fired at the Batronians.

"Just grazed me," she answered as she shouldered her Ll-29 and began firing. Several troopers were down in the clearing either squirming and screaming in pain or, worse yet, laying silently and perfectly still. Dave and Karen fired as a team, covering for each other as charge packs were changed. Four Batronians were down. The other four had taken cover and were firing at the humans.

"Grenade!" Karen yelled. She dove as Dave did. The explosion rattled Dave's teeth but he managed to dive clear of it. Now bolts from one of the Batronians were passing just inches above his head. Dave pressed his body to the ground trying to avoid getting hit. Karen fired a shot killing the Batronian that had Dave pinned down.

A few minutes later, the fight was over. All eight of the Batronians lie dead. But, it had cost the humans six more troopers. The six remaining troopers managed to make gurneys using tree branches and blankets. They placed two bodies on each gurney and carried them as they set off again.

One hour later, the troopers arrived at the road. Zelerod was only a quarter of a mile away. Second Platoon's Sergeant had located the remaining two troopers from Second Platoon and had taken command of the fourteen troopers from Third Platoon. Altogether, there were only 22 survivors from Company C. As the rest of the regiment arrived, the troopers began to set up for one final stand.

* * * * *

Command Vehicle
Zelerod, Omar IV
June 7, 2487, 1839 Local, 1539 UT

The Usian River passed through the middle of Zelerod, flowing north to south. Colonel Nelson's command vehicle was position in the middle of the bridge that crossed the river, looking through his binoculars at what remained of Third Regiment as they were setting up. He could hardly believe his eyes. The regiment had started with 648 troopers and he had just learned he was down to just 289. He pulled the binoculars down and pushed a button on the comm unit. "Eagle Eyes, this is Top Dog. Give me an estimate on the enemy's strength"

"Top Dog, Eagle Eyes. Approximately 900 to 1000 enemy combatants," the Communications Specialist onboard the EWC-2 reported. *A three to one advantage*, the Colonel thought before connecting to the Command Center.

"What can I do for you, Colonel?" Captain Harrington asked. She was two years senior to the Colonel, but right now she felt confined and that the Colonel was doing the real leading.

"Ma'am, I need every spacecraft that you have available. If we don't stop them here, we won't stop them at all," Colonel Nelson said. There was a distinct pause as Harrington discussed it with the wing commanders.

"They'll be there in ten minutes," Amber said.

"Thank you, ma'am," the Colonel said disconnecting. He lifted his binoculars to his eyes just as mortar rounds began falling on the capital.

* * * * *

Third Regiment/First Battalion/Company C/Combined Platoons
One-Quarter Mile West of Zelerod, Omar IV
June 7, 2487, 1841 Local, 1541 UT

The mortar shells forced Company C and the rest of the remnant of the Third Regiment to seek cover. The explosions were powerful and continuous. The mortar rounds were soon joined by bombs from Batronian spacecraft and 400-mm laser fire from the orbiting battleships. The rain started falling again as troops sought shelter in water filled bunkers, foxholes and drainage ditches.

Several minutes into the attack, spacecraft from the Naval Base streaked over Zelerod and the Third Regiment. SA-18s bombed enemy positions as SF-112s engaged enemy spacecraft.

"We're going to advance," the Sergeant yelled to the troopers of Company C as bombs, mortars and 400-mm bolts continue to fall on them. By advancing toward the enemy, the Sergeant reasoned, the enemy could not continue to bombard the troopers without risking their own soldiers.

Dave and Karen advanced together and began firing near the maximum effective range of the L-29 or two hundred yards. Firing on fully automatic, the Third Regiment watched as enemy soldiers fell. But, the enemy was fighting just as effectively and slowly, the Third Regiment not only stopped advancing, but began to retreat.

At 1920, the Third Regiment entered Zelerod. The city seemed deserted with the residents hiding in bunkers. Several buildings were already burning. The buildings were not tall by Earth's standards, but here they were Omar IV's tallest. Two collapsed when they were struck by bombs from Batronian spacecraft. Third Regiment was in a fighting retreat, engaging the enemy for a few minutes and then retreating some through the city. They crossed the Usian River and blew up the bridge behind them attempting to slow down the Batronians.

As Dave fired across the river at the Batronians, a black dog crossed the street with its tail tucked between its legs. Dave nearly shouted at it. Despite all the troopers and Batronians dying around him, seeing the dog killed would have bothered Dave in a way that was impossible to explain. Bolts from both sides passed over the dog who made it across the street, while a man to the dog's right fell over with a wound to his chest.

The retreat continued as the Batronians managed to somehow cross the river and at 2005 locally, the Third Regiment pulled out of Zelerod.

* * * * *

Governor's Office
Zelerod, Omar IV
June 7, 2487, 2025 Local, 1725 UT

"Citizens of Omar," the Governor began. Off camera stood ten Batronians soldiers, weapons in hand. They were led by an officer who spoke English and watched as the Governor spoke to the people of Omar IV. "Today, in response to Earth's continuous interference in Batron's affairs, Batronian forces have occupied major cities on Omar IV. Although, Earth's Naval Forces opposed the peaceful forces of the Batronian Army, the Batronians have rightfully taken control of Omar IV. I urge all citizens to lay down their weapons and allow the Batronian soldiers to safely do their job. The Batronians government is pleased to welcome us as citizens of Batron."

* * * * *

Remnant of Third Regiment
One Mile East of Zelerod, Omar IV
June 7, 2487, 2100 Local, 1800 UT

The 116 remaining troopers began the march toward Naval Base Quebec at 2100, exhausted and beaten.

CHAPTER THIRTEEN

ESS London (CSV-7)
226 AMU from Omar
June 7, 2487, 2312 UT

"Flight Quarters! Flight Quarters! All hands man your Flight Quarter stations for the launching of spacecraft," came the announcement over the ship's intercom. In the flight bay, men and women moved around, preparing the bay and the spacecraft for launch. This was the moment everyone on the ship had been waiting for since the invasion began. Now, they moved with determination, ready to help those on Omar IV.

Chris Davenport lowered his 5'9" frame into his spacecraft looking over and seeing Donald Franklin strapping himself into his SF-112. The pilots were ready. For the past two days, all they could do was wait. Now, they could finally do something and Chris was pumped. Chris started his LX-15 engines and began to go through his preflight checklist. As he worked his way down the list, checking various systems and configuring the spacecraft for flight, he felt the clamp lock onto his SF-112. The clamp pulled his spacecraft into the line of other craft waiting to be launched.

"Charlie Flight, this is Charlie Leader, report," Chris ordered over the flight's comm frequency. All five of the other pilots, four men and a woman reported that they were ready to launch. "Okay then Charlie Flight, let's go get them."

An alarm sounded as the Flight Bay's light turned from green to flashing amber and the bay crew cleared the bay. Minutes later, the SF-112 shook as air was removed from the bay and the flight bay doors were opened. The light turned read and, in pairs, the spacecraft were launched from the carrier.

It took almost ten minutes for all the craft to be launched, but finally the twenty-four SF-112s and twelve SA-18s turned toward Omar and accelerated to 100 AMU. The pilots settled in for a flight that would take over two hours with nervous anticipation of the upcoming fight.

* * * * *

Transport Vehicle
Twenty Miles Southwest of Naval Base Quebec, Omar IV
June 8, 2487, 0318 Local, 0018 UT

It had taken hours to coordinate the transports from Naval Base Quebec to pick up the survivors from the Third Regiment. At first, only a few transports were available, but no trooper would leave until there were transports for everyone. Colonel Nelson was proud of his troopers for maintaining their unity despite their defeat.

Dave sat beside Karen Baker. Both were muddy and exhausted. However, the more he got to know about her, the more impressed he was. She was a good trooper, an excellent shot, brave and well-disciplined. And, despite the mud and sweat, very attractive. She seemed to be just as impressed by him. For now, however, they sat in silence, minds struggling to deal with all that had happened in the past couple of days. Now that the fight was over, Dave struggled with the fact he had killed so many Batronians. How many? He didn't even know. He remembered Phil's body, practically cut in half. The images kept flashing through his mind as he struggled to stay awake.

An explosion snapped everyone back to reality. The transport came to a jerking stop and the troopers began to jump out. Dave, filled with dread, grabbed his L-29 and jumped out of the vehicle. Dave heard and saw the Batronian spacecraft as they attacked the convoy. *Will this ever end?* Dave asked himself.

* * * * *

Command Center
Naval Base Quebec, Omar IV
June 8, 2487, 0320 Local, 0020 UT

"I'm sorry ma'am, we have only two SF-112s left. Sending them out would be sending the pilots to a meaningless death," the Commander of the Thirteenth Fighter Wing told Amber. He was right, of course, but that did not make in any easier to her. She looked around the table hoping to hear any suggestions on how to help the nearby troopers, but there was none.

"Okay. Then let's do this. Load anyone we can find with an SL-21s into a transport and get out there and help our troopers," Amber ordered.

"Aye, ma'am," a Lieutenant at the table said. He got up and moved to a comm unit.

* * * * *

Remnant of Third Regiment
Twenty Miles Southwest of Naval Base Quebec, Omar IV
June 8, 2487, 0322 Local, 0022 UT

Dave Roberts felt completely helpless. As far as he was concerned, the battle had been lost and they were withdrawing. Now, the Batronians were bombing again. They seemed to not be content with just beating the troopers, but seemed intent on annihilating them. And there was nothing anyone could do about it. They had no anti-spacecraft missiles or guns. All they could do was wait it out. Several of the transports had been destroyed and no doubt even more troopers had died. Karen was beside Dave in the ditch trying to keep herself as low as possible as bomb after bomb fell.

The sound of a larger spacecraft approaching caused Dave to raise his head and look. The bombing ceased and Dave watched as Batronian soldiers jumped out of the larger spacecraft descending rapidly toward the ground on repelling ropes. He nudged Karen who looked up and watched dozens of Batronians descending.

"Let's go!" a Sergeant ordered as troopers rose from the ditch and moved to defensive positions along the road. Several of the troopers began firing at the Batronians as they continued to repel from the spacecraft. Dave and Karen took cover behind an undamaged transport and began firing; Karen from a kneeling position and Dave firing from a standing position over her.

The Batronians began to return fire as soon as they hit the ground. They, also, were using abandoned vehicles for cover. The enemy began to spread out, entering the woods to the left and right of the road. Third Regiment countered the move as various Platoon Sergeants ordered part of their forces into the woods determined to keep the Batronians from flanking them.

Karen and Dave were left in their position behind the transport, firing at the enemy. Karen shot two Batronian soldiers as they attempted to move into the woods. Bolts hit off the transport forcing Dave and Karen to duck behind the vehicle.

"Damn, we're so close to the base," Karen said changing out a charge pack.

"I know," Dave replied. He peered around the corner of the vehicle and more bolts hit the transport forcing him to take cover again. Then, he heard the Batronian spacecraft returning and bombs began to fall once more.

* * * * *

Transport Vehicle
Twenty Miles Southwest of Naval Base Quebec, Omar IV
June 8, 2487, 0348 Local, 0048 UT

Naval personnel from Naval Base Quebec jumped out of the transport. Unlike Assault Forces Troopers, regular naval personnel did not use night vision goggles normally, so many moved awkwardly as they set up a dozen SL-21 shoulder launched missiles systems. They launched the missiles as soon as they got tone and within ten minutes, the sky was cleared of Batronian spacecraft.

* * * * *

Remnant of Third Regiment
Twenty Miles Southwest of Naval Base Quebec, Omar IV
June 8, 2487, 0402 Local, 0102 UT

Seeing the Batronian spacecraft being shot down motivated the remaining troopers from the Third Regiment.

"Cover me," Dave told Karen as he moved from behind the transport and fired at a group of four Batronian soldiers who were using another vehicle as cover. He killed two before return fire forced him back behind the transport with Karen.

"That was stupid," Karen said as she shot one of the remaining Batronians who stuck his head out too far while firing at Dave. Dave moved back into position firing from a standing position above the kneeling Karen once again.

"Yeah, but it…" Dave began before he felt a punch to his chest. He looked down and saw a wisp of smoke coming from a hole in his chest. He tried to breathe, but found he couldn't inhale as if the wind had been knocked out of him. He looked at Karen, who was looking at him with a shocked stare. Blackness overcame him and he fell, dropping his weapon as he did.

"Medic!" Karen shouted as she dragged Dave's limp body behind the transport. Her hand trembled as she covered the wound.

* * * * *

Charlie Flight
Omar System
June 8, 2487, 0132 UT

"Charlie Flight, this is Charlie Leader. Let's keep the SA-18s safe," Chris Davenport ordered over the Flight's comm frequency.

"Roger that, C-Dog," Donald Franklin replied. "Let's light them up!"

The fighters streaked toward the enemy. Chris' sensors detected the enemy fighters launching from their carriers. The SF-112s stuck close to the SA-18s as the enemy fighters quickly closed the distance. Chris selected his AM-2 missiles, set them to thruster only mode and obtained a lock on one of the enemy fighters. He released the missile, then selected his lasers and began firing. Donald stuck with Chris, holding position on his right wing as they dodged enemy fire. Don managed to hit one of the Batronians as they flashed past them. The flight banked hard and came around toward the Batronians again.

A warning tone indicated that one of the enemies had locked onto Chris. He toggled his release, dropping three decoys as the Batronian fired the missile. He waited until the last second, pushed his control down and then broke left allowing the missile to hit one of the decoys.

He pulled into a turn with Don on his right. An enemy fighter dropped in behind him firing 35-mm bolts. Instinctively, he pressed down on his left rudder pedal activating thrusters that spun his spacecraft laterally and cut his throttle to neutral. He found himself facing the enemy, flying backwards under the inertia of his fighter. He toggled an AM-2 and fired it at point blank range, destroying the enemy. He spun the SF-112 back around and advanced his throttle.

"Damn, C-Dog, where did you learn to do that? That was unbelievable!" Don exclaimed.

"I haven't shown you all of my tricks, Dreamer," Chris said, his heart pounding. Actually, he had never even thought about doing that before, but there was no way we would admit that to Don. He brought his fighter back around for another pass at the enemy. Several 35-mm bolts hit his spacecraft along the left side, fired from a nearby destroyer. *Damn*, the thought as he tested his flight controls. Everything seemed to work still, so he continued engaging the enemy.

* * * * *

Remnant of Third Regiment
Twenty Miles Southwest of Naval Base Quebec, Omar IV
June 8, 2487, 0438 Local, 0138 UT

The medic was working Dave while Karen provided cover, firing sporadically at the enemy when she could and glancing down to see what was happening with Dave when she couldn't. The roar of spacecraft flying above her in the predawn sky drew her attention as she wondered how the remaining troopers could survive another bombing. She was pleasantly surprised when the SSA-18s from *ESS London* began bombing the enemy. With air support, the Third Regiment was able to engage and kill the remaining enemy soldiers. After bombing the Batronians, *London*'s spacecraft banked hard, flying toward Zelerod.

With the Batronians dead, transport vehicles from the Naval Base were able to move up to supplement the remaining transports that the Third Regiment possessed. Dave was loaded into the transport that Karen and he had used for cover. Without hesitation, Karen jumped into the transport with him.

"How is he?" she asked the medic.

"Not good, but he's alive. His lung has collapsed and he is in shock, but he was lucky that the bolt missed his heart." Karen bowed her head silently praying.

* * * * *

Charlie Flight
Omar System
June 8, 2487, 0154

Chris continued to dodge enemy fire as he protected the few SA-18s that still had missiles left to fire at the enemy ships. The attack craft had managed to destroy a cruiser and destroyer and several other ships were damaged and on fire.

Don felt his fighter jolt as a bolt struck him on the left side, punching a hole into his fighter and damaging his left engine. Warning lights flashed on his HUD and alarms rang out. He quickly shut down the left LX-15 engine. A fire warning light flashed and then went out.

"C-Dog, I lost an engine," Don reported.

"Okay, Dreamer. How's the other one?" Chris asked as he fired a burst of laser fire at a Batronian fighter.

"It's okay," Don said, checking his display. His right engine seemed to be running fine. A warning light and alarm warned him that a missile was locked onto him. He banked and dove, launching three decoys as he did. The missile detonated above and behind him, shaking his fighter. He rejoined Chris who had a Batronian on his tail. Don selected an AM-2, fired it and watched the fighter chasing Chris explode.

"Thanks for the help, Dreamer," Chris said.

"No problem, C-Dog," Don said confidently.

"Okay Charlie Flight, form up. We're out of here," Chris said.

* * * * *

Transport Vehicle
Arriving at Naval Base Quebec, Omar IV
June 8, 2487, 0516 Local, 0216 UT

The transports entered the main gate of Naval Base Quebec just a half an hour before sunrise and headed directly to the Naval Hospital. Most of the 78 survivors from the Third Regiment had wounds that needed battle dressed, including Karen. She reluctantly left Dave's side, her sense of duty overcoming her desire to remain with him.

First, she had her armed looked at by a nurse. The nurse put a fresh bandage on it after applying an ointment to aid in the healing process and prevent infection. Next, she went out, found the Sergeant and reported for duty.

"I'm sending everyone to chow. Get yourself something to eat and then get some rest. If the sirens go off, report to the Space Center and I'll assign you to a gun or SL-21."

"Thanks, Sergeant," Karen said. She walked over to the chow hall, then headed to the hospital to check on Dave. She found him unconscious in a bed. She sat in a chair beside him and within minutes had dozed off, exhausted physically and mentally.

* * * * *

ESS London (SCV-7)
56 AMU from Omar
June 8, 2487, 0241 UT

Chris was the last in his wing to land on the carrier. After the flight bay was repressurized, Chris was helped out of his fighter. He looked at the scorch marks on the left side where enemy bolts had struck his fighter. It made him nauseous knowing how close he came to being killed. When he saw Don's fighter he was shocked. A 35-mm bolt had hit the fuel line for the left engine of his friend's SF-112.

"Can it be fixed?" Don asked desperate to get back into the fight.

"Yeah," the Second Class Spacecraft Technician said. "We'll get it ready for you, sir."

As the pilots moved toward the exit of the flight bay to get food and drink, as well as to be briefed on the next mission, the crew surrounded each craft and began getting them ready for the next mission.

On the Flag Bridge, Rear Admiral Kilgallon looked over the results of the strike. The results were good: two Batronian ships destroyed and several others damaged with minimal loss to the task force. But, the situation on the planet was bad. Omar IV was practically in Batron's hand and all Kilgallon had was a regiment of troopers. Plus, Batron had reinforcements coming. The Rear Admiral considered his options then reached for the comm unit.

"Get me the Captain of *Iwo Jima*," he ordered.

* * * * *

Naval Hospital
Naval Base Quebec, Omar IV
June 8, 2487, 0726 Local, 0426 UT

Karen woke at the sound of the sirens. She looked at Dave who was still unconscious, then grabbed her L-29, exited the hospital and headed for the Space Center at a good run. The sun was out and bright in the sky and the blacktop was drying out from yesterday's rain. The sirens wailed as she saw others rushing toward their stations. Bombs began to fall from the sky as Batronian spacecraft bombed the Space Center.

The Sergeant handed Karen an SL-21 shoulder launcher and a heavy canvas bag containing ten of the three-foot long missiles. Karen quickly loaded the first missile, turned on the targeting system and raised the SL-21 to her shoulder. The first missile she fired was fooled by a decoy, but the second one found its mark destroying a Batronian attack spacecraft.

One of the fighters that was escorting the attack craft that Karen had destroyed dove at her, firing 35-mm bolts and forcing her to dive to the ground. As it passed her, she rose to her knees and fired a missile which the fighter easily avoided. Spacecraft from the second wave from *London* joined the fight over the Naval Space Center, helping to disrupt the Batronians and allowing Karen to shoot down two more spacecraft before the Batronians broke off their attack.

* * * * *

ESS Iwo Jima (AS-38)
Near Omar System
June 8, 2487, 0430 UT

"Set condition One Alpha for assault operations. ACU crew man your craft. All personnel not involved, stand clear of the assault bay while the ship conducts assault operations," the announcement came over the ship's intercom. Men and women responsible for the ACUs moved to the assault units, conducting final checks and starting the engines. The ship's crew checked the bay to ensure everything was secure and ready to launch the ACUs.

Max Finley and the rest of second squad from his platoon had been assigned to security on ACU-17. The eight members of the squad boarded the mainly empty assault unit. Minutes later, air was vented from the bay, the doors opened and the assault units backed out of *Iwo Jima*.

* * * * *

ESS London (SCV-7)
Near Omar System
June 8, 2487, 0435 UT

The spacecraft from *London*, having been rearmed and refueled, had been launched. Rear Admiral Kilgallon sat on the busy flag bridge coordinating his resources for this final action.

"Sir, the ACUs are away. Fighters are escorting," a Communications Technician said.

"Very well," Kilgallon replied as he pictured the plan in his head. He turned to his Operations Officer. "Is the battleship still hanging back at Omar VII?"

"Yes, sir," the Operations Officer replied.

"And our friends are in position?"

"Yes, sir."

"Good," Frank said as he continued to picture the operation unfolding, trying to ensure every detail was covered.

* * * * *

Charlie Flight
Near Omar System
June 8, 2487, 0451 UT

Charlie Flight was tasked with escorting the three ACUs from *Iwo Jima* to Omar IV. They moved toward the Omar system. The ACUs were equipped only with thrusters, so the fighters were on thrusters only as well. It would take almost an hour to reach Omar IV.

Chris watched on his sensor display as the other spacecraft from London attacked the Batronian fleet. He saw the Batronian battleship at Omar VII turn and head for him. With no attack craft with them, Charlie Flight could not take on the giant, well-armed ship.

* * * * *

Naval Space Center
Naval Base Quebec, Omar IV
June 8, 2487, 0752 Local, 0452 UT

Karen Baker scanned the sky looking for any spacecraft, but none appeared. She thought about going to check on Dave now that the attack to be over, but the all clear signal had not been sounded. The morning air was crisp and, other than the smoke from the bombing, the sky was clear.

"Baker, I need you to go to the hospital and assist with the wounded," the Platoon Sergeant said, seeming to appear out of nowhere.

"Sure, Sergeant," Karen said. She looked at the Sergeant's face and realized something was going on. "What's up?" she asked. He told her and all she could do was stare in shock.

* * * * *

In the Air
Village of Lansing, Omar IV
June 8, 2487, 0754 Local, 0454 UT

The pilot of one of the few remaining SA-18s from the Fifteenth Attack Wing flew just north of the village of Lansing over a cornfield. The corn was high this year, which was an advantage, considering. As she banked, she saw three flashes of light below her. She double checked to make sure she had made the proper selection, then circled around, descending as she did and triggered the release.

The object fell, a parachute opening and slowing its descent. No one noticed the object falling nor the 400-pound farmer, who while tending his field, recovered the package and took it to his home.

Chapter Fourteen

Charlie Flight
Omar System
June 8 2487, 0455 UT

Chris watched the battleship moving toward Charlie Flight and the assault crafts that they were escorting as they passed Omar VIII.

"C-Dog, you know that I hate to ask stupid question, but have you noticed that large Batronian ship moving to intercept us?" Don Franklin asked.

"Yeah, I see it Dreamer," Chris said smiling as he thought of Don. Like Chris, Don would know that fighter spacecraft would be no match for the behemoth.

"Again, with the stupid questions, but umm…do we plan on doing anything about it?" Don asked.

Chris had to practically bite his cheek to keep him from laughing. "That's an affirmative, Dreamer."

Don looked at the battleship that was getting larger as it rapidly got closer. "Umm, may I ask when?" Don asked. Just as the question came out of his mouth, a bright flash appeared in space as a missile struck the battleship.

"I would say about now," Chris said no longer able to contain his laughter.

* * * * *

ESS Armstrong (SS-16)
Omar System
June 8, 2487, 0455 UT

"Bring her about!" Commander Carl Adams ordered as he watched two of the four missiles he had fired hit the Batronian battleship. *Armstrong* was in stealth mode and had managed to close in on the enemy and fire without being detected.

"Left thrusters at full, coming about," the helmsman replied as the stealth ship began to turn.

"Fire missiles five through eight," ordered Commander Adams.

"Missiles five through eight away, sir," the Weapons Officer replied as the 200-foot-long ship continued to turn.

"Reload all missile launchers! Thrusters down full!" the Captain ordered.

* * * * *

ESS Argentina (D-868)
Near Omar System
June 8, 2487, 0456 UT

Yeoman First Class Andrew Wilson and Boatswains Mate Apprentice John Bennett were both asleep in the forward berthing on the fifth deck of the destroyer, located aft of the missile launchers and one deck above Repair Locker Two.

"Hostile spacecraft inbound! General Quarters! General Quarters! All hands man your battle stations! This is not a drill!" a voice shouted over the intercom followed by the clanging of the klaxon.

Andrew jumped up, adrenaline pumping, as he quickly pulled on his uniform. The berthing area grew loud as men and women opened and shut lockers, yelling and encouraging each other to hurry. Andrew pushed his way through other crewmembers as he hurried to get to his battle station. John Bennett noticed the black man who forced his way by him. Although, John did not know Andrew, he was aware that the First Class Yeoman was new and always seemed to be tense and didn't interact with anyone else, but John figured that would be normal. Rumor had it that the Yeoman had been on Kylar II when it was attacked and no one could imagine what it was like on the ground during the attack.

John Bennett finished dressing and headed down to the sixth deck to Repair Two where he dressed in his pressure suit quickly as he tried to finish waking up.

Andrew reached Mount 54, powered up the gun, tested the controls and then pressed a button on the comm unit. "CIC, Mount 54, manned and ready," he announced hoping that the Batronians would show up this time.

On the bridge, Al Singleton arrived at the sensor display. He looked over the data. "Captain, I have 76 Batronian craft inbound. ETA six minutes. Recommend course 141 by 306," the Ensign calmly said.

* * * * *

ESS Armstrong (SS-16)
Omar System
June 8, 2487, 0456 UT

Carl Adams watched as three of the four aft missiles struck the battleship. The exhilaration quickly changed to concern as he watched the guns of the giant ship turn and fire 400-mm bolts toward his invisible ship. Fortunately, *Armstrong* was not where the Batronians had anticipated and the bolts passed aft and above the stealth ship. But still, Carl knew that it would only take one hit from a bolt of that size to destroy *Armstrong*.

"Sir, *Glenn* just scored two hits with their missiles," a Sensor Technician reported. Carl loved working with *Armstrong*'s sister ship and was beginning to appreciate the advantages of stealth ships operating in pairs.

"Very well," Carl said. As Captain, Carl generally allowed his officers to remain in charge during operations, but taking on a battleship was a tall order, one he intended to handle himself. The battleship had sustained seven missile hits and was heavily damaged. Exactly how badly was hard to tell.

"Missiles one through four are loaded and ready in all respects," the Weapons Officer reported.

"Come to 217 by 296, thrusters ahead one-half," Carl ordered the helm.

"Come to 216 by 296, ahead one-half, aye, sir," the Second Class Quartermaster at the helm answered. His hand moved over the controls carrying out the orders. "Thrusters are ahead one-half. Steady course 217 by 296, sir," he announced twenty seconds later.

"Target the battleship and fire missiles one through four," Carl ordered.

"Aye, sir," the Weapons Officer said. He gave the orders through the comm unit to the forward missile room. The missiles were pushed out of the ship by pressurized air. Once outside of the ship, the thrusters on the missile fired (the engines of the missile would be fired instead in interstellar space). The targeting computer then would guide the missile to its target.

"Reload forward missiles," the Captain ordered as he watched the trails from the four missiles thrusters heading for the Batronian ship. The damage to the battleship seemed to be affecting its maneuverability. All four missiles struck the huge ship, bringing it to a halt. Carl observed the guns falling silent as he recommended a course change.

* * * * *

ESS Argentina (D-868)
Near Omar System
June 8, 2487, 0502

Andrew Wilson's heart was pumping hard as he closed his eyes, picturing Kaitlyn's face. "Fire at will," a voice ordered over the comm unit. Following the guidance of the targeting computer, Andrew swung the gun toward a Batronian spacecraft and fired. The bolts passed behind the spacecraft.

"Damn, they're fast," Andrew said out loud. He began firing again, but still didn't lead enough. Fortunately, the 75-mm guns on a ship fired more rapidly than the land-based BA-75. While a good team could fire 45 round per minute on a BA-75, the ship based 75-mm guns could fire 65-70 round per minute.

Andrew selected another spacecraft and fired, holding the trigger and rotating the gun as he did. Bolts chased the Batronian spacecraft, but just as they were closing in on it, the spacecraft dove and spun, fooling Andrew. *Damn it*, Andrew thought. *This is much harder than firing at targets in practice.*

* * * * *

Charlie Flight
Omar System
June 8, 2487, 0504 UT

Chris and the rest of Charlie Flight escorted the three ACUs passed the disabled Batronian battleship. As they streaked by, Chris kept an eye on the drifting ship. Even though it was damaged and appeared to no longer be functioning, the sheer size of the ship and its massive guns was intimidating. Chris could see fires burning inside the ship and secondary explosions occurring. Escape pods began to appear around the ship. Ahead, Chris could see on his sensor display that other spacecraft from *London* were attacking the Batronians creating an opportunity for Charlie Flight to escort the ACUs down to the naval base.

* * * * *

ESS Argentina (D-868)
Near Omar System
June 8, 2487, 0505 UT

"Don't let them get near *London*," Captain McCollum ordered the Officer of the Deck.

"Aye, sir," the OOD replied

Argentina and the other three destroyers of Task Force One (*France, Ukraine,* and *Norway*) were working together to protect both *London* and the battleship *Newton* from enemy spacecraft. Although they were not hitting as many spacecraft as they should be, the laser fire was forcing the enemy to break off attacks or fire their missiles at the destroyers rather than the carrier or battleship. Two flights of SF-112s from *London* joined the fight, destroying several Batronians who had somehow avoided the destroyers.

"Missile inbound, port side," Ensign Singleton said calmly from the sensor console. It was noted by Captain McCollum how far the young officer had come in such a short time.

"Decoys!" the Captain ordered. "Port thrusters to full!"

In Gun Mount 54, Andrew Wilson was becoming increasingly frustrated. The enemy spacecraft was fast and difficult to hit. Andrew had managed almost a perfect score against drones during training. The Batronian spacecraft seemed to easily dodge his bolts as if toying with him.

Trying a new tactic, Andrew intentionally led too far ahead of a Batronian attack craft. Holding the trigger, he fired a half a dozen bolts ahead of the Batronian allowing the Batronian to fly directly into his laser fire and watching it as it exploded in a brilliant flash. But, instead of feeling satisfaction at killing one of the beings responsible for Kaitlyn's death, he remained frustrated by the training he and the others had received. Earth needed to get its act together or they were going to lose this war.

Andrew lined up a shot for another Batronian when the ship shook and power failed briefly as a missile struck *Argentina*.

"Sir, missile hit near Repair Two," a Communications Technician reported to Captain McCollum on the bridge.

* * * * *

ESS Newton (B-39)
Near Omar System
June 8, 2487, 0506 UT

Newton, like all the ships in Task Force One, was at General Quarters. Unlike the destroyers, however, the massive battleship was not engaging the enemy. Battleships were designed to destroy other ships and to bombard planets with their 400-mm guns. Against spacecraft with missiles, they were vulnerable. Although *Newton* had sixteen 35-mm anti-spacecraft guns, those were used only if spacecraft penetrated the shielding destroyers and fighters as a last line of defense.

Nevertheless, Kendra Allgood paced the silent bridge impatiently. She wanted to get into the action and felt that Rear Admiral Kilgallon was being foolish by not taking Task Force One into the Omar system and destroying the enemy. She had served patiently for a long time to get an opportunity to engage in combat, and now a weak leader was holding her back. Captain Allgood studied the sensor display. She saw a gap and, what she considered, an opportunity.

"Come right to 217," she ordered. The Executive Officer looked up at her. He knew better than question her order, but wondered what she was doing. The course change would bring them between *Ukraine* and *Argentina*. The purpose of having the destroyers there was to protect *Newton* and *London*. *Why would the Captain want to move outside of that protection?* the XO wondered.

"Standby on the forward 35-mm guns," Kendra ordered over the comm to the Combat Information Center (CIC).

"Mounts 31 through 38 are standing by, ma'am," a voice replied.

Again, the XO wondered why. Few spacecraft were getting into the range of the battleship and those that did were being quickly destroyed or chased away by the fighters from *London*.

"Fire at will," Kendra ordered. 35-mm laser fire flew outward from the battleship. Two SF-112s from *London* banked hard to avoid the bolts fired from *Newton*, aimed at the very Batronian spacecraft that they were chasing, but almost hitting the SF-112s instead.

* * * * *

ESS London (SCV-7)
Near Omar System
June 8, 2487, 0506 UT

"What is she doing?" Rear Admiral Kilgallon asked aloud. He reached over and pressed a button on his comm unit connecting him with the communications shack. "Signal *Newton* to get back in position. And for God's sake tell her to cease fire!"

Kilgallon had met Kendra Allgood about six years ago while serving as Captain of *ESS France*. She was serving as Executive Officer of *ESS Einstein*. He remembered her as a very ambitious officer. She had served as Commanding Officer of a destroyer before that and the job of an XO on the battleship was a step by her to take command of a battleship herself. He remembered her as a stern disciplinarian, pushing her crew. *Maybe, she was thinking the war is another opportunity to advance her own career*, Kilgallon though. If that was the case, Kilgallon knew that he would have to reel her in. The battleship ceased fire and turned heading back to her assigned position within the task force. *At least she is obeying orders*, the Rear Admiral thought.

* * * * *

Command Center
Naval Base Quebec, Omar IV
June 8, 2487, 0807 Local, 0507 UT

"Ma'am, the Batronians are a mile outside of the base. I'm moving the remaining troopers to the Space Station. The ACUs will be here in less than a half an hour. We can defend ourselves there," Colonel Nelson, now back in the Command Center, said.

"Very well," Captain Harrington replied. Like Colonel Nelson, she knew that they simply did not have the manpower to defend the entire base, so taking a section of the base, such as the Space Center, and defending themselves from there would be the best solution. Still, Captain Harrington hated giving up even an inch of the base to the Batronians.

"Ma'am, I would suggest we move there, too," Nelson said. "It is easier if we have everyone in position"

Amber looked around the room. It truly was time to go, but it didn't make it easier. Still, they had to protect each other and those ACUs. "Very well, Colonel," Harrington said, rising from her chair. "Hand me an L-29."

"You heard her," Colonel Nelson said to a trooper standing at the entrance to the Command Center. The Private, shocked at the request by a senior officer, especially a Naval Officer, handed Amber his weapon. She loaded a charge pack and flipped off the safety.

"Let's move out," she ordered loading a charge pack and leading the way.

* * * * *

ESS Argentina (D-868)
Near Omar System
June 8, 2487,0511 UT

It was John Bennett's turn as nozzleman on the number one fire team. He entered the dry goods storage area on the seventh deck and began sweeping back and forth beating down the flames. His pressure suit's pressure remained steady so there was no hull breach in the compartment, just fire caused by the heat of the explosion of the missile that impacted two decks up. It was exhausting work, pulling the heavy hose through the narrow passageways and doors of the ship while trying to hold it steady as a stream of water at 250 PSI flowed from the nozzle.

The fire in the compartment was quickly extinguished. John turned to leave the room when he saw a cook, in his white uniform, laying on the deck.

"Hey! We have a cook in here! Send the stretcher bearers and the corpsman," John said using the speaker in his suit to communicate with the team leader. John made his way over to the man. He was unconscious with no obvious burns or injuries. "I think he was overcome by smoke," John said through the speaker.

On the bridge, Ensign Singleton watched the ongoing battle on the sensor display. Thanks to the coordinated effort of the four destroyers, the enemy had only scored a few hits on the destroyers and none on the carrier or battleship. But, then a bright flash filled the bridge windows and pieces of metal struck *Argentina*'s hull.

"What was that?" Captain McCollum asked.

"Sir, several missiles hit *Ukraine*. Apparently, she exploded," Al reported.

"Shit," Command Pete Williams said.

The bright flash had briefly messed with Andrew's vision and for several seconds he was forced to stop firing as he blinked his eyes to clear them.

* * * * *

Naval Space Center
Naval Base Quebec, Omar IV
June 8, 2487, 0825 Local, 0525 UT

Tents had been set up for the wounded around the Space Center and Karen helped transport the wounded, including Dave, from the hospital to the temporary shelters. After the wounded were in the tents, the remaining troopers from the Third Regiment gathered near the center of the Space Station. Only 61 of the 78 remaining troopers were able to fight.

Naval Personnel had also gathered at the Space Center, assembled by their units. Everyone was armed, some with L-29s, some with SL-21s and a few with handguns. Three BA-75s were still operational and being manned. Only 220 people remained from the Naval Base that had been home to over 2000.

Captain Harrington looked around at what she had left. The base was very heavily damaged, although the Space Center was in relatively good shape. *Why?* Amber asked herself. The only answer that made sense was obvious. She went and found Colonel Nelson.

"Colonel, we need to get charges ready to blow up the Space Center," Amber said.

"Already done, ma'am," Byron said. He had reached the same conclusion as Amber. And if it was the Batronian's goal to use the Space Center, then they were in for a surprise.

"Very well, Colonel," Amber said. She moved to a position where she could monitor the main gate to the base. Attack craft from *London* were attacking enemy positions just outside of the base. As she watched, a human craft got shot down by a Batronian Fighter, the crash sending a ball of fire into the sky.

"I need a bull horn," Amber said. One of the officers handed her one. "Listen up. The Batronian troops are just outside of the gate. I know it's been a long few days. We're tired and hurting. We don't have to hold out long. Just long enough for the ACUs to get here. Task Force One is doing their part, now we need to do our part."

* * * * *

Batronian Attack Spacecraft 1842
Near Omar System
June 8, 2487, 0526 UT

The Batronian knew they would have to break off the attack soon. The attack was not going well and the spacecraft would have to rearm and refuel soon. The pilot broke left and right dodging fire from the human's destroyers. He broke right heading directly for one, arming one of his missiles.

A bolt clipped his right wing causing the craft to yaw. He pushed his control stick to the left to compensate and try to recover as a second bolt, which he never saw, struck the craft. The 75-mm bolt passed straight through the cockpit, through the pilot's chest and into the engines in the rear of the craft, causing the craft to explode.

Unbeknownst to Andrew Wilson, he had just got his revenge against the Batronian who had killed Kaitlyn.

* * * * *

ESS Argentina (D-868)
Near Omar System
June 8, 2487, 0727 UT

Andrew watched the spacecraft explode having no clue who the pilot had been and having none of the joy he expected to have as he killed his second Batronian. Instead, his mind was on protecting the ship. He knew that they had taken a hit and was trying to keep the Batronians from scoring anymore hits. But, he also realized just how bad the training that he had received had been. Real pilots flew faster and more aggressively than the drones he had been trained with.

Since arriving on *Argentina*, Andrew realized, he had been totally focused on himself and his revenge. He had not gotten to know his shipmates, even the ones he supervised. All he had care about was killing the enemy. That had to change. Admiral Morris had been right. Killing Batronians to avenge Kaitlyn's death was not the answer and Kaitlyn would not have wanted this need for revenge to consume him.

Fewer spacecraft were approaching now. The Batronians were obviously done here. The order to cease fire came a minute later. Andrew took a deep breath and wiped a tear from his eye.

* * * * *

Naval Space Center
Naval Base Quebec, Omar IV
June 8, 2487, 0831 Local, 0531 UT

Captain Amber Harrington saw the tall thin form of a Batronian breach the main gate of Naval Base Oscar. She raised the L-29 and fired a three-round burst, killing the first soldier through. Barriers had been placed surrounding the Space Center both to slow the Batronian advance and to provide cover for the humans. As more Batronians entered the main gate, laser fire chewed them down. The fire came from different directions preventing the Batronians from being able to concentrate their fire on one target and cover their soldiers as they entered the base.

Five minutes of Batronian troops trying to enter the base resulted in five minutes of failure. So, the Batronians changed tactics. Artillery fire rained down on the humans forcing them to take cover. Amber flipped her L-29 to auto and fired a sustained burst at a group of Batronians heading roughly in her direction. Dozens of the aliens made it through the gate of the base. Most of the Batronians avoided the space center, choosing instead to secure the remainder of the base and occupying the major buildings.

As the mortar fire slackened, the humans tried to prevent more enemy soldiers from entering the base by concentrating their fire on the main gate.

At 0849, several SF-112s swooped down from the skies above the base.

* * * * *

Charlie Flight
In Air Above Naval Base Quebec, Omar IV
June 8, 2487, 0849 Local, 0549 UT

Chris Davenport led Charlie Flight into a dive after passing over Naval Base Quebec. Several hundred Batronian soldiers were along the road leading to the Naval Base. He could see some had entered. He couldn't do anything about them, but he could do something about the hundreds waiting.

"Charlie Flight, this is Charlie Leader. On me," Chris ordered. He passed low over the enemy firing 35-mm bolts into the enemy lines.

"Yeah!" Don Franklin shouted over the comm as the rest of Charlie Flight followed Chris, firing their guns as they did. The strafing fire scattered the enemy, throwing them into chaos as they looked for a way to protect themselves. Chris looked down, pleased with the results as he swung around to make another pass.

* * * * *

Assault Craft Unit 17
Over Naval Space Center, Naval Base Quebec, Omar IV
June 8, 2487, 0851 Local, 0551 UT

Max Finley waited nervously for the ACU to touch down. The ACU had no windows, therefore, the troopers had no way of knowing where they were or what was going on outside of the craft.

"Prepare to move out," a Sergeant ordered. Max tightened his grip on his L-29, flipping the safety off as he did. The ACU touched down and the back door opened, a ramp deploying as it did. The eight troopers on the ACU moved out, L-29s at the ready. As they exited, naval personnel began loading stretchers and assisting the walking wounded onto the ACU.

Captain Harrington glanced back over her shoulder while continuing to fire as more Batronians attempted to enter the base. "Pass the word down the lines. Pull back and load up into the ACUs."

Bolts started coming down from a building to Max's right. Max aimed his L-29 and saw several Batronians firing down on the ACUs from a third-floor window. The small arms fire could not penetrate the armor of the ACUs, but it was a danger to the people trying to get into them. Max and the rest of his squad made quick work of it, either killing the Batronians or at least forcing them back into the building.

As the survivors from Omar IV were being loaded, Max scanned people's faces searching for Dave and Phil. He had no way of knowing that Phil was dead and the Dave was critically wounded and had already been loaded onto ACU-14. Nor did he realize that a female trooper who passed him could have told him Dave's whereabouts. He had never even met Karen Baker.

The ACUs were loaded just seven minutes after they touched down. They lifted off with Charlie Flight forming up to escort them back to *Iwo Jima*. Seconds after lifting off, a series of explosions at the Space Center destroyed much of the tarmac and many key buildings.

* * * * *

Main Gate
Naval Base Quebec, Omar IV
June 8, 2487, 0902 Local, 0602 UT

The Batronians watched the ACUs lift off and the series of explosions at the Space Center. Troops began to move through the gates and into Naval Base Quebec. It took almost 45 minutes for them to complete a search and secure the base. Once they knew the base was secure, the celebration began as the Batronians met in large groups and celebrated.

Omar IV was now in Batronian hands.

* * * * *

Charlie Flight
Omar System
June 8, 2487, 635 UT

The outbound flight was uneventful. Attack spacecraft from *London* kept the Batronian ships busy allowing Charlie Flight to escort the ACUs past the Batronian ships orbiting Omar IV. Chris Davenport took the time to contemplate what happened. The Batronians had won another battle. Earth had to find a way to start winning and soon.

At the same time, Chris realized, this time the humans had done some real damage. They had destroyed or severely damaged ten Batronian ships as well as an unknown number of spacecraft and of Batronian soldiers killed on the planet. It wasn't a victory, but it wasn't Kylar II neither.

CHAPTER FIFTEEN

ESS London (SCV-7)
In Orbit, Travos I
June 9, 2487, 0912 UT

Rear Admiral Frank Kilgallon sat on the flag bridge of *London*, looking out at Task Force One now orbiting the only planet in the Travos system. The planet was an uninhabitable mass of super-heated gas surrounding a mainly iron core. It was moonless and of now value, making it an idea place to hide the task force.

ESS Mexico had been assigned officially now to Task Force One, replacing the destroyed *ESS Ukraine*. Still damaged, *Mexico* waited for the arrival of a supply ship and a repair ship that was enroute from Kylar II. All the ships in the task force needed resupplied and some of the destroyers needed some minor repairs for damage incurred during the battle. While waiting for the ships to arrive, the ships of Task Force One began repairing what they could and training their crews. Frank watched as fighters flew by providing cover for the task force.

As Frank watched, he was considering what to do next. *Where do I begin?* Frank wondered. It was a good question, an important one. It was much easier at Masic Point where others made those decisions and he simply went to where he was told and did what he was ordered to do. Now it felt as if he had to decide how to fight a war which, of course, was exactly what he had to do.

* * * * *

ESS Argentina (D-868)
In Orbit, Travos I
June 9, 2487, 0931 UT

Yeoman First Class Andrew Wilson made his way through Officer's Country on the third deck of the destroyer. Officer's country was the nickname for the section of the ship where the officer's quarters were located. The quarters lined the passageway that was spotlessly clean, walls bright white and a deck that was highly polished. The wardroom, where the officers ate and held meetings was located at the end of the passageway. Andrew arrived at a door labeled "Gunnery (3rd Division) Officer" and knocked.

"Enter," a voice said loudly. Andrew opened the door and stepped in. A Lieutenant opened the door and stepped in. A Lieutenant sat at a desk along the wall to the right with the desk light on and a stack of papers in front of him. A bunk and a locker were to Andrew's left. The room was small and utilitarian, but lavish compared to the cramped berthing areas that enlisted crewmembers lived in.

"Sir, could I have a moment of your time?" Andrew asked.

"You're the new guy on Mount 54, right?" the Lieutenant asked.

"Yes, sir. YN1 Wilson, sir," Andrew replied.

"What's on your mind?"

Andrew stood thinking for a second. "Sir, I think we have a problem," he said finally. The Lieutenant raised an eyebrow. "When I qualified on the 75-mm gun, I scored a 97, almost perfect. But the targets were moving slowly and tracked in a straight line. They were easy to hit. During the battle, the Batronian fighters were fast and very evasive. I struggled, sir. I only hit two targets. A person who scored a 97 in qualification, could only hit two spacecraft during a battle of that size. Something must be wrong, sir.

"I thought maybe I was just rusty. But every gunner that I've talked to has said the same thing and had similar results. If that had been a larger force, sir, we would have been in serious trouble. We wouldn't have been able to protect ourselves let alone *London* and *Newton*.

"Has anyone looked for a way to update our training? Maybe using faster drones? Ones that try to evade our fire? I we don't, gunners like me, who score high in training and feel confident are going to get a reality check that we don't want to have. Sir, we have to prepare ourselves for real battles, not just for a high score in qualifications."

"Have a seat, Wilson," the Lieutenant said. He took a drink of his coffee as he studied Wilson. "You used to work for Admiral Morris, right?" he finally asked.

"Yes, sir," Andrew replied.

The Lieutenant looked coldly into Andrew's eyes. "Well, you are not on an Admiral's staff now, son. You are on a ship of the line and here you will not question how officers do their job or how they train you. You will follow orders; do as you are told and keep your mouth shut. Learn your place, son. Do you understand?"

Andrew stared at the Lieutenant in disbelief. *Why was he acting this way? I'm not criticizing him. Why would he take it personally?* Andrew asked himself. Still, Andrew recognized that he was being dressed down and self-discipline kicked in. "Aye, sir," he replied.

"Now, if you are having trouble hitting spacecraft, perhaps you should go back to being an Admiral's errand boy. Is that what you want?"

"No, sir."

"Then get out of here and do your job. Understood?" the Lieutenant asked, his voice dripping with poison.

"Yes, sir," Andrew said rising from his chair. He stepped out of the cabin, shutting the door behind him. He was angry. He had been in the service for over six years, had a stellar reputation and had never had an officer talk to him that way. And worse yet, Andrew knew that he was right. But he had no idea what he could do about it.

* * * * *

ESS Iwo Jima (AS-38)
In Orbit, Rankus I
June 9, 2487, 1028 UT

His eyes flickered open in the bright light. At first all he could see were shadows before he was forced to close his eyes again to shut out the bright light. Again, he opened them. This time shapes began to form before again his eyes closed. *Where am I?* Dave Roberts asked himself. His head ached. He tried to take a deep breath and found a new source of pain. Something was seriously wrong. He struggled to open his eyes again.

An image flashed in his mind. A puff of smoke coming from a hole in his chest. *Oh my God,* he thought. *I was shot!*

He forced his eyes open again. A nurse was standing over him. He was in a hospital he realized. *No, that's not quite right,* he thought to himself.

"Where am I?" Dave asked. His voice was week. He was having trouble drawing a breath.

"You are in sick bay aboard *Iwo Jima*," the nurse, a woman in her late thirties replied. "Do you remember what happened?"

"I was shot…on Omar IV," Dave said. "Can I have some water?" His lips were dry and cracked. The nurse poured him a drink and handed it to him. As he drank, he noticed the nurse looked to his left. He turned his head and saw Karen Baker sitting in the chair beside his bed, sleeping.

"She wouldn't leave your side," the nurse said. She leaned over to Karen. "Karen, he's awake."

Karen looked over at Dave. Her eyes brightened and she smiled broadly. "About time you woke up, lazy," she teased Dave as she stood and moved to his side.

"You saved my life," Dave said. He looked at her. She was in uniform, but for the first time since meeting her, she was cleaned up, not running around in the hot sun and sweating, firing her rifle. She was uncovered, her blond hair clean and silky. She was wearing a little makeup, especially around her blue eyes. *She's beautiful*, Dave realized.

"You saved mine, too," Karen reminded him. There was a moment of awkward silence as the two admired each other hoping the other one didn't notice. They were interrupted by a figure appearing in the doorway.

"Hey, you're awake," Max Finley said as he entered the room. He walked over to Dave, bent over and hugged him. The two friends from bootcamp finally reunited.

"Hey, what are you doing here, Max?" Dave asked surprised to see his friend out here.

"First Regiment has been assigned to *Iwo Jima* and we were sent to help evacuate the base on Omar IV," Max replied.

"We evacuated?" Dave asked looking over at Karen.

"Yeah. Just after you were shot. We couldn't win. There were only 78 of us left from the whole regiment and most of us were wounded, many of those like you, were no longer able to fight. Six died since we arrived here. We just couldn't hold out any longer," Karen said, her face downcast as she remembered those last moment of the battle.

Dave remembered too. The firefights. The death around him. The struggle and the fear. He remembered it all. He would never forget the sights, the sounds or the smell of his first battle. He remembered Sergeant Pachenko and carrying his body back to the line. And, of course, the third member of the group that went through bootcamp together, Phil.

"Phil didn't make it," Dave said, tears filling his eyes.

"I know," Max said softly.

"He died right beside me," Dave said as he relived that moment. Karen reached over and squeezed his hand. The three troopers fell silent as each recalled their personal battles.

* * * * *

Headquarters Destroyer Squadron Ten
Naval Base Oscar, Kylar II
June 9, 2487, 0817 Local, 1437 UT

Admiral William P. Morris sat at his desk reviewing the final report from Captain Harrington and Rear Admiral Kilgallon. Admiral Morris had taken a lot of heat over the loss of Omar IV, but he knew it couldn't be avoided. Actually, he was pleased with how the battle had went. True, Batron did capture Omar IV, but Morris was certain it cost the Batronians more than they wanted to pay.

Morris got up and walked over to the window. He looked out at the activity on the base. Construction was proceeding quickly, beginning to replace what Batron had destroyed just over three weeks ago. A new Fourth Fleet Headquarters was already rising out of the ground where the old one was. A new control tower already stood at the Space Center and new hangers were being erected at an incredible rate. Debris from the attack had been almost completely removed. What few pieces of ships that came crashing down on land were being recovered. Wrecked spacecraft were being broken up and prepared for shipment to a recycling facility.

In orbit, docks were being repaired and new docks were being constructed. Plans were to increase the capability to support over one hundred ships in orbit. Due to the war, the Fourth Fleet would be greatly increased in size and strength. Naval Base Oscar would also be expanded to support both more ships and more troopers as the Naval Assault Forces began to move addition units into the sector. A new army base was being constructed to support the planned four divisions the army would be moving into the Young-Wise sector to support war efforts.

Work also continued on ships damaged during the attack on Kylar II. With more docks available, Morris was able to send the repair ship *Appalachian Mountains (RS-3)* and the fleet supply ship *LaSalle (FS-2)* to Rankus I to resupply Task Force One and make repairs to *Mexico*. But as Admiral Morris stared out the window, he realized what he really need was a mission for Kilgallon and Task Force One.

* * * * *

Home of Tony Fillmore
Village of Lansing, Omar IV
June 9, 2487, 2003 Local, 1703 UT

Jack Mitchell approached Tony Fillmore's house just after dark. Now that Omar IV was under Batron's control, he had to be careful. Movement of humans was restricted to begin with and a curfew had been established at 1800 local. But, Jack Mitchell's years in the navy had taught him how to remain under the radar. The Batronian soldiers in Lansing, seemed to trust him. *But they shouldn't*, thought Jack. He tapped lightly on the door and was let in by Amy.

"He's in the basement," she whispered. Whispering was unnecessary but seemed appropriate for what they were doing. Amy closed the door as Jack entered. He headed for the basement. The basement of Tony's house consisted of a large open room. It was okay for now, but they would have to find an alternate place soon. Jack found tony at the workbench studying the portable sensor display that the Navy had dropped off just prior to the end of the battle. Jack had set up the small sensor array, hiding it in the growth of the fields. It had a very limited range, extending just beyond the Omar system, but with it, Tony and Jack could monitor the movement of enemy ships around the Omar System.

"Any luck?" Jack asked.

"It's working," Tony replied taking notes on what he as seeing on the sensor display. "They have moved a huge number of soldiers here already. Maybe 100,000 even."

"Damn! Have you told Fourth Fleet?"

"Not yet," Tony replied. "I want to get an accurate count on everything they have here and send it all in one message. No reason to risk the tall and uglies getting lucky and detecting messages going out from here." Tall and uglies was a term that the humans on Omar IV had started calling the Batronians. It was derogatory, sure, but it was hard not to think of an enemy who had violently taken control of your planet in anything but derogatory terms.

"Let me see," Jack requested. He looked at the display and was shocked by the sheer number of ships in the Omar system. Not just a dozen, but scores of ships. He wondered how many additional ships were just outside of the system or on their way here. "Wow," he said to Tony as he backed away.

"Yeah. Obviously, they are planning on using Omar as a major forward base. They aren't done doing whatever they are planning," Tony said. He looked up at Jack. "How is your part going?"

"I better prepare the message," Tony said.

```
060924871708U

From: Hawkeye 12
To: Fourth Fleet Intelligence...
```

the message began.

* * * * *

ESS London (SCV-7)
In Orbit, Travos I
June 9, 2487, 1928 UT

Chris Davenport sat in his stateroom. He had just finished the final draft of his Action Report on the Battle of Omar IV. He was shocked and saddened by the way the war was going. Not only had the Batronians captured Omar IV, but now, Earth was completely cut off in the Young-Wise Sector from anything beyond the Omar system. Batron had occupied many smaller systems as well. Only Antron was still fighting and it was unclear how long they could hold out without Earth's support. For the normally cocky fighter pilot, this realization was sobering. Earth was losing. During his time in the navy, Chris had steadfastly believed that his navy was indestructible. And slowly his cockiness was being replaced by somberness.

He leaned back in his chair taking a deep breath. On the bright side, they did have a couple of stealth ships operating between Omar and Batron. He knew through unofficial channels that they were having some success intercepting cargo ships heading to Omar and destroying them. He didn't know exactly how the stealth ships were able to be in exactly the right place at the right time. Obviously, someone had a source of intelligence, but no one seemed to know exactly where that intelligence was coming from.

And, of course, there was Task Force One. It wasn't much, but in Chris' opinion it was a start. He hoped that once repairs were complete to *Mexico* and the ships were resupplied, that they would get back out and, well, do something. Anything. This war had to start changing soon or Batron was going to win. His thoughts were interrupted by a knock at the door.

"Enter," Chris said. The door opened and Donald Franklin entered the stateroom.

"Busy?" Don asked

"No, just thinking," Chris replied as Don sat in the chair beside his desk.

"Yeah, my mind has been racing. This isn't how war I thought war would be. I thought we were the toughest beings in the universe, but now, it just seems that we keep losing," Don said.

"I know what you mean. But, this is just the beginning of what will likely be a long war. Two lost battles don't mean anything. It's what we do from here. After all, Masic Point started off worse than this in many ways. But in the end, we won. And we'll do it again. Remember, Kilgallon, Morris and the others fought in that war. They know what they are doing. We will win," Chris said.

"Well, we're flying the patrol at midnight, so I better get some sleep," Don said.

"Me too," Chris replied. "And Don, you're doing great."

"Of course, I am. What did you expect, C-Dog?" Don said, his cockiness still there despite all that had happened. "Don't worry, we're going to get them."

EPILOGUE

Naval Brig
Naval Station Oscar, Kylar II
June 12, 2487, 0915 Local, 1535 UT

The duty officer led Carol Anderson to the interrogation room surprised to see her holding a basket of fruit. *I wonder exactly what she's up too?* He knew better than ask of course and he wasn't sure he wanted to know. Right now, like most of the brig's staff he just wanted to beat the daylights out of the Batronian pilot. Get the win that they hadn't been able to achieve in any other way. Eventually, he would talk. All this keeping him isolated stuff didn't seem to be accomplishing anything and certainly didn't help the people on Omar IV. Still, seeing the way she could get the Batronian to react was impressive.

Carol sat at the interrogation table and sat the basket of fruit in front of her. She saw the look of confusion on the duty officer's face, but for now didn't comment. Two guards led Shonze into the room. The transformation that had taken place in the Batronian pilot's appearance was significant. She studied him, not saying a word. She noticed that he kept glancing over to the basket of fruit. She knew that, for a Batronian, fruit was a delicacy. Before the war, Batron imported as much fruit from Earth as Earth was willing to provide. She sat silently for a full two minutes before she began to speak.

<<The fruit is yours, of course,>> she told Shonze. He looked at her. She knew he was suspicious of what would motivate her to make such a gesture.

<<Another game? You are so inefficient,>> Shonze told her. Despite his physical appearance, he still spoke with his typical arrogance.

<<No game. A token of our appreciation,>> she replied. She watched as he studied her, knowing he was confused by the statement. She waited just enough time. <<Without your help, we would have lost Omar IV to Batron. But, thanks to you, we still have it. And Batron is in almost as bad of shape as we are. Oh, we haven't won yet. But at least we've leveled the playing field.>>

<<You expect me to believe that your pathetic fleet stopped our glorious forces? You must think that I'm a fool.>>

<<Not at all, Shonze. I think you're a lot of things but not a fool. But, I have no questions for you now. Just a gift and my personal thanks,>> Carol said. She nodded to the Duty Officer who summoned the guards.

"Make sure you put him in the best cell you have available. The guards should be polite. They should pretend to sneak him extra portions of food, smile at him and attempt to communicate politely. I will be sending more fruit over and your guards should sneak him some occasionally. They do not need to understand why. But, they must act as if he is their ally, not enemy," Carol instructed the duty officer.

The duty officer could not contain his anger. He knew and had served with people who had died at Omar IV and more that were not accounted for. And now this woman expected him to treat a Batronian like he was an ally. *This woman must have lost her mind*, he thought. He tried to bite his tongue, but found he couldn't stop from speaking out as soon as the alien left the room. "Why are we treating him as if he were our friend? I lost friends on Omar IV and I have no idea why you would treat a prisoner of theirs in this way. I have done everything you have asked, but this is too far," the Duty Officer said.

"No, it isn't. We're thanking him for his help that prevented Batron from taking Omar IV. He needs to know that if it ever came out that he was the reason that Batron lost there, that his exile would be complete."

"What are you talking about? Batron didn't lose! We did! We didn't save Omar IV, we lost it!" he shouted.

"True, but the prisoner doesn't know that, does he?" Carol said as she headed for the door leaving the Duty Officer speechless.

Please continue reading the short story "Collision Course – An Earth@War Short Story".

Prior to the attack on Kylar II, Admiral James Morris received a report that *ESS Mexico (D-866)*

collided with a stealth ship that was operating in the Omar system. This is the story of that collision.

Collision
Course

An Earth@War Short Story

By John J. Knox Jr.

Collision Course

ESS Mexico (D-866)
Entering Omar System
May 21, 2487, 2214 UT

"You got this!" a voice shouted from the crowd surrounding the man on the bench. Yeoman First Class Bruce Tivis strained as he attempted to press the barbell from his chest, his arms shaking from the effort. 545 pounds would not only be his personal best, but also the ship's record. Of course, the record didn't really matter to the crewmembers who had wagered on Bruce's success or failure. Money was on the line after all. Sweat beaded on the dark brown skin of Bruce's forehead as inch by inch, the bar rose from his chest.

"Ughh!!!" Bruce cried out as he extended his arms completing the single rep and resulting in a loud cheer from the crowd surrounding him. Two men grabbed the bar and helped Bruce rack the barbell. Bruce sat up, breathing heavily as he received congratulations from those around him – even those who had lost money because of his success. After catching his breath, he rose to his feet. At 5'4" he was among the shortest crewmembers on *Mexico,* an aging destroyer assigned to Earth's Fourth Fleet and currently forward deployed to Naval Base Quebec on Omar IV. But, despite his short frame, he was perhaps the strongest person on the sip, as evidenced by his new record. At one time, Bruce planned a career in boxing. But once he joined the Navy, he never looked back. He loved the comradery of the fleet, the trips through space and the visits to other planets.

"Damn, Bruce," Quarter Master First Class Trevor Ryan said. The 34-year-old was Bruce's best friend. They had gone through Naval Boot Camp together sixteen years ago at Naval Base Bravo on Mars and had served together planet side at Naval Base Delta on Lucai II from 2480 to 2482 before meeting again last year when Bruce reported for duty on *Mexico.* Trevor slapped Bruce on the Back. At 6'1" and weighing only 145 pounds, Trevor was physically the opposite of Bruce. "That was amazing."

"Thanks," Bruce replied. He flexed his arms trying to release the tension from his chest as more crewmembers made their way over to congratulate him.

Three decks up, Captain James Allen, commanding officer of *ESS Mexico* stepped onto the ship's bridge.

"Captain on the bridge!" Lieutenant Clark Baxton, the Officer of the Deck shouted at noticing the Captain's arrival. On the bridge, due to the nature of their duties, the crew did not come to attention when the Captain arrived on the bridge, but instead simply acknowledged his arrival. Captain Allen made his way to his chair located forward on the starboard side of the bridge allowing him a clear view out of the angled windows. Several displays and a comm unit were on the bulkhead forward of the chair within easy reach for the Captain.

He looked out of the windows, then down at the monitors noting the ship's current heading and speed. He then noted the ship's position just inside the limits of the Omar System. It was the largest system in the Young-Wise sector, consisting of eight planets, only one of which—Omar IV—was inhabited. Omar IV was a terraformed planet with a varied climate similar to Earth but consisting of a single large continent surrounded by a single ocean. Despite the similar atmosphere and climate, the planet remained sparsely populated. It was, however, the home of Naval Base Quebec, the forward most of Earth's two naval bases in the sector. Since the War at Masic Point, Naval Base Quebec had been largely ignored by Earth and the Navy which kept most of the fleet at Naval Base Oscar at Kylar II and a Masic Point since the war ended there over twenty years ago. Only a small force of three destroyers (including *Mexico*) and the cruiser *Lake Erie* were homeported at the naval base along with a battalion of Naval Assault Forces troopers.

But, with the war between Batron and Antron in its second year and tensions increasing between Batron and Earth over Earth's continued trade with Antron—including sales of weapons, the four aging ships were increasingly being ordered to escort cargo ships through increasingly dangerous shipping lanes. Not that Captain Allen was complaining. The escort duty gave *Mexico* and the other ships at Omar IV more time in space than almost any other ship in the Navy and the experience showed in the increasingly efficient operation of *Mexico*.

Down in the ship's gym, the celebration of Bruce Tivis's accomplishment began to break up. Once again, Trevor Ryan approached Bruce, this time carrying two bottles of water.

"Man, congratulations again," Trevor said handing Bruce one of the waters.

"Thanks," Bruce replied thankful for both the words as well as the water. He opened the bottle and took a large drink.

"Do you ever regret not getting out of the Navy and having that boxing career you wanted?" Trevor asked.

"No, why?" Bruce replied.

"Just, if I was you, I might have done that. Man, you could have been the champ. You are stronger, faster and have more heart than any of those chumps boxing right now."

"Yeah," Bruce said after a moment of thought. "But, do you know where I got that heart? Right here, from guys like you. The Navy is my life. I have no regrets." Bruce drank the last of the water and put the bottle in the recycler.

Trevor put his in the recycler too. "Well, I hate to do this, but I need to get some rack time. I have the four to eight watch."

"Understood," Bruce replied. The two men headed out of the gym. Trevor turned right heading toward the forward crew berthing, while Bruce turned left, heading aft toward the ladder that led up to the Mess Deck, where he grabbed a snack as the ship continued toward Omar IV.

* * * * *

Batronian Stealth Ship 1821
Near Omar VII
May 21, 2487, 2236 UT

The Commandant of the Batronian Stealth Ship watched Earth's approaching destroyer from the bridge. The ship, like all Batronian ships didn't have a name. To the Batronians, a ship was simply a tool and didn't need a name. The stealth ship was in stealth mode making it practically invisible to sensors and sight. This was important since the ship was operating illegally inside of Earth's territory.

The Commandant watched the destroyer approach with the bridge alive with activity. He maneuvered the ship in front of the destroyer, facing it. All four forward missile tubes were loaded with Batron's newest anti-ship missiles and were locked onto the destroyer. Of course, today the Commandant

4

would not give the order to fire. Today was just training—making sure his crew could get into position, making sure they could lock their missiles onto the human's ship and making sure the humans did not detect the stealth ship. So, today, he would not fire. The war hadn't begun yet. But when it did, his mission would be to eliminate the four ships the humans had in the Omar system. He watched as the destroyer grew larger in the bridge window.

<Thrusters to full. Come right to 184 by 229,> the Commandant ordered. Time to get out of here, he thought.

<Sir, thrusters not responding!> the helm replied just before electrical power failed on the bridge.

What? the Commandant asked himself as he checked the status of the stealth field generator. Fortunately, and to his relief, the generator was still working, and his ship was still invisible. Now he just had to figure out how to get his ship out of the way of the rapidly approaching destroyer.

* * * * *

ESS Mexico (D-866)
Near Omar VII
May 21, 2487, 2239 UT

Captain Allen took a sip of coffee as he looked out at the uninhabitable ball of ice that was Omar VII. Around him, his crew efficiently performed their duties that over the past two years had become routine. As he looked out of the bridge window, he saw the bow of the ship begin to mysteriously crumble.

The sound of the hull giving way reverberated throughout the ship. The ship shook violently, throwing many of the officers and crew of *Mexico* off of their feet—those who were awake that is. Those who were sleeping their bunks were thrown out and tumbled to the deck. A Machinist Mate fell from the ladder leading to the Number Two Engineroom breaking his neck.

On the bridge and in damage control central, alarms rang out and lights flashed as forward compartments on decks one through four were opened to space. Emergency bulkheads closed sealing off compartments that were venting air into space. Fires broke out in several compartments where the air wasn't vented.

Captain Allen had been flung forward but managed to remain in his seat. He straightened himself off as the collision alarm rang out and looked forward just as the Stealth Ship came out of stealth mode and returned to normal mode becoming visible. The stealth ship, smaller and more lightly armored than *Mexico*, had been severely damaged, the bow of the ship almost completely separated from the rest of the ship. *Why is there a stealth ship here?* Captain Allen asked himself. While Earth's Stealth Ships occasionally entered the system, they never entered it in stealth mode to prevent collisions like this. *Why?* James asked himself again. Despite his confusion, Captain Allen reacted instinctively. "I have the con," he said taking command of the bridge and control of the ship. "Sound General Quarters."

"Aye, sir," the Boatswain's Mate of the Watch replied, her eyes wide in shock. She triggered the ship's main intercom on the comm unit located on the aft bulkhead of the bridge. "Collision forward near frame ten! General Quarters! General Quarters! All hands man your battle stations! This is not a drill!" she shouted over the intercom. Following the announcement, she pressed the button sounding the klaxon throughout the ship.

On the mess decks, located aft of frame 90 on the fourth deck, two decks below the bridge, Bruce Tivis and the other dozen or so crewmembers who were either eating or playing cards together picked themselves up off the deck the collision knocking them all off of their feet. Bruce had hit the deck hard, smashing his nose on the table as he went down, dazing him. Through the daze, he heard the collision alarm sound. The lights flickered but remained on. Blood flowed from his nose as he looked around the room, his mind struggling to make sense of what happened. *What the hell did we hit?* he asked himself. He grabbed a handful of napkins from the dispenser on the table and pressed them to his nose just as the

Boatswain's Mate's voice came over the intercom ordering the crew to General Quarters. Bruce exited the mess decks to the port side making his way to the ladder leading down to the third deck.

He made it to the ladder and quickly descended and started moving forward. His Battle Station was Repair Locker two about ninety feet forward of the ladder. Emergency bulkheads had already closed along the passageway leading forward. Bruce arrived at the first one and felt the hatch with the back of his hand. Cool to the touch, he opened the hatch and moved into the next compartment, closing the hatch behind him. A light whisp of smoke lingered in this passageway along with a burnt odor, not strong, but certainly noticeable. *Fires nearby*, Bruce noted.

Bruce moved through the corridor coming to the door leading to Repair Two to his right. Opening the door, Bruce stepped into the repair locker. Repair Two was a beehive of activity. On the wall display console located along the aft bulkhead, flashing lights and blaring alarms indicated the severity of the damage to the forward part of the ship. As he donned his pressurized damage control suit, Bruce noticed that several of the forward compartments were open to space. *What did we hit?* he asked himself again as he finished suiting up and waited for instructions.

Back up on the bridge, Captain Allen looked out of the window noting both the damage to his ship as well as the stealth ship they had hit. The bow damaged from the thinly armored stealth ship obviously even more seriously damaged in the collision than *Mexico*. The stealth ship was slowly drifting away from *Mexico*, carried by inertia and not under its own power. Despite the chaos around him and his own confusion, he quickly scanned the other ship looking for any markings to identify it but found none. He reached down and pressed a button on his comm unit.

"Damage Control Central, Bridge," he said contacting the Damage Control Assistant (DCA) Lieutenant Pamela Barnes, who was the officer in charge of damage control on *Mexico*.

"Central, aye," Pamela responded over the comm.

"Damage report," the Captain inquired.

"Repair Two is just manning up. We'll have damage control teams on the scene shortly and more information then. However, sensors indicate several comparts on decks one through four open to space. High temp alarms indicate several fires have broken out. There are going to be personnel casualties, but I have no idea how many. Obviously, this is a major catastrophe, but I'll know more when damage control teams are on the scene," Pamela reported.

"Very well. Keep me informed," Captain Allen replied.

"Captain, helm is not responding," the helmsman reported, his fingers moving rapidly over the helm's control pad.

"Very well, secure main thrusters," the Captain quickly ordered.

"Secure main thrusters, aye, sir," the helm answered pressing the appropriate controls to carry out the order and stopping the ship. "Main thrusters secured, sir. Forward thrusters are offline."

"Very well," Captain Allen replied. The Captain turned as the XO arrived on the bridge. "XO, send a message to Naval Base Quebec and Fourth Fleet. *ESS Mexico* involved in a collision with a stealth ship that was operating in stealth mode and give our position. Both ships are heavily damaged. More to follow."

* * * * *

Batronian Stealth Ship 1821
Near Omar VII
May 21, 2487, 2241 UT

Less than two minutes after the collision and the Batronian Commandant already knew his ship was in grave danger. From the forward bridge window, he watched as the bow section of his ship finally broke loose of the rest of the ship and began to drift away. Like *Mexico*, alarms blared, and warning lights flashed on consoles around the bridge. Engines, thrusters and the stealth generator were all offline. It took less than two minutes since the collision for the Commandant to realize all was lost. Around him, he could feel the pain and anxiety of his crew through the social bond that connected Batronians. But his crew and himself had one last duty to perform.

<Weapons Officer, detonate all missiles immediately,> he ordered sentencing his crew and himself to death. Detonating the weapons loaded in the tube would destroy the ship and it was important that Earth had no evidence that a Batronian stealth ship was operating in the Omar system. The weapons officer stared at the Commandant in shock. <Hurry before the bow drifts too far away.>

* * * * *

ESS Mexico (D-866)
Near Omar VII
May 21, 2487, 2241 UT

Captain Allen had his head down changing his comm unit when *Mexico* was rocked again when the mysterious stealth ship suddenly exploded. A pinging sound came from the hull as pieces of the stealth ship struck *Mexico*.

"What the hell was that?" he heard someone on the bridge yell. A screeching sound from *Mexico's* hull could be heard as metal twisted, followed by a large crack as something within the ship snapped.

Down in the Number One Engineroom on the first deck, Engineman First Class Jimmy Forbes was trying to keep the number one engine running. Although the engines weren't used for ship's propulsion while in system (thrusters were used instead due to the gravitational stresses created by faster than light travel), the engines still ran to provide the ship with power for electricity and water.

A pipe burst behind Jimmy, the second coolant pipe to rupture since the collision. "Close that valve Becky!" Jimmy ordered Engineman Apprentice Rebecca Pierce, pointing to a cutout valve. At eighteen, Rebecca was just two months out of Engineman "A" school and was still qualifying for watches on *Mexico*. As she strained to close the valve, the "low coolant pressure" alarm sounded.

Jimmy touched a button on the engine's control pad silencing the alarm. Seconds later, a "high temperature" alarm went off. "Shit!" Jimmy shouted, silencing the new alarm. He watched the temperature gauge climb as the coolant pressure gauge dropped to zero. A squealing sound could already be heard coming from the engine's overheated bearings. Jimmy toggled the comm. "Main Control, Engine One. I have to shut her down," he told the Chief Engineer whose battle station was Main Control located at the forward end of the Number One Engineroom.

Jimmy pressed the large red emergency stop button and the engine screeched to a stop. Smoke and an odor of hot metal came from the engine. The overhead lighting went out and the emergency lanterns came on dimming the space and casting long shadows around Jimmy.

"Get me a round of readings," Jimmy ordered Becky. "Temperature and pressure."

"Aye," Becky responded. To her credit, her voice remained calm despite the unfolding catastrophe occurring around her and her inexperience on the ship.

Bruce Tivis had just finished donning his Damage Control Suit when the stealth ship exploded, rattling the ship and knocking him and several of his shipmates off their feet and setting off more alarms in Repair Two. *Damn, what was that?* he asked himself as the emergency battle lanterns came on. But there would be time to figure that out later. Now was the time for action and his team was ready.

"Let's move out," Bruce ordered the Number Three Damage Control Team, the damage control team that he led. The team consisted of ten members, including himself and was divided into two five-member hose teams (numbered one and two). Each member of the team was loaded down with gear including hoses, axes and patches for temporarily sealing hull openings, as well as various other hand tools. The Number Three Damage Control Team exited Repair Two and headed forward.

* * * * *

Private Home of Captain Amber Harrington
Naval Base Quebec, Omar IV
May 21, 2487, 1942 Local, 2242 UT

The comm unit chimed as Amber Harrington, Commanding Officer of Naval Base Quebec, had just finished dishes from the dinner she had enjoyed earlier with her son Howard and daughter Anne Marie. Howard and Anne Marie. It was the last day before Howard and Anne Marie would return to Kylar II where Amber had been stationed before taking command of Naval Base Quebec eighteen months ago. Her children, who had both been born and raised on Kylar II, were enrolled at the University of Natasha there. They had arrived a week ago during a break between semesters and would be leaving on an early flight tomorrow morning and had returned to their hotel in Zelerod, the capital of Omar IV.

Amber looked over to the comm unit, a realization coming to her. A long, shrill single note continued to be emitted from the comm without interruption. This indicated an emergency call from the base's operation center where the Command Duty Officer was stationed.

She walked over to the comm unit and toggled it to receive the heavily encrypted signal. "This is Captain Harrington," she said.

"Captain, this is Lieutenant Command Dawson, Command Duty Officer," a voice reported formally. "We have received Emergency Flash Traffic from *ESS Mexico*. She reports that she has collided with a stealth ship that was operating in stealth mode near Omar VII heavily damaging both ships. The stealth ship has since exploded and has been destroyed."

"What stealth ship?" Amber asked, stunned by the report. Any stealth ship should have requested permission to conduct operations in any system and Amber would have been informed if any had. Any stealth ship Captain in any of Earth's fleets knew the rule which existed to prevent an accident like this.

"It wasn't one of ours," Dawson reported.

"Not one of ours," Captain Harrington repeated considering the consequences of those words. Even in her shock, she issued orders decisively. "Order the base to Alert Delta. Notify *Lake Erie* to get underway with her destroyers. Launch all available fighters and four flights of attack craft. I'm on my way." If it wasn't one of Earth's stealth ships, then it shouldn't have been in the Omar system at all. And only one other race of beings had stealth ships in the sector—the Batronians.

* * * * *

ESS Mexico (D-866)
Adrift Near Omar VII
May 21, 2487, 2243 UT

The first injured crew member arrived at the Forward Battle Dressing station just four minutes after the collision. Quarter Master Apprentice Ralph Graham screamed out in pain as he was moved from the stretcher to the exam table, his leg clearly broken. The injured man was wearing only boxers and a T-shirt and had blisters on his hands. The 19-year-old had to be strapped down the examination table as he writhed in pain.

"What happened to him?" Hospital Corpsman Peter Sheffield asked as he stepped up to the table pulling on fresh gloves as he did.

"Fell off the top bunk," one of the stretcher bearers reported. "Tried to get up and burnt his hands on the deck. Apparently, a fire in the compartment below him."

Ralph screamed in pain as Peter began his assessment. The Forward Battle Dressing Station, manned only when the ship was at General Quarters and located just forward of the Chief's Lounge on the fourth deck of *Mexico*, was a triage center, designed to treat injured or wounded crewmembers during emergencies and return them to their Battle Station or move them to Main Medical once they were stabilized if the person was unable to return to duty. Peter quickly realized that Ralph Graham would need to be moved to Main Medical once Peter had stabilized him.

Peter began by hooking up an IV and starting a morphine drip. The effect was almost instantaneous as Ralph's screaming suddenly ended. The burns on Ralph's hands received an antibiotic spray and his hands were wrapped in fresh bandages. Next, Petter moved to Ralph's leg. The leg was clearly broken, but the bone had not penetrated the skin. A simple fracture, Peter quickly diagnosed. It would need x-rayed then set. Peter pulled out an air splint and wrapped it around Ralph's leg as another injured man, this one unconscious, was brought in and placed on the other exam table. As soon as the air splint was inflated, Peter told the stretcher bearers to transport Ralph to Main Medical. Peter changed his glove as he moved to the man laying on the other exam table.

Bruce Tivis led the Number Three Damage Control Team forward on the third deck through the dimly lit passageway. The lights from the damage control suits sliced through the smoke-filled air. He arrived at the door at frame 22 that led into the Forward Crew Berthing. The hose teams took up position behind him as he opened the air-tight hatch. A whooshing sound and a buildup of air pressure in his suit were all the indicators Bruce needed to realize that there was a hull breech in the compartment. Bruce entered the space, shocked at the sight before him.

The Forward Crew Berthing compartment began with the forward bulkhead at frame 6 and extended to the aft bulkhead at frame 22, a total distance of 32 feet. Now, however, everything forward of frame 12 was simply gone—opened directly to space. *You could walk straight out of the ship*, Bruce thought awed by the sight. Bruce could see debris flashing outside of the ship through the opening and some bodies drifting by. The remainder of the compartment was a mass of twisted metal from the deck plates and the bulkheads, twisted bunks and lockers thrown about. A few bodies were trapped in the debris, but with no air in the compartment, there were obviously no survivors.

"Backing out!" Bruce shouted to the rest of the team as he began backing to and then through the hatch. He resealed the hatch and slapped a bright yellow square sign on it. "OPEN TO SPACE! DO NOT

ENTER!" the sign warned. The Damage Control Team's messenger then commed Repair Two which would pass the information on to Damage Control Central.

In Damage Control Central, located aft of the ship's gym and forward of *Mexico's* four aft crew berthing compartments, Lieutenant Pamela Barnes was beginning to receive the initial damage reports from Repair Two's five damage control parties and was piecing together a picture of the damage to *Mexico*. And the picture was not good. She reached over to the comm unit in the darkened room, illuminated only by the emergency battle lanterns.

"Captain, Damage Control Central," she said into the comm unit.

"Captain, aye. What's the story Lieutenant?" the Captain replied.

"Sir, we have major damage to the entire forward part of the ship. The forward thrusters, forward missile launchers, forward emergency generator, turret one and gun mounts 31 through 34 all destroyed or heavily damaged and out of commission. There are numerous fires forward of frame 40 and the ship is open to space at frame 10 on decks one through four. The number one engine is down. Engineering is trying to find a way to restore electrical power to the forward half of the ship. The ship is severely damaged, nearly catastrophically," Pamela reported.

"Estimated time we need to get underway?" the Captain asked

"Sir, we can't even begin to repair this type of damage until we reach dock. Without the forward thrusters, we can't steer or control the pitch of the ship. All that the damage control teams can do for now is put out fires and isolate the vented compartments. There may be a few compartments that we can seal the breeches in and repressurize, but most need dock work. I hate to say it, sir, but we're going to need towed," Pamela reported.

* * * **

Delta Flight
Breaking Orbit, Omar IV
May 21, 2487, 2248 UT

Just nine minutes after the collision, Commander Terrance Franklin led Delta Flight, consisting of four SA-18s, the Earth's latest attack spacecraft out of Omar IV's atmosphere and into the darkness of space. Terrance kept his thrusters to full power and the nose of the spacecraft pointed away from the planet as the broke free of Omar IV's gravitational field. Delta Flight's SA-18s were armed with eight AM-2 short range missiles and fully charged 20-mm lasers.

"Delta Flight, this is Delta Leader, arm your missiles," Terrance ordered his flight over the comm. Like everyone else, he had no idea why a stealth ship was in stealth mode while inside the Omar system, but he knew that Naval Base Quebec wouldn't have ordered Delta Flight to take up position and defend *ESS Mexico* from any threat had it been any of Earth's own stealth ships.

He toggled his missiles to armed and selected the outboard missiles on each wing of the spacecraft as Delta Flight raced toward Omar VII

* * * * *

ESS Mexico (D-866)
Adrift Near Omar VII
May 21, 2487, 2449 UT

Flames flared out from the hatch as soon as the hatch was opened, forcing Yeoman First Class Bruce Tivis to a crouch as the flames passed over his head. He turned on the nozzle of his hose, sweeping it back and forth spraying a stream of water at the base of the flames. The Personnel Office he worked in was fully engulfed by fire—the first fire that Damage Control Team Three had encountered since the collision.

Bruce advanced slowly, the remainder of the team on Hose One dragging the hose behind him. The heavy smoke reduced his visibility to almost nothing in the empty office. The only real source of light came from the lights on his Damage Control Suit. He continued to sweep at the pale orange glow of the flames, carefully advancing further into the compartment. Desks, computer consoles and cabinets were strewn throughout the compartment, thrown around by the force of the collision. Toward the forward end of the office, Bruce noticed the deck had been bent slightly upward. Bruces light revealed scorching on the bulkheads as the result of the fire. The heat in the compartment penetrated his suit and sweat formed along his brow.

The number two hose team had moved to Bruce's left working the fire from another angle, both teams working together silently and efficiently because of steady training. They quickly brought the fire under control and just five minutes after entering the compartment, they had the fire out.

Down in the Number One Engineroom, Engineman First Class Jimmy Forbes continued to assess the damage to the Number One Engine. The bearings on the engine were shot and it would take hours to replace them assuming that the bearings were in stock. Otherwise, the bearings would have to be fabricated in the machine shop and that would take several days more. *Shit*, Jimmy thought. There was no way that the Number One Engine could be restarted.

Jimmy looked up and saw Perry Goodwin, a First Class Electrician's Mate, approaching him. Perry and Jimmy had much in common. Both had joined the Navy in May of 2472, though they were in different companies in boot camp. Both had attended "A" school on Mars, though different schools—Jimmy to Engineman's "A" school while Perry attended Electrician's Mate "A" school—to learn their trades. And ten years later, they had served together on the cruiser *ESS Salt Lake* for two years, becoming good friends. Both were "snipes"—Navy slang for Engineers. They had reconnected when Jimmy reported for duty on *Mexico* a year ago.

"Well, Jimmy, how bad?" Perry asked. As the Electrician's Mate of the Watch, he was responsible for the two generators in the Number One Engineroom. Unfortunately, the generators required power from the engine to generate electrical power for the forward half of the ship when the ship was at Battle Stations. At Battle Stations, the ship's two engine rooms were placed in "split-plant" operation to prevent damage from systems in one engine rooms causing damage to the systems in the other one. Normally, the engines were "cross-connected" with the systems working together for both engine rooms.

"It's bad," Jimmy said, sitting down a wrench. He picked up a rag and wiped the grease from his hands. "We may need to dock just to begin repairs."

"We need to get electrical power restored,' Perry said. He thought briefly. "What's the status of the Number Two engine?"

"Hell, I haven't even thought about what's going on back there. Let me check," Jimmy replied. He went to the comm unit at his station and pressed a button and connected to the Number Two Engine's station located in the Number Two engine room directly aft of the Number One engine room. "Number Two, Number One. What's your status?"

"Number One, Number Two. It was shaky for a minute but we're still running. What about you?" came the reply.

"Number Two, Number One. We're out of commission and probably won't be back up for some time," Jimmy replied. Jimmy thought for a second, then pressed a button correcting the comm unit to Main Control to speak to the Chief Engineer. "Main Control, Number One. Sir, I recommend that we cross-connect the plants. Number One engine is OOC for the foreseeable future. If we cross-connect we can at least restore electrical power forward."

"Understood," the Chief Engineer replied. He gave it a moment's thought. The ship wasn't in battle and with the other ship gone, further damage was unlikely. "Cross-connect the plants," he ordered. A minute later, the lights flickered back on in the forward compartments of the ship including the bridge.

* * * * *

Operations Center
Naval Base Quebec, Omar IV
May 21,2487, 2010 Local, 2310 UT

Captain Amber Harrington walked into the Operations Center of Naval Base Quebec, now in uniform and with questions running through her mind. *Where did the stealth ship come from?* and *were there more of them out there?* were possibly the two most important questions. It seemed cruel to think that the condition of *Mexico* and her crew were not at the top of the list. While Amber was concerned with the loss of life, her primary duty was the security of the Omar system, which had been compromised by the unknown ship that *Mexico* had accidently discovered.

The main room of the Operations Center was large and open with rows of terminals where operators sat communicating with other commands within the base or in orbit above, monitoring the status of defense systems, reading displayed sensor data and monitoring comms. The large central room was surrounded by offices and conference rooms, most of which were empty at this time of night. But the main room was buzzing with activity as the red-headed Commanding Officer moved toward her station at the rear of the room. A man wearing the insignia of a Naval Commander approached her.

"Captain," Commander Luke Wilholm, Naval Base Quebec's Executive Officer and Amber's second in command said. "*ESS Lake Erie* and her destroyers have detected no other ships in the system and the System Monitoring Center is not detecting any unusual activity inside or outside of the system. *Mexico* has reported that she has suffered serious damage and is adrift. I recommend that we dispatch tugs escorted by two for the destroyers to prepare *Mexico* for towing to dock."

Amber took a minute to study the system's sensors on her monitor. All civilian ships were being held outside of the Omar system and those inside of the system were being held in docks. Only Earth's four warships and spacecraft appeared on the sensor display. *Of course, there wouldn't be anything else on the display if there was a stealth ship out there*, Amber thought as she considered her decision.

"Are we sure that this isn't a major screwup and it's one of our stealth ships?" Amber asked.

"Stealth Squadron Ten reports that they have no stealth ships operating in or near the Omar system," Luke replied bringing up the message on his comm unit and showing it to her. She studied it for a minute and then turned her head toward the Executive Officer.

"Very well. Dispatch two of the destroyers to escort the tugs to *Mexico*. Let's get her docked and find out exactly what happened," Amber ordered.

"Aye, ma'am," Luke responded and then moved off to carry out her orders.

* * * * *

ESS Mexico (D-866)
Adrift Near Omar VII
May 21, 2487, 2320 UT

The fires were out, at least that was what had been reported to YN1 Bruce Tivis when Damage Control Team Three changed out air supplies in Repair Two ten minutes ago. Now he led the team forward along the third deck, retracing the route they had taken earlier. With the fires out and depressurized compartments isolated, the damage control party's mission would shift. Now they would concentrate on patching the hull where possible and recovering injured and dead crewmembers. After seeing the amount of damage to the ship, Bruce did not look forward to this part of the operation.

With electrical power restored returning light to the passageway leading to the door at frame 22, things looked almost normal, like the collision had been a bad dream. But the yellow sticker warning of the danger beyond the hatch remained on the door. It wasn't just a bad dream. Bruce stopped at the door, officially door 3-22-2. He waited until the hatch behind the damage control team was closed and sealed. He then had one of Damage Control Team Three's members set up the Compartment Decompression Unit. Commonly known as the "Big Red Sucker" due to its bright red color, the machine was box shaped, measuring approximately 8' x 6' x 8'. It would pull the air out of space, creating a vacuum. The unit would hold the air until they were ready to repressurize the space. This would allow the damage control party to pull the air of this passageway and enter the already vented forward berthing compartment without venting more precious air into space.

The Big Red Sucker was turned on and Bruce Felt the air pressure in his suit start building up in response to the change of air pressure in the passageway. Ito took several minutes for the Bed Red Sucker to shut down, a light on it signaling that the air had been removed from the passageway. Bruce opened door 3-22-2. Lighting, as expected, was out in the berthing compartment, but light from the passageway combined with the lights on his damage control suit allowed Bruce clear visibility as he entered the compartment.

Bruce had served 17 years in the Navy. During that time, he had seen fires on ships and even once, while serving on *ESS Japan*, had been in a minor collision. But, as he looked at the ruins of the Forward Berthing Compartment, he realized he had never seen damage like this. With air no longer being vented from the compartment, debris had settled to the deck. Bruce stared through the gaping hole at the forward end of the compartment seeing a spacecraft flash by. As he looked around, he saw the deck and bulkheads were buckled. Bunks and lockers were strewn around the compartment, laying amid clothing and personnel items belonging to the crewmembers who lived here. There were several bodies tangled in the remains of bunks, and one caught between two lockers. Bruce again looked at the opening on the other side of the compartment, knowing that most of the crew who had been in the compartment when the collision occurred were pulled out of the ship and into space.

It was the third body that Bruce was helping remove caught beneath a collapsed bunk. The face was swollen and discolored which caused Bruce not to immediately recognize his friend Trevor Ryan. Once he realized who it was, he froze staring. His stomach tightened and rolled. Just an hour ago, his best friend had been cheering him on while Bruce pushed himself to set the bench press record. *He couldn't really be dead.* He began shaking violently, so violently that he had to allow someone else to help remove the body. He watched with his vision blurred with tears as they placed Trevor in a body bag.

* * * * *

Naval Tug 2214
Approaching ESS Mexico (D-866) Near Omar VII
May 21, 2487, 2357 UT

It was nearing midnight when the four naval tugs approached *Mexico* with Omar VII in the background and two destroyers escorting them. Chief Quartermaster Douglas Henry carefully piloted his tug, numbered 2214, through the debris field surround *Mexico*. The 53-year-old Chief was a veteran of the War at Masic Point and unlike Bruce Tivis, had seen damage like this before during that war. Seeing the ship adrift, dead in space, brought war memories to his mind. The screams and the smell of a damaged ship were something never truly forgotten.

Douglas pushed the memories aside as he concentrated on getting the tug into position, zigzagging his way through debris from both *Mexico* and the mysterious stealth ship. His tug was a one-person spacecraft. Visually, it resembled a large cargo shuttle. It consisted of a pilot house with just enough room for the controls and the pilot to take a few steps to look through portholes on both sides and the rear, and a large engine compartment located behind the pilot house. The large engines on a craft that was only 30' long gave the tugs the muscle power to move the much larger ships they towed.

Chief Henry maneuvered his tug alongside *Mexico*. He liked operating the tug. It was a great way to end his career. *Just six months until retirement*, he thought as he pressed a button on his comm unit. Of course, the Chief had no way of knowing that in less than two weeks, his contract would be extended for "the duration of the war."

* * * * *

ESS Mexico (D-866)
Adrift Near Omar VII
May 22, 2487, 0008 UT

"Captain, Tug 2214 reports ready for docking clamp five," the Communications Technician handling the short-range voice comm unit reported.

"Very well," Captain Allen replied. He turned to another member of his crew who manned internal an internal comm unit. "Have them extend docking clamp five."

Captain Allen moved to the Starboard Bridge Bubble, a clear enclosure that gave a view of the starboard side of the ship. The bubble's clear deck, bulkhead and overhead gave the illusion of floating in space. Captain Allen faced aft and watched as docking clamp five extended then attached to the tug. He then looked forward to where docking clamp three was already attached to a tug on the port side and that the last tug was maneuvering into position to take docking clamp six. Together, the four tugs would pull *Mexico* back to dock 27L above Omar IV. Satisfied that docking clamp five was securely attached to the tug, Captain Allen reentered the bridge, crossed over and entered the Port Bridge Bubble to watch the last tug move into position.

Two decks below, in the Forward Battle Dressing Station, Hospital Corpsman Second Class Peter Sheffield finished stitching a deep cut in his last patient's forehead. Peter removed his gloves and looked around the Battle Dressing Station. Three bodies, two men and a woman, were waiting for stretcher bearers to transport them to the refrigeration locker on the first deck, the lowest deck on the ship. Puddles of blood lay on the deck, as well as some of the equipment. Peter pulled on another pair of gloves and filled a bucket with disinfectant. It would take him an hour to make the Forward Battle Dressing Station spotless.

On the second deck, nearly all the way to the forward end of the ship, Bruce Tivis led Repair Team Three into the forward thruster control room. The forward thrusters provide *Mexico* with steering and elevation control. Bruce was aware that the thrusters were not functioning before he entered the compartment. Like most spaces this far forward, the forward thruster control room's air had been vented to space. Fortunately, since the compartment was normally manned only during Battle Stations, no one had been in the compartment when the collision occurred.

The heaviest damage to *Mexico* had occurred on the third and fourth decks, so the damage to the forward thruster control room was relatively minor. A three-foot gash caused by separating armor plates looked like the only breach to the hull in the compartment. A four-foot by eight-inch patch was muscled into position. Bruce and another member of the repair party. Valves were opened by a third member allowing air to fill the space. The pressure of the air combined with the vacuum of space outside of the hull held the patch in place while a Hull Technician welded the temporary patch in place.

Unfortunately, the damage to the thrusters wasn't going to be dealt with by a simple patch. Bruce knew virtually nothing about thruster mechanics, but even he could see that the thrusters were too badly damaged to repair outside of a dock. The piping connected tot the thrust control unit had been ripped open, fluid dripping from them. The unit itself was deformed and partially ripped from the deck. Along with all the other damage that Bruce had seen, he wondered how long it would take to fix *Mexico*. As Bruce surveyed the damage, a large groan emitted from the hull causing the members of Damage Control Team Three to look around nervously.

"Tugs have us underway," the First Lieutenant—the officer in charge of the Deck Department and third in command of *Mexico* reported to Captain Allen who was studying damage reports on a console in front of him. The Captain looked out of the bridge windows and saw the slow forward movement of *Mexico*.

"Very well," the Captain replied formally. Again, he looked at the damage report. Hidden among the reports of damage to the various systems onboard *Mexico* were the casualty figures. Eighteen dead, thirty-three missing, presumably pulled out of the ship into space after the collision. Fifty-one letters to write; fifty-one families whose lives would be shattered.

The Captain looked up and out of the bridge window again, watching the debris floating by as the ship was towed slowly toward Omar IV. The hull groaned and creaked from the stress of the towing on the damaged sections of the hull. *It had to be a Batronian Stealth Ship, but why?* Captain Allen asked himself. *Why was it out there?* Of course, there was no answer forthcoming. The only thing Captain Allen felt sure of was that this would not be the last time he would be dealing with the Batronians.

* * * * *

Batronian Carrier 211
Nearing Target System
May 22, 2487, 1321 UT

Commandant Shonze, Command of Strike Force 7-2—commonly known as the Strikers—looked out at the stars as the Batronian Task Force closed in on the target from the observation deck of the carrier. He would lead the attack craft making up Strike Force 7-2. He was a combat veteran, heavily decorated and had led many strikes during the war with Antron. Now, Earth would also be attacked for their continuing support of Antron. A weak enemy, not truly worthy of him while the battles with Antron continued. Still, he would do his duty. Just three more days.

www.ingramcontent.com/pod-product-compliance
Lightning Source LLC
Chambersburg PA
CBHW080719020726
47502CB00009B/2473